FIRE IN HIS KISS

Abby could not move as Mike's fingers fumbled at the ribbons of her sopping bonnet. When he stripped the bonnet slowly from her head, she felt bared, vulnerable; her face was fully open to him.

Nothing in all Abby's experience of seeing visions, of healing people and observing their pain and pleasure, could have prepared her for that kiss. Mike's lips were tentative at first, testing her. She could not help but respond; then she was drowning in a flood of emotions.

His kiss robbed her of her breath while filling her body with a heat stronger than fire. He pulled her closer against him, and she was aware not only of heat, but of strength and hardness. She had never been so close to a man, and she was shocked at the lascivious urges that ran through her. No virtuous woman could feel as she did; no lady permitted such liberties until marriage. But all she had ever believed was pushed aside by that one wonderful kiss. She could not question why; she could not think at all with Mike's lips on hers.

A GLIMPSE OF FOREVER

LINDA O. JOHNSTON

LOVE SPELL ◆ NEW YORK CITY

For Fred, my romantic hero.

LOVE SPELL®

December 1995

Published by

Dorchester Publishing Co., Inc.
276 Fifth Avenue
New York, NY 10001

Printed in the United States of America.

Acknowledgments

My gratitude forever to all the wonderful writers who've critiqued and encouraged me. Thanks especially to Karen Pershing, Julie Hurwitz, Hermine Kopp, and Betty Moss; Janie Emaus, Marilyn Dennis, Susan Williams, and John Vornholt; and Paul Gillette and his Wednesday night crew.

A GLIMPSE OF FOREVER

Prologue

The desert was never quiet, not even now, in the middle of the night.

Mike Danziger stood motionless to avoid rubbing his running shoes against the gritty walkway, for he was listening.

A breeze whistled softly. The sand it whipped about scratched at the wooden walls of the cabin beside him as small animals scuffled in sparse brush—most likely mice, jackrabbits, snakes, or scorpions. In the distance, a coyote yipped and an owl keened a mournful "hoo."

Despite the length of time Mike had spent here, he never tired of comparing these sporadic wilderness sounds with the cacaphony left behind in Los Angeles: freeway traffic, burglar alarms, phones, beepers, radios, television . . . civilization.

He squinted and looked about but couldn't see the creatures that were his only company. Without the blaze of city lights snared in the haze of pollution, the night was dark. Not pitch-black, though. The moon, little more than a crescent, illuminated a pale, narrow swath that began as a pinpoint in scrub-shrouded sand and ended at the gleaming windows of his unlighted cabin.

This was his fifth month here. He had hauled wood from his truck for his many projects. He had hiked uncounted miles on the desert floor and in the weathered mountain range at whose foot he had built his cabin. The exercise had hardened his body enough that his muscles now strained against all the T-shirts and jeans he had brought.

Many nights he strolled outside to listen and commune with the serene display of nature at peace, even though he knew the tranquillity was an illusion. The nocturnal animals did not wander for the supposed joy of it, as he did. This was when they foraged for food—which was, most often, each other. There was, in fact, no peace here.

But that was why Mike had come: a quest for serenity.

He crossed his arms to retain some heat in his thin leather jacket. The dark brown hair he had not cut since leaving town rippled in the breeze. Cool air blew through his light jeans. The desert at night was cold—as cold as many eyes in the town he had left behind. At least his face was warmed by the mustache and beard he had grown since arriving here. The air was dry and smelled of the wind-disturbed creosote bushes.

The cabin had been his haven for years. Previously he had come for a week or two to escape, now and then, what his life had become. This time he had planned to stay as long as it took to escape his life's most bitter irony. But he had learned here instead that the old maxim was true: you could escape nothing when what you ran from was yourself.

Should he go back? Not yet. If he found no peace here, he certainly would find none back home.

Heading toward the cabin, he sighed aloud, a near-moan escaping his lips. Before he reached the door, an unnatural hush settled over the desert.

Startled, he turned. As if a voice commanded him, he looked up. A countless array of stars speckled the sky. While he watched, the stars seemed to rearrange themselves in a slightly different configuration, the change so minor that he half believed he was dreaming it. Surely it was an illusion—like the peacefulness here in the desert.

But he was awake, and there was more.

Somehow he felt he was watching the heavens through someone else's eyes. His throat ached suddenly with a terrible dryness, and he sensed someone else's yearnings—for peace, like him, and something beyond. There was a sadness, a loneliness, a longing, all of which he himself had experienced over and over, yet now they were not his own.

Impossible . . . ridiculous . . . but Mike could

not shed the feeling of sharing another's vision, another's emotions. He did not believe in ESP or any of that supernatural garbage. Where, then, could these feelings have come from—his own overwrought mind? But he did not consider himself an imaginative man.

In a few moments, the sensation vanished, and he felt abandoned. He heard the faint droning of a plane overhead and looked up. Its triangle of blinking white lights traversed the sky like the speeded-up passage of stars in a planetarium display.

He shook his head. What a strange hallucination! The solitude was getting to him. Or maybe he was going crazy. Maybe he was already crazy. That might solve all his problems. He would either die here or someone would drag him back to town and commit him to a loony bin.

Somehow, though, whatever it was that had happened reminded him that seeking peace was not a fool's mission. Maybe, someday, it might even be attainable. That and an end to loneliness.

No, damn it! He kicked the toe of one running shoe hard against the walkway. There would be no peace for him. He would find no forgiveness from anyone—least of all himself.

He had killed his wife.

Chapter One

1858

Her thirst woke Abby Wynne. Until a few days ago, she had never imagined such dryness. Her skin seemed like brittle paper wrapped about her body, and she felt sluggish, as though her blood had thickened for lack of moisture. She sat up in her bedroll beneath the high base of the covered wagon. Sleep had provided a temporary respite, but now that she was awake, her misery had returned.

For the past eight days, the caravan had rolled through the desert along the Spanish Trail in the state of California. The wagons had carried ample water for the first five days, and the Indian guide, Hunwet, had assured the emigrants he knew of a small stream that would allow them to replenish their supply.

But the stream had been dry. Hunwet, of the

southern Cahuilla tribe, had asked local Mojave Indians for water—but there was none. This year was one of severe drought, and the Indians who made the desert their home could not help the white travelers, even had they wanted to.

Abby pulled on her boots without lacing them, then slipped out from beneath the wagon and stood. A wind blew through her blue flannel nightgown, rippling the cascade of long, pale brown hair that she wore pinned up during the day, and making her shiver. Abby had thought deserts to be hot, yet she had felt cold every night.

She considered taking a sip of water from their precious, dwindling supply—just enough to wet her lips. But that might deprive others. Besides, tasting it would add to her guilt. She, of all people on the wagon train, should be able to find water—for she frequently had visions. If only she could control them . . . but over the years that had proven impossible. And none of the herbs and medicines she used could cure thirst.

She thought about trying to get back to sleep. Maybe she could again escape her discomfort. But she was wide-awake. If she lay back down and told herself to think of anything but her thirst, all she would think about would be . . . her thirst.

She looked around in the faint light from the crescent moon. The inside of the circle of wagons was quiet. The only movement she saw was near the main campfire in the center. Lighted from behind by the fire's dying embers, two men on watch sat whispering, heads together.

She knew that other men patrolled the perimeter of the wagons and around the livestock. This night, which had almost ended, their task had been more difficult than usual, for the day before the train had reached the base of a mountain range. The emigrants had hoped to find comfort in its shadow, if not water running from its heights. The men had to be on guard to make sure the cattle, oxen, and horses did not venture up the dangerous slopes.

As Abby took a step forward, she heard a sleepy whisper. "Abby? Are you all right?"

Angry with herself for having disturbed her sister, Abby replied softly, "Everything's fine, Lucy. Go back to sleep."

But in a moment, she felt a shawl being slipped about her shoulders. "You'll get cold," Lucy said quietly.

Abby turned to look down at her petite older sister in the light of the distant, flickering fire. Lucy's waiflike eyes were drawn down in concern. Her dark blond hair drifted about her face like unbaled cotton, and her muslin nightgown shone in the faint light.

Abby gave her a hug. "I'm sorry I bothered you. Is Father still sleeping?"

"I think so."

They both peered into the still shadows beneath the wagon. "At least I didn't rouse him," Abby said in relief. He had not been well since they had reached the desert. She paused, studying her fragile-looking sister, then said, "Why don't you take a drink?"

"I don't want any," Lucy replied too hastily, but Abby, holding her nightgown away from her boots, climbed into the tall wagon as silently as possible to get their precious canteen. She made Lucy take a sip but refused any herself. "But, Abby—" Lucy protested.

"I'm fine," Abby insisted. "Really." Then, replacing the canteen, she said, "I need to take a walk."

"By yourself?"

"Yes."

Despite a frown, Lucy did not argue, for Abby had long since convinced her sister of her need for snatched privacy along the trail. "You'll call if you need me?"

Abby assured her she would. She watched Lucy duck back under the wagon; then she slipped carefully over the tongue to which the oxen were chained during the day, hugging the shawl about her. It had once been their mother's and was therefore not very long. Abby did not recall Catherine Wynne but knew she had been more petite than Lucy. Their father, now stooped, was also small. He often commented how Abby, tall and willowy, was their changeling, resembling no one in the family—especially with her unusual abilities. His thoughtless remarks added to her sense of isolation.

Abby walked swiftly toward the expanse of sand away from the mountains, listening to the whispers of wind and men and the muffled noise of the livestock.

Without warning, all sound ceased. Startled by the utter silence, Abby stopped abruptly. She shivered; her extra sense told her something momentous was about to happen. Compelled by a force beyond volition, she looked into the sky—and, as she watched, everything changed. The stars of the constellations were suddenly spaced a little too far apart, as though someone had drawn a spoon gently through the usual flour-sprinkling of lights and skewed them just a bit.

There was more. There was a feeling of sadness, of loneliness mirroring her own, of longing and undefined need that seemed somehow to belong to someone else. She heard a mournful sighing—the wind? Yet all was still. She reached up as if trying to touch the stars, then dropped her hand to her side. Her own fears and sorrows felt overshadowed by similar, yet different, emotions to hers—except, all at once, there was anger. It would have frightened Abby, but it was tempered by so much despair that she ached to comfort the person whose emotions she sensed.

Suddenly a strange growling caught her attention, and she looked toward the eastern sky. A great bird made the noise, gliding swiftly toward the west without flapping its wings. The sky was too dark for Abby to make out any more than its large, soaring shape. It appeared to carry a lantern in its mouth and on each wing, all flickering evenly.

Abby called softly, "Wait!" But the large bird continued on. If only it could pick up the dehydrated travelers and carry them from this terrible place! As it disappeared from her sight, the stars returned to where they belonged—and the strange, shared feelings ceased. Such a wonderful vision, she thought, despite the anger and despair. But what could it mean?

She stared after the bird for a long while. When she finally thought of returning to her wagon, she felt impelled instead to hurry in a different direction from the way she had come. Having learned from experience to obey such urges, she found herself moments later in the area where the livestock were herded.

The oxen, cattle, and horses were dark silhouettes against the faint glow of impending dawn, their restless stamping punctuating soft lows and nickers. Abby trod surely toward her right. There, on the ground, lay two oxen. She bent down. They were dead. She could not tell in the faint light whose they were, but she was nevertheless sure her family had just lost two of the six precious beasts that were to have pulled their belongings through this desert.

She stood looking at the motionless hulks on the ground, cursing herself for the futility of her visions. Why could they not give her the ability to be of use?

That wasn't fair. Several weeks ago, she had saved little Mary Woolcott when she envisioned the four-year-old being crushed by her family's wagon. The next day, her alerted mother, Cora, had snatched Mary from beneath the wheels.

Of course, Cora and Jem, her husband, now suspected Abby of somehow having caused the near-accident, perhaps by witchcraft. And Abby had not foreseen little Jimmy Danziger's deadly reaction to a mere bee sting. She had been with the boy when he died, suffering along with his agony, for none of her herbs and cures could battle his inability to catch his breath. Jimmy had been buried alone beneath the unforgiving desert.

A footfall behind her startled Abby, and she jumped. A deep, drawling voice asked, "Abby, what's wrong?"

Without turning, Abby knew who had joined her. She whirled to face Arlen Danziger.

Arlen, the elected wagon master and uncle of poor, orphaned Jimmy, was not much taller than Abby. Although he had been somewhat soft of build when the train had set off, hard work had turned him lean and muscular beneath his usual wrinkled white shirt and leather vest. The outdoors had changed a handsome but somewhat unformed face into one with resolute character. His formerly fleshy cheeks now clefted into hollows beneath silvery eyes that squinted even when, as now, there was no searing sun. His dark hair was long and straight.

He had been a cook in his former life; now he was a leader. From the time they met at the train's formation in Independence, Missouri, Abby had felt an affinity toward him. At this moment, she was flooded with an impulse to throw herself into his arms.

That was, of course, impossible. Nearly every unmarried woman on the wagon train had set her cap for Arlen, a kind man who had been taking his dead sister's son to a new life. Emmaline

Woolcott, Jem's niece, had been the most obvious. She was also the most spiteful when Arlen fell in love with Abby's sister, Lucy.

Now, looking into Arlen's keen gray eyes in the faint glow of daybreak, Abby had a vague feeling that it could have been he with whom she had shared her emotions in that strange vision of moving stars and the growling bird.

She closed her eyes, trying to reestablish the inexplicable contact she had had with another's mind. Had it been Arlen? No; her special sense told her that Arlen was not the one, after all—but at the same time it filled her with an immutable certainty that her destiny and Arlen's were intertwined. She shook her head in disgust. Once again, her powers were odd and useless.

His voice tight with concern, Arlen said, "Abby, are you all right?"

He would be embarrassed if she cried in his arms as she suddenly wanted to do—for herself; for her flawed powers; for her fears for the thirsty emigrants; for little Jimmy lying beneath the ground. She answered simply, "I'm fine, Arlen. No," she amended, "I'm frightened. How can my family go on without a third of our oxen team—particularly with the rest so weak from lack of water?"

"We'll find a way, Abby. Don't worry." He took her arm and led her back toward the wagons. "Other livestock have died, too," he said. "We will let the remainder rest today. You'll all wait here while I go with Hunwet to find water."

"But if there isn't any?"

"We'll find some," he said with determination.

Arlen and Hunwet had been gone less than an hour when the argument started. Surprisingly, its source was not the usual complainers of the wagon train, often led by the ornery Woolcotts. Instead, normally soft-spoken Daniel Flagg gathered a group of travelers into the center of the wagon cluster. "We shouldn't lose the day of progress," he insisted. "We must keep going toward the West and water."

"But we don't know if there's more water ahead than in the dry stream we left behind," Abby's father, Lucius, said. In Arlen's absence, he often assumed the role of deputy wagon master. Abby was concerned about him, for his wizened face looked pale and his stoop was more pronounced. He had once been spritely, reveling in the attention of many women during the years since his wife's death. His sense of adventure and desire for a better life had led the Wynne family west. Now he looked old and frail.

Lucy spoke up beside him. "Arlen will be back, and he'll bring water, you'll see." Her small, upturned nose had become sunburned at the tip despite a broad-brimmed bonnet much like Abby's. Even though she was older than Abby, she looked like a determined child. Her large eyes were deep, sparkling brown, as were Abby's, and Lucy wore her favorite day dress—a blue flowered print with a lace-covered yoke, now faded from months on the trail.

"Even so, I say we go on," Flagg said stubbornly. "Arlen and Hunwet will catch up. If they have water, so much the better. If not, we will be closer to finding some than if we just sit here drying up." Flagg's pregnant wife Molly looked into his face and nodded nervously. "Who's with us?"

"Wait!" Abby cried out in alarm. Flagg was suggesting that the wagons split up. "Let's take a vote."

Those inclined to obey the wagon master agreed that a vote was necessary, but the disgruntled faction disagreed.

"No vote," Elisha Parks said. "Except maybe to elect a new wagon master for those of us heading out."

The result was the division of the wagon train. Nothing could stop the group determined to go forward. The others did not want to overwork the thirsty oxen or to disobey Arlen.

After the dissenters recommenced their journey along the base of the mountains, only twelve wagons remained. Abby was surprised at first that the Woolcotts' two were among them. On further reflection, it was not so surprising, for Emmaline, with her frilly skirts and flirty eyes, had insisted with strident vehemence on their staying. Abby watched the Woolcotts argue in muted tones among themselves, with Cora's gaze fixed longingly on the defectors. Sighing, Abby surmised that Emmaline had not yet lost hope of captivating Arlen.

Lucy stood beside Abby as they watched the dust kicked up by the departing wagons and listened to their rumbling grow fainter. "What will happen to us now?"

"We'll be fine," Abby assured her sister, pulling at the bonnet ribbons that irritated her chin. She nodded toward the wagons that rolled away. "They're the ones who will be in trouble. We can rely on Arlen."

"Of course," Lucy said with a shy smile. Then she turned to Abby. "You seem . . . well, quiet today. Are you feeling all right?"

"Me? Certainly," Abby replied. She usually told Lucy about her visions, for Lucy was the only person who seemed to understand. But how could she tell her sister that she had had an experience that led her to believe her fate, and that of the man Lucy loved, were joined in some incomprehensible way? "Let's take advantage of the day of rest, shall we? I'm going to gather plants growing around here that Hunwet says have medicinal properties." She had been unable to collect seeds, berries, and stalks as the wagon train pressed forward through the desert. This pause would give her the opportunity she had hoped for.

"Plants? Haven't they all died?"

"If so, it will be even easier to dry them for use," Abby replied. "Do you want to help?"

Lucy shook her head. "No. I have fallen behind in my writing, and I've much to describe. I've nearly completed my third journal."

Abby asked, "Have you another to begin?"

Lucy nodded. She had loved writing since she was small. Abby marveled at her sister's dedication and her ability to snatch time from their arduous journey—and now from Arlen's wooing—to maintain the record of their trip as she had sworn to do when they set off.

Holding up her beige skirt, Abby climbed into the wagon. The belongings of the Wynne family were packed tightly inside, from the important farming tools to help them begin their new life to the precious silver tea service cradled in a large pocket inside the wagon's canvas cover. The tea set had belonged to their mother and was Lucy's now. By habit, Abby touched its pocket for luck as she extracted from a neat stack beneath it a reed basket and small knife. She stared at the canteen hanging in one corner, then allowed herself the tiniest sip of water. After all, she rationalized, she would be looking for materials that could benefit all the travelers. Before she could find an excuse for drinking more, she left the wagon and ventured from the encampment.

The towering mountains shone in parched shades of gold and brown in the beating sun. The defecting travelers had headed in the direction of the known pass through the mountain range, perhaps ten miles to the south. Abby walked the opposite way, where the plant life seemed more plentiful. She had been surprised, when the wagon train had entered the desert, to learn that the arid ground produced abundant plant life. Some vegetation was tall, like the green, prickly cactus and gnarled joshua trees. Most, though, grew low in shades of dusty brown and dark green that would have meant, on the farm back in western Pennsylvania, that the plants had died. Not here, though. There were often dainty little flowers on the most grim-looking plants. Life here had adapted to the sparseness of rainfall.

Abby sought the goat nut plant, called *jojoba* by the Indians. The oil pressed from its seeds would help heal the parched skin of the emigrants. Hunwet had told her that palo verde, with its yellow flowers, and similar-looking cassia shrubs might grow in this vicinity. Abby knew they were members of the senna plant family and could therefore be used as cathartics. Abby also hoped to find desert lavender. If it was similar to the lavender with which she was familiar, it might aid queasy stomachs and help heal wounds. Desert buckwheat might be useful as a coagulant.

Abby had been a healer on the farm the Wynnes had left behind. She had treated both livestock and people, and neighbors had often come to her for help. She had never been taught; she simply picked up cures here and there from rumors and intuition. Her abilities, plus her visions, had set her apart from other people. As much as others sought her aid, they avoided socializing with her, for despite all her efforts to be friendly, they were afraid of her.

Abby suspected that her father's decision to move west was partly to help her start over. It was for Lucy's benefit, too, for Abby's reputation seemed to have tainted her older sister. Lucy was 24 years old, and although she had had a beau or two, she remained unmarried. Abby, two years younger, was sure she would never marry. Certainly no man had ever shown any interest in her, and she understood why. Although her healing skills might be useful, who would want a wife who saw things that weren't there or had strange feelings that came true? She could not even hide her visions; how could she have kept silent and let little Mary Woolcott die?

The sandy ground was uneven, so Abby had to pick her way carefully. She stooped to see the low-growing plants, but had to use caution not to trip on her long skirt. She straightened frequently to avoid stiffness, tugging in irritation at her bonnet ribbons. When she found a plant she sought, she cut off sprigs or seeds with her knife and put them into her basket. Now and then she discovered plants that were interesting but that she did not recognize. She took along samples for Hunwet to identify later.

She saw little in the way of animal life—a scorpion, which she avoided; the winding trail made by a snake. There were many insects, though, and she had to keep swatting them from her damp skin.

The sun beat relentlessly. Its fierce glare reflecting on the sand hurt her eyes. Her skin burned, and the heat made it difficult for her to breathe. She craved a drink. Occasionally she thought she saw distant pools of water but realized they were illusions caused by the heat rising from the desert.

After about an hour, Abby looked behind her.

The wagon train was quite a distance away. She had to start back soon, and yet something inside told her to go farther along the base of this mountain.

There were many plants she could not use, such as spiny cholla and twiggy paper bag bushes. Soon she came to a clump of dried-looking branches that she recognized as smoke trees. Nearby were the low-growing white flowers of chia bushes. There was something about these plants that she knew she should remember . . . and then it came to her. They grew in washes. And washes meant—sometimes—water.

Abby looked around. She was perhaps half a mile from the wagon train. She had veered around a bulge in the base of a mountain and could barely make out the white covers of the wagons.

She swayed on her feet, suddenly dizzy. Closing her eyes, she reveled in the unfulfilled sensation of taking a long, refreshing drink of water. She opened her eyes and saw a hazy, shimmering vision of a small wooden cabin at the base of the mountain. As she had the night before, she felt as though she peered through someone else's eyes, experiencing someone else's reflections of sad and angry solitude. That someone was not thirsty, as she was.

Her mind raced suddenly to Arlen, with a thought that his emotions were the ones she shared. But she knew she was wrong. Arlen was far away on horseback, looking for water. He was nowhere near this loop in the mountain. He was not hallucinating cabins or disembodied emotions in the desert.

Abby blinked, and the cabin was gone. For no rational reason, except for trusting her intuition, she suddenly felt hope. She sensed survival. She knew her body would soon drink the water it craved.

She circled the area a few moments longer, then realized this wash was hidden from the wagon train. In fact, it would be difficult for anyone to find between the crevasses of the mountain. She realized that washes originated from runoff from rare rainstorms. This wash formed a groove in the mountain. She walked along it for a while into the pass it created, then grew excited. The wash seemed wide enough for the wagons to pass through. Maybe this would form a route to speed the wagons reaching the other side of the mountain—and water.

Arlen and Hunwet returned at dawn the next day, empty-handed.

"My people cannot spare any water," Hunwet explained, his voice heavy with sorrow. Hunwet's name meant *bear* in the Cahuillas' language. He had the appearance to Abby of a picture-book Indian, with high cheekbones, a broad nose, and full lips, yet he looked and acted more civilized than some of the white men Abby had known. He wore woven shirts and buckskin pants as did the emigrants he guided. Now there was a haunted expression in his somber ebony eyes that Abby had not seen before.

"There were so many of his tribe who had died from thirst," Arlen explained as the Indian walked off by himself. "The children, the old—everyone was suffering, and he could do nothing to help. He nevertheless asked for water for us, even though I could see how much it hurt him to suggest taking anything from his dying people."

Abby had told the others of her discovery of the wash, and now she revealed it to Arlen. The wagon master looked excited but, calling to Hunwet to rejoin them, deferred to him.

The Indian seemed puzzled. "I thought I knew all ways through the desert," he said. "Although this area is not of my people, we have learned what we could from other tribes. But we will see."

Abby mounted a horse, and Arlen, Hunwet, and she rode in the direction of the wash. When they reached it, the two men looked at the winding path that severed the mountain, growing more and more excited.

"It is a way that should not be taken in the rain," Hunwet cautioned, "for in such a wash there would be quick floods that kill all in their paths."

Arlen looked up at the blue, cloudless sky. "Not much likelihood of that," he said. He turned to Abby and smiled. "Let's find out where it leads."

The three began their way along the wash, their horses at a walk. The sides of the canyon twisted and turned, sloping gradually at first, then stretching to the towering cliffs rising starkly above. Abby thought of the irony of the thirst Arlen, Hunwet, and she shared; their path had been etched over centuries by water that was no longer there. At least the air seemed cooler here in the shadows in the protected wash, and Abby felt she could breathe more easily. She imagined—prayed—that, at the other end of the trail, they would find a green, wet Eden.

After a few minutes, Arlen reminded her of their last conversation, when Abby had found the dead oxen. He asked, "Are you still frightened, Abby?"

She looked up at the cliffs looming over them and shuddered as they seemed to draw menacingly closer. She nodded. "What if I was wrong to suggest this way?"

"Did a vision lead you to this hollow?"

Abby looked at him. She knew Lucy had told him about her special abilities. "Does it matter?"

"No. But do you have any thoughts about whether we'll find water there?" He pointed toward the far end of their path between the mountains.

"There'll be water," she said. "There has to be." But her extra sense was silent, neither confirming nor denying.

Two hours later, when they came out on the other side of the mountains, Abby stared out at the flat, empty—and horrifyingly dry—expanse of desert that stretched before them. "Oh, no," she whispered.

"It's all right, Abby," Arlen consoled her. "We knew there would be desert on the other side. But there still might be water."

Arlen and Hunwet began combing the slopes of this side of the mountains for a sign of moisture. Abby, distraught, lagged behind.

At first she rode her horse around the base of the mountain, looking up at the slopes and out at the desert and praying that she had simply missed seeing a trickle of water somewhere in the vastness that unfolded about her. All she found of interest was a dry groove in the earth that had been carved by streams running from the mountain.

She dismounted and tied the horse to the branches of a smoke tree. At the rut's sides were rounded rocks from which protruded shapes like tiny seashells. She had seen similar formations before.

"They are the remains of little sea creatures," Hunwet had told her. "Part of the desert was once, in ancient times, beneath a large ocean. Some native people believe the areas where such long-ago creatures and plants are found to be sacred. They are said by some tribes to connect the past with the present and future. Some believe they hold great power that a *pul*—a shaman who uses dreams to make magic—can use." He had looked at Abby intently. Maybe her powers of vision were similar to a *pul's*. Maybe she could use the magic to help the others if it were anything but a myth.

Holding her skirt out of the way, Abby sat down in the shallow gully. She leaned her back against one of its sides, touching a jutting rock embedded with clumps of small fossilized shells.

Loosening her bonnet ribbons, she closed her eyes, hoping to feel the magic that Hunwet had described.

"Please," she whispered aloud. "I have to find water. So many are suffering. . . . " Now, of all times, she wished she had the ability to conjure up a vision on demand. But all she saw behind her closed eyelids was the glare from the desert sun.

Were they to die there? What of her sense of shared destiny with Arlen—had it only meant they would cross the wash together with Hunwet and find nothing on the other side?

She thought of her ill father. She pictured lovely, petite Lucy, looking up with adoration at Arlen's face to the same expression mirrored on his. Abby had to save them.

"Please," she said again. "Spare the others. I would do anything, give anything—even my life—if only they could find water."

Her mind reached out for the magic—and all at once she felt it, so strongly that it made her skin tingle. She let herself be swept into it, laughing aloud. The fossil-laden rock that she touched seemed to shift without her moving it, burning her fingers, freezing them—she was not sure which, but she held on.

The gully in which she sat shifted. With no warning, she became dizzy. The world spun about her in a crazy whirl, and fear shot through her. This was not the light-headedness that presaged one of her visions. The magic here was potent and irresistible, and she was suddenly

certain that she was hurtling to her destiny as
surely as if she were caught in the vortex of one
of the tornadoes the travelers had spotted across
the Kansas plains. Her eyes opened, but she saw
nothing. Sand pelted her as though she were lost
in a desert gale. Before she lost consciousness,
she thought she heard the sound of the growling
bird.

Chapter Two

The morning was cloudy and cool. Mike Danziger had not slept well; he had been plagued
with dreams he could not remember.

Sitting up in bed in his cabin, he realized how
incredibly thirsty he was. Clad only in blue boxer
shorts, he threw himself from bed, downing two
glasses of water from the chilled pitcher in the
refrigerator before he felt comfortable. He
started a pot of coffee brewing as he dressed in
jeans and an L.A. Rams T-shirt. Then, on an impulse, he stood before the small mirror over the
sink and shaved off the mustache and beard he
had been wearing for three months.

When he was finished, the face that looked
back at him, once arrogant and handsome
enough to attract nearly any woman, was drawn
and solemn. His gray eyes looked lifeless. He did
not like the reflection of the stranger who
watched him from the mirror; the guy appeared

to have no sense of humor.

With a deep sigh, Mike sat down with a filled mug at the small wooden table in the cabin's kitchen area. Had he been home, he would have opened the *Los Angeles Times*, delivered to his door, to check the business section for any stories on Arlen's Kitchens before turning to the stock market's shenanigans. Here he did not even have a television. He was addicted to working with his hands, and he picked up the only magazines he subscribed to—on do-it-yourself projects—at his weekly visit to his post office box in Barstow. He had no idea what was happening on Wall Street or in the rest of the world. He still didn't care.

Yet maybe he had been here too long. His mind kept flashing back to his strange hallucinations of stars that moved and emotions that did not belong to him—gentler emotions that did not fit his frustration and anger. Maybe his overwrought subconscious was telling him to return to civilization.

No! Mike slammed the mug on the table. He did not want to go back, not even to all that was waiting for him: his business, Arlen's Kitchens, the quickest-growing fast-food chain in the West. And all the money it made him that had enabled him to afford the house in the Hollywood Hills and his wife, Dixie.

He still had the house to go home to. But what he had done to Dixie . . .

No, he was not ready to go back. He had left reliable deputies in charge, and if they ran the whole company into the ground, who cared?

Forcing his mind to change the subject, Mike considered what to do that day. He went through the same process every morning. His answer was inevitably to build another table or chair or birdhouse, or to do nothing.

Except recently he had discovered an interest in paleontology after finding a few fossilized creatures and plants. On one of his trips to town, he had bought a couple of volumes on desert paleontological finds, and he now had maps of dry lake beds and other areas where prehistoric Indian sites and fossilized ferns, shells, and skeletons—both animal and human—had been excavated. He had an urge that morning to visit an uncharted site he had found the week before at the far side of the mountain pass near his cabin. The afternoon had been late when he had found his first trilobites and brachiopods, and Mike had started back immediately so he could reach his cabin by dark. He had been meaning to return to the site. He felt, suddenly, that this was the right day.

Mike put on thick socks and boots. He packed a couple of sandwiches in his backpack for lunch and set out toward the wash. The clouds in the sky formed a high, fluffy ceiling over the canyon. Along the shadowed, twisting path beneath the mountains, Mike's hike was pleasant and cool. He found himself wondering how many other people had made this journey. The gorge was wide enough to admit cars, if a road had been cut this way—but he was glad it hadn't. The solitude of the area was much too pleasant for the intrusion of civilization.

But maybe a wagon train or two had ventured this way during the last century.

Mike was suddenly certain of it. After all, his cabin was not far from the Old Spanish Trail— one of several routes taken by settlers of the West. Still, why was he so sure now that the pass had been a wagon train route?

It wasn't important. For a moment, he allowed his mind to wander to Arlen's Kitchens. No—no business, no worries. He forced himself to stare at the rock formations on the dry mountain slopes, the plants that grew along the path, the strange shapes in the shifting clouds above him. He inhaled the dustiness of the desert air. There were few sounds to listen to: the droning of an occasional plane, a whooshing of the increasingly gusty wind through the canyon, the clicking of insects. Now and then he stopped for a swig of water from the plastic bottle clipped to his belt.

After he had walked for nearly three hours, the light brightened as he neared the far end of the path. Soon he stepped from between the mountains. A vista of rolling, arid desert fanned out before him.

As Mike recalled, he had found the trove of fossils about a hundred yards to the left and about nine feet up the mountain. He headed in that direction.

He didn't notice anything else until he was nearly at the area—for the figure lay in a gully.

As soon as he realized someone was there, he cried out, "Hey!"

The motionless form did not respond. Mike called out again while scrambling the rest of the way up the hill, his eyes fastened on the female figure. "Hey, lady," he yelled in concern, but she did not stir. As he reached her, gasping for breath, he understood why he had not seen her sooner, for her beige skirt and golden brown hair blended into the earth tones all around. Her eyes were closed; her long, thick lashes feathered over her cheeks. She was slumped to one side—and she was as pale and still as death.

Mike touched the woman's face. Her skin was warm—was it from the heat of the desert, or from her own inner warmth? Her full lips appeared split and parched. Her face was unburned, but an old-fashioned bonnet lying on the ground beside her explained why.

Old-fashioned—that described the rest of her clothing as well: her laced boots, her long, high-necked dress. She looked like a refugee from the sixties in her granny gown. Maybe she was from some strange religious cult. But Mike did not have time to speculate further. He felt her neck; fortunately her pulse was strong.

"Miss?" he said, pulling off his backpack and sitting on the ground beside her. He patted her soft cheek. "Can you hear me?"

The woman moaned.

"Miss," Mike said again, cradling her limp body in his arms. "Wake up. Please."

The eyelids, with those lovely, thick lashes,

fluttered, and Mike found himself staring into large and soulful deep brown eyes. They seemed unfocused and immediately fell closed again as her head lolled.

"Hey!" he said, knowing his voice sounded tinged with desperation. "Hang on, please." This woman was beautiful, perhaps the most stunning woman Mike had ever seen—even though she was ashen and she wore no makeup.

He couldn't let her die. He had enough death on his conscience—but it was more than that. Looking at the fragile woman now clutched to his chest, he was suddenly filled with an irrational certainty that, if he did not save her, his own life, as pitiful as it had become, would be even less worth living.

No matter that the feeling was dumb, macho, and totally out of character; he felt utterly protective of this woman. It was as though she had called to him for help, and he was bound to save her. He had to do something. But what? CPR? But that was only good if her heart had stopped and she wasn't breathing. He knew she had a pulse, but was she getting any air?

He put his cheek to her mouth and felt her warm, faint breath feather against him. He was relieved. Surely she would be all right—wouldn't she? "Okay, miss," he repeated, his voice urgent. "You've got to wake up now." He pulled back to look at her.

Her facial structure was exquisite with its prominent cheekbones and delicate jaw and chin, needing no camouflage from the wisps of her light brown hair that had escaped in charming disarray from the bun fastened on top of her head. There was something familiar about her—yet Mike was certain he'd remember if he had met this woman before. Her poor lips were so dry. . . .

Still holding her, he worked his water bottle from his belt and, after awkwardly unscrewing the cap, held it to her mouth. She stirred and gasped, swallowing involuntarily. Water ran over her cracked lips, and as her tongue appeared from between them to lick at errant drops, her eyes opened again.

This time they stayed open, catching his. Her smile seemed painful, but her eyes softened in an apparent pleasure to see him that incredibly, inexplicably, made his heart soar. Until she spoke.

"Arlen," she whispered in a cracked yet pleased-sounding voice.

Mike started, his excitement plummeting. How would this strange, barely conscious woman, in the middle of the desert, know of his connection to Arlen's Kitchens? He replaced the lid on his water bottle while he waited to see what she would do.

More alert now, she stared at him, puzzlement etching her brow. "You're not Arlen, are you? But . . ." She stopped. The expression on her lovely face looked so crestfallen and confused that, just for a moment, Mike wished he were anyone she wanted him to be.

Inside, he laughed sardonically at himself. Where had the cautious, suspicious nature he'd nurtured for years fled to so suddenly? Hadn't he learned from his wife to trust no one? Not her, and certainly not a stranger. Whatever he had felt for this woman in those brief, effervescent moments had been imagination, wishful thinking— an illogical lowering of his guard. She seemed to know him, and she was up to something. Whatever it was, it would be of no benefit to him.

He realized he was still holding her. He lowered her gently to the ground, feeling strangely abandoned. If only the first impression of a fragile, lovely creature who would be important to his life could have been real. He shook his head, tossing off the unwarranted whimsy. Then, looking down at her, he demanded, "Who are you?"

Abby, now fully awake, sat up. She felt frightened. This man looked much like Arlen, but his face was yet more gaunt, with deeper hollows in his cheeks. His jaw was stronger, the dark hair that hung below his collar much wavier, his eyes grayer and more expressive. Right now they appeared confused and angry. She could not tell for sure whether he was as much taller than Arlen as he looked, or whether she was simply feeling intimidated as he placed her gently back on the ground, then rose to tower over her, his broad hands on his hips.

In any event, his body appeared even more muscular than Arlen's beneath clothing that looked . . . well, foreign. His blue pants looked like pictures she had seen of the Levi's worn by gold miners, but surely no prospector would wear them so tight. He had a pack of some sort

41

Linda O. Johnston

strapped to his back. His shirt had words and symbols on it: *L.A. Rams*. She had never seen a shirt decorated that way before. Rams . . . was he a shepherd? But where, here in the desert, could he support his flock?

The shirt clung to every bulge and sinew as if it were wet. A shiver ran through her—of fear and of something else. Surely she could not be physically attracted to this man who wore his clothing so indecently snug.

Where had he come from, way out here in the middle of the desert? He did not look Indian. Was he not a shepherd but a prospector? Was he from some other wagon train? She glanced around, but she saw no horse—not even her own, she realized in dismay.

As she turned back to the man, she looked up into the vast depths of his angry gray eyes—and beyond them as, suddenly, a premonition of terrible danger stabbed through her. Icy claws ripped at her spine as a drape of fiery red closed over her eyes, her nose, choking her, suffocating her, warning her of . . . what?

She nearly screamed. She wanted to stand, to flee, but she could not move.

In a moment the feeling was gone. She blinked, noting how ragged her breathing had become. She sat very still until she felt more composed, aware that the man, again kneeling beside her, was staring at her.

What had that terrible sensation meant? She knew it was an omen. It had been different from any vision she had ever experienced, yet even more frightening, for it was unfocused, and she had no idea in which direction the danger lay.

Except it involved the stranger who looked so like Arlen.

He was watching her with a perplexed scowl. Did the danger come from him? She didn't know—although that was the logical conclusion. Looking once more into eyes the color of cold granite, she had a sense that the man hid a darkness, a rage, deep in his soul.

But right now she was in no condition to run away. She asked tentatively, ready to hush if his anger seemed to increase, "Did you see Arlen or Hunwet? They were looking for water, too. Oh, yes—thank you for the drink." Her throat was still dry, and, after saying so much, she coughed.

"Here," the man said, taking something from his belt. "Have some more." He held out a container that resembled a bottle. If this was what he had used to give her a drink before she had not known, for her eyes had been closed. She reached for it. Its milky blue translucence looked as though it were made of glass, but its smooth texture was unlike anything she had ever felt before. It did not pick up the heat of the air as glass would. But it was clearly a bottle, and as she turned it one way, then another in the cloud-muted sunlight, she was certain she saw a liquid inside—water.

In her eagerness, Abby fumbled with the top, crushing the sides just a little, but they returned to their original shape as the man knelt and took the container from her gently, unscrewed it, then handed it back.

What a strange bottle—but Abby did not care. She took a sip, closing her eyes in utter ecstasy. She licked her lips. Then, trying not to look too longingly at the peculiar container, she returned it to him.

The man asked softly, "Is that all you want? I thought you might still be thirsty."

That was the longest speech he had made since Abby regained consciousness, and she realized his voice was deeper and more resonant than Arlen's. It seemed to caress her with its low vibrance, and she looked with surprise into his eyes. The darkness she had sensed in their slate depths had not disappeared, but it now was tempered by something resembling compassion. She felt herself smile, just a little, as she relaxed for the first time in this man's presence.

"I am still thirsty," she admitted. "But I cannot take all your supply." She glanced at him, not quite keeping the hope from her voice. "If you care to share any more, there are many others who need it."

He looked puzzled. "Others?"

"My family and the other people with whom I am traveling."

He asked, "Where are they? Where's your car?"

Abby stumbled over her words in her confusion. "My . . . what?"

He sat on the ground beside her, regarding her intently with those eloquent gray eyes. "Are you feeling all right now?"

Abby thought for a moment. She was no longer dizzy, and her thirst had been temporarily eased. "I think so," she finally said.

"Then tell me exactly what happened to you."

She could hardly explain to this stranger that she had attempted to invoke magic in order to find water. "I . . . don't know."

His brow furrowed; clearly he did not believe her. Still, he seemed more concerned now than angry, and he did nothing to renew her initial impression of danger. "All right, just tell me how you got here."

She suddenly felt as though she wanted to pour out all her troubles to this man, for she sensed he would care. But then she shook her head. Where had that thought come from? He had not indicated any affinity toward her beyond basic human kindness. She, on the other hand, had felt an unwarranted attraction to him from the moment she awakened and looked into his changeable gray eyes. Perhaps it was a result of his resemblance to Arlen.

She said simply, "Three of us rode our horses through the wash looking for water. We became separated. I suppose the others have returned to the wagon train."

"Wagon train?" His obvious incredulity puzzled Abby. And then his handsome features lightened. "Oh, you're with one of those reenactment camping groups. That explains your clothes." He paused, frowning again. "I can't say I'm thrilled to hear of expeditions like that starting up around here; too many people. I don't suppose your group travels with radios or cellular phones so we can find them and get you back to them."

He seemed to want a reply, but his speech had bewildered Abby. "I don't think so," she said hesitantly, trying to keep the quaver from her voice. What was he talking about? He did not seem to be speaking a foreign language, yet she could not understand him at all.

He watched her for a moment. Then he asked coolly, "What aren't you telling me? And how did you know of my connection with Arlen's Kitchens?"

"Arlen's . . . kitchens?" Arlen was a wonderful cook, but there were no kitchens on the trail.

"The restaurants," he snapped. "My business. You called me Arlen when you woke up, so I know you somehow recognized me."

She said nothing, upset with the gibberish he spoke and by his angry change of mood.

"Well, look." His voice sounded aloof. "You can tell me more later. Meantime you can't stay here alone, so you'll have to come with me to my cabin. It's through there." He pointed at the gap between the mountains. "We'll have to walk; I didn't drive. Tomorrow we'll find a way to locate your group. Okay?"

Something was dreadfully strange here. She did not understand his comments about the wagon train or Arlen. She did not understand a lot of what he said. And then she remembered her last thoughts before she had fallen unconscious. She had promised the magical essence surrounding the fossilized shells that she would suffer anything, even the sacrifice of her life, in exchange for water being found for the others.

Maybe she was dead.

But she had been terribly thirsty when she had first awakened. Surely the dead did not feel thirst. And why had she felt that panicky sense of danger when she first saw the stranger? The dead would not feel danger—would they?

This man looked like neither angel nor devil. He looked like Arlen. But he wasn't. That earlier impression of danger must have been imagination—maybe a result of her loss of consciousness—for she trusted her instinct. It told her now that this man would do her no harm. In fact, she felt drawn to him, as though . . . how silly. She was the one who seemed to be lost right now. Yet she had a feeling that she would help this man find his way.

After tying on her bonnet, Abby took the man's proffered hand as he pulled her to her feet. His grip was firm, and the contact felt alarmingly intimate. She let go quickly.

She was glad to find she was not too shaky. Finally recalling her manners, she said, "My name is Abby Wynne."

He smiled a little, and his craggy features softened. "I'm Mike, Abby," he told her. "Mike Danziger."

Abby gasped, and his expression narrowed suspiciously at her reaction. Danziger was Arlen's last name.

Since they had just met, etiquette demanded that he call her "Miss Wynne," but she was too startled to react to his use of her first name. Besides, this man had some connection to Arlen—and, perhaps, to her.

But who was Mike Danziger?

Mike considered leaving Abby Wynne here; maybe he shouldn't take her to his cabin.

Nevertheless, he found himself saying gruffly, "Come on." Hefting his backpack to his shoulders, he walked toward the path, glancing back to see if she followed.

The woman was exquisitely lovely, with her high cheekbones and lips that seemed lusciously full despite their dryness. The fit of that antique-looking dress hinted of curves in all the right places. Still, she wasn't model perfect. She had a slight, sexy overbite and the merest of spaces between her front teeth that indicated she must have escaped the torture of braces as a child. When she stood, he found her taller than he expected.

But so what if he had a hard time keeping his eyes off her? There was something strange about her. He was right to be suspicious of her. None of her reactions seemed to fit anything he said or did. He felt as though he were participating in a television show in which someone played the wrong sound track with the picture.

Unbidden, he thought again of how sweet and delicate she had felt in his arms—and how he'd had a strange, fleeting sense of her importance to him.

He shrugged it off. His imagination had gone

haywire, that was all. Still, speaking of imagination, why had she seemed to panic when she first saw him? Later, her response to their discussion about her wagon train camping expedition was odd, as though she had never heard of such a thing, even though she just claimed to have come from one.

And what was that strange reaction when he mentioned his name?

He turned for an instant—long enough to see her first wobbling steps. But as she caught his eye, her chin rose as though in defiance and she began striding forward until she passed him. Her speed picked up, and he found himself following her—filled with admiration. Well, whatever and whoever she was, the lady had guts.

"Abby," he called, "you can have some more water if you'd like."

She stopped until he had passed the bottle to her. She took a swig—and this time, she did not hand the bottle back.

He kept pace with her so that they walked side by side through the narrow gorge, the golden slopes of the mountains towering above. Noon had passed, and the sun, although no longer straight overhead, had left a trail of heat that surpassed the warmth that had surrounded Mike that morning. At least he wore a light T-shirt; he realized that Abby must be very uncomfortable in the high neck, long sleeves, and full skirt of her period costume.

But he had to hand it to her. She still did not complain. In fact, she looked right at home striding through the dust, her arms swinging at her sides, her face shining in the heat.

Mike had never been particularly attracted to athletic, outdoorsy women; Dixie, his wife, had been a sophisticate who only deigned to exercise in the comfort of an air-conditioned gym. Maybe that was why he found Abby's attitude so refreshing, so . . . enticing. Despite himself, he had an urge to get to know her better.

Trying to make conversation, he commented, "I've never been on one of those wagon train expeditions, although they do sound fun."

She glanced at him. Her expression seemed, for some reason, incredulous. "I have learned a lot but found our journey most difficult, myself. I suppose an adventurer might enjoy it better. How did you travel here?"

"I drove," he said.

"Cattle?"

That silenced him. Again, her response was off.

He asked finally, "Where did your wagon train come from?" Maybe he could get some information from her that way—like where he could drop her tomorrow.

"Independence, Missouri," she said.

"Oh, come on now," he exploded. At her frightened expression, he tried to calm himself. "Look, I asked a simple question. All I want is the truth."

"I gave it to you," she said in a hoarse whisper, her brown eyes wide and wary.

For the moment, he gave up. Either she was working very hard to keep up a role in order to hide something, or she was a few bricks shy of a load.

Whichever it was, he reluctantly admitted to himself that he found this mysterious, beautiful woman intriguing. Maybe he was just captivated by the challenge. In any event, he determined to pry the truth from her.

But as they walked, she answered no more questions about herself or the wagon train. All he was able to get from her were pleasantries about the scenery, the heat, and their progress.

Soon their progress slowed as Abby began to lag. She still did not complain, though. In fact, he was finding her lack of bitching quite touching and brave, for she was obviously tired. No other woman he knew would have kept so silent about her discomfort, even if Mike could do nothing to help it; certainly his late wife wouldn't have.

"Let's rest for a few minutes," Mike said. "I have some food in my pack. We'll have a little picnic."

The look Abby shot him was full of gratitude—which he also found appealing. He unstrapped the backpack from his shoulders and offered her a sandwich.

"Thank you," she said. She pulled the plastic bag from it, studying it carefully. She even looked through it before putting it down.

Then she turned the sandwich over in her hands, staring at it, too. The hands holding the sandwich were somewhat rough, as though she worked with them; the nails were short and unpolished. Mike found himself enjoying the sight of her grace of movement, her strange inquisitiveness, even though he wished he knew what she was thinking.

What the heck was getting into him?

"This bread is rather unusual," she said. "Its texture is so smooth, and the slices so even. And what is this inside the two pieces? I have heard of bread used this way, but never have I eaten it."

Mike rolled his eyes heavenward and sighed, shaking his head. Again, he determined to learn this woman's game. "It's plain white bread," he said. "You're eating a chicken salad sandwich."

"Oh," she said, digging in once more with gusto. Mike kept watching her. When she was finished eating, she thanked him. "I will have to try to make a chicken salad sandwich when next I have a chicken to slaughter," she said. He merely shook his head without otherwise responding.

They continued forward through the wash, Abby, obviously feeling peppier, again in the lead. They had been walking for nearly two hours total when Mike noticed that the darkness of the gray sky was deepening. He did not believe his watch had stopped, but the time seemed much later than he had thought.

A lightning flash in the distance gave him an unwanted explanation: a storm was coming. They were still a good hour away from his cabin. A few moments later, the air began to crush him with the odor of ozone, and rain began to splatter all about.

Abby exclaimed, "Rain!" She began to laugh and whirl, stretching her arms out as the drops pelted down. "My family. The others. They are saved!"

Mike stopped in his tracks. "What are you talking about?" He watched her lithe movements with an intensity that surprised himself, feeling a heat rise through his body that had nothing to do with the temperature. The rain had begun to plaster her clothing to her. Even though he had concluded she must be athletic, she had lovely, full curves rather than being determinedly, exercise-consciously skinny like most women he knew. Her breasts were lush and high, her waist small, her hips rounded. He tore his gaze from her body to her face as she stopped whirling.

Apparently oblivious to his admiration of her body, she looked for a moment as though ready to hug him, to get him to join in her dance—but she shyly dropped her hands. "I must get to them quickly, help put out vessels to trap the water." She began to hurry again along the path.

Mike inhaled deeply, following her. He was beginning to have a terrible feeling that this lovely woman was serious in all she said. And that meant . . . no. He was not willing to accept that she was crazy. He yelled, "I can't believe your expedition leader was stupid enough to come unprepared without enough water for a trip in the desert."

She turned back for only an instant, her eyes fierce enough to make Mike hesitate. "He is not stupid; he is a fine leader. He has done all he can to find water, but even he cannot control the weather."

For just a moment, Mike wished that he had done something to inspire Abby's loyalty the way her trail leader had. Was she in love with the guy? The thought made his whole body seem to deflate.

The wet sand beneath Mike's feet became soft and squishy beneath his boots. His own clothes stuck to him. Water poured from his too-long hair onto his face, and he brushed its sopping length away from his eyes. He was glad he had shaved off his mustache and beard that morning, for they, too, would be soaked by now.

He glanced at Abby's back. Her bonnet drooped, and her skirt hung heavily about her legs, impeding her progress. But still she did not complain. In fact, she seemed determined to keep moving as quickly as possible to the other end of the gorge. His admiration grew nearly as intensely as his sensual awareness of her.

But as the rain began to come down in sheets, Abby's steps finally faltered. Once more she turned back toward Mike. Her beautiful face, wet despite the bonnet, frowned in worry. "This is a wash," she said. "It may flood."

"We'll be fine," he said. "The rain has just begun."

The rain intensified, and he took her hand. Looking at him as though surprised, she tried to withdraw it. "I want to help you," he yelled over the storm. The truth was, he did not want to let her go; he wanted a physical connection with her as they faced the elements together.

Her hand was cold and wet, and it was very small in his. It felt almost fragile. But Abby seemed anything but fragile as she managed to keep pace with him without complaint.

After perhaps half an hour, she stopped suddenly, and their joined hands halted him, too. Her dark brown eyes seemed to stare into the distance. They were as unfocused as when she had first regained consciousness.

Worried that she was suddenly going to go soft on him, Mike ordered, "Let's go, Abby."

Her hand was still in his, and instead of going slack, it gripped him with determined pressure. "Up!" she shouted. "Can't you hear it? Look!"

"What are you talking about?" he demanded. He listened but heard nothing other than rain and wind and her voice. He looked around but saw little but grayness and the water sheeting around them. Nevertheless, he allowed her to pull him along as she began to climb the slope.

Fortunately the incline here was more gradual than in other parts of the gorge. Still, his calves ached with the effort of climbing. How must she feel, in her rain-sopped, dragging dress and uncomfortable-looking boots? But despite her hampered progress, she did not stop.

And then Mike heard it, too—a roar. He looked down. Quite suddenly, the gorge below them in which they had been walking was a raging river. The water level increased relentlessly, until, with a speed swifter than a pouncing cat, it rose to within mere yards of the spot on which they stood.

Chapter Three

"Come on!" Mike yelled, scrambling up the slope—but Abby wasn't following quickly enough. Not that she wasn't trying; with a look of terror in her eyes, she propelled herself forward. Her hand was no longer in his, and she held her skirt off the ground, but her progress was much too slow. The water already swirled about her feet and rose with a speed Mike would not have thought possible.

Half running, half sliding in a frantic rush, he careened back down the slope to her. He grabbed her skirt at the waist and ripped it off. He could not hear the fabric tear, for the roar of the water was everywhere, punctuated by angry crashes of thunder. Lightning flashed all around, bare seconds before the thunderclaps; Mike and Abby were in the center of the storm. The light revealed that she was still wearing a long, frilly thing resembling pants. He prayed that the lightning would find things to strike other than the two wet people.

Mike could understand why the skirt had impeded Abby's progress; the sopping pile of material must have weighed 20 pounds. He dropped it and put his hand on the small of her back, pushing her ahead as his pumping adrenaline gave him strength to climb. Daylight had all but given up to the storm-generated darkness, but he spotted, in one particularly bright lightning flash, a huge boulder perhaps two dozen yards ahead. If it were high enough so the water would not reach them, it might provide some shelter from the wind-driven rain.

Mike kept looking behind them. Their minutes of scrambling felt like hours as he continued to push Abby before him. By the time they reached the uphill side of the rock, the rain had tapered off. He thrust her behind the boulder.

The torrent sparkled in the dim light as it continued its raging rush, but it was still some distance below. Soon it seemed to stop its perilous rise.

Mike returned to Abby. Huddled near the ground, she shivered. He wished he had a sweatshirt or jacket, anything to warm her. All he had was himself, and he was cold, too. Still, their bodies together might generate enough heat to keep them from becoming too chilled. He sat and held her close. She pulled back at first. "For warmth, Abby," he said, tightening his grip. She stopped struggling.

A short while later, she even nestled close to

him. She was as wet as he, and she smelled vaguely of cinnamon and potpourri. To his surprise, he liked feeling Abby Wynne so close—and he hated it. His body was reacting treacherously. Months had passed—maybe longer—since he had been aroused by a woman. He had been content to feel nothing. Now, despite himself, he enjoyed the combining and strengthening of their body heat.

Soon she stopped shivering—but he did not let her go. He did not want to release her, not yet. Amazed, upset with himself yet filled with a compulsion impossible to ignore, he realized he might not ever want to let go of this strange yet lovely young woman.

The man who held her close made Abby feel small and protected. It was not a sensation she was used to—and despite her upbringing, which forbade unmarried men and women to act in such a manner, she discovered she liked it. The warmth radiating from his large, firm body even helped her take her mind off their peril—and the fact that she huddled there half nude with a strange man who had ripped her skirt right from her body.

He had done it, of course, to save her life. Still, she could not help feeling humiliated, for it appeared now that they would live.

She looked up, intending to thank him—and found herself gazing again into the depths of those gray eyes that so resembled Arlen's. But they were not Arlen's. They were deeper, more intense, more . . . carnal. Abby flushed, wanting to look away, but instead she felt as captive as the oxen yoked to her wagon.

She could not move as his fingers fumbled at the ribbons of her sopping bonnet. When he stripped the bonnet slowly from her head, she felt bared, vulnerable; her face was fully open to him. She stayed utterly still, unable to move, as his head lowered toward her and his lips found hers.

Nothing in all Abby's experience of seeing visions, of healing people and observing their pain and pleasure, could have prepared her for that kiss. Mike's lips were tentative at first, testing her. She could not help but respond; then she was drowning in a flood of emotions.

His kiss robbed her of her breath while filling her body with a heat stronger than fire. He pulled her closer against him, and she was aware not only of heat, but of strength and hardness. She had never been so close to a man, and she was shocked at the lascivious urges that ran through her. No virtuous woman could feel as she did; no lady permitted such liberties until marriage. But all she had ever believed was pushed aside by that one wonderful kiss. She could not question why; she could not think at all with Mike's lips on hers.

But he pulled away, his breath short, his expression bewildered. "I . . . I didn't . . ." His deep voice tapered off. He brushed long, wet strands of his hair away from his face. "I think we should go on now."

He rose to his feet, and Abby began shivering once more. She felt cold and bereft, but obviously he was right. They had to find shelter, and they should not stay here to continue what had been so impetuously begun.

They said little as they picked their way over water-soaked sand, slippery rocks, and patches of mud as Mike led her along the mountainside. She carried her wet bonnet. Now and then they had to traverse wide, but fortunately shallow, rivulets that had fed the gushing stream below. The sky lightened as the storm clouds finished their passage above, then darkened again as the day waned. Luckily they had nearly reached the other end of the gorge before the wash had flooded, for their progress was slow.

Abby could not still her thoughts as Mike and she trudged forward. She had behaved so uncharacteristically, so wantonly. What must Mike Danziger think of her?

Yet she knew her reaction had been involuntary—perhaps predestined. Her special sense was telling her that she was where she needed to be, that something extraordinary had happened—and that something even more remarkable was yet to come.

She sneaked glances at Mike as they walked. He was quite good-looking despite the way he unnerved her by scowling each time their gazes met. The hollows at his cheeks lent him a haunted appearance, emphasized by eyes as gray and stormy as the clouds still scudding above.

She had met few men who exceeded her unfeminine height by as much as he, fewer still who carried such height so proudly. Full of masculine grace, he strode as though unaware of the discomfort of his clothes; their tight fit was made tighter still by their wetness, their clinginess revealing even more the extent of the muscular frame she'd found so forbiddingly appealing not long before.

Night had nearly fallen by the time the route began to slope downward. "We're almost there," Mike said in a reassuring voice.

And then Abby saw it—the wooden cabin of her vision. Or at least it resembled it, in the faint light that still remained. It was nestled at the base of this mountain, where she had first headed into the gorge—but how could that be? The cabin had not really existed; Arlen and Hunwet had not seen it. Abby was confused—but she was too exhausted to worry. Maybe she would ask Mike Danziger some questions, but not now. Not until she had had some sleep and some time to think. She could look for the wagon train in the morning.

To one side of the house was a second, smaller building—the stable, Abby presumed. Near it was a row of tilted panes of glass that resembled large mirrors. Abby puzzled over their use—for growing plants? But even if the harsh elements usually kept at bay by greenhouses existed here in the desert, this glass was flat and not the shape of a sheltering building.

Still musing, Abby stumbled after Mike to the cabin door, which he unlocked. He reached inside and immediately the place was flooded with light, both inside and out. It was nearly as bright as daylight. She gasped. "What did you do?"

He looked at her strangely. "I turned on the lights. Didn't you see the solar panels? I have electricity out here."

"But . . ." She would not meet his gaze. What was he talking about? Once again, his words sounded foreign, incomprehensible, but she was afraid to ask more questions. Mike Danziger was already staring at her as though she were crazy—or worse. She recognized that look; she had seen it often when she had revealed one of her visions to anyone but Lucy, when she had been labeled evil, blasphemous, a witch.

But these lights—they seemed to radiate from lamps that did not flicker as oil lights would. There were no flames that she could see, and how could they all have lit at once? Another mystery, like the flat glass panes, the oddly flexible water bottle, and the very existence of this cabin outside her vision. What was happening to her?

She stepped inside, feeling terribly self-conscious in the light with her wet blouse clinging to her and nothing on below save bloomers and boots. Mike's eyes ranged over her and widened in what appeared to be appreciation, and she felt herself redden. Still, she raised her chin. She could not help feeling ashamed, but she did not have to show that to him. She hoped he would soon offer her extra clothing.

She had preceded him inside the cabin, and she began to look around. It looked homey and inviting. A large, plaid divan faced the stone fire-place. There were two comfortable-looking chairs and several bare, carved tables. The walls were painted white, and on them were attractive sketches of desert scenes. Doorways indicated there were at least four other rooms.

Mike said, "Why don't you take a nice, warm bath or shower while I get us something to eat? The bathroom is in there." He pointed toward an open door near where they stood. "There are fresh towels under the sink, and I'll get you something to put on."

A bath or shower here, in the middle of the desert? How wasteful of precious water that would be . . . but a warm bath certainly sounded heavenly. And after that day's storm—well, he probably had a cistern to collect water. She would simply be careful not to use too much.

She realized, then, that she had not spotted the privy when they were outside. Perhaps she would be expected to use a chamber pot. Too uncomfortable to ask, she decided to find out for herself. She went into the darkened bathroom and looked around for the lantern. There was none that she could see—not in a wall sconce or on any surface.

Looking at her as though she were quite peculiar, Mike reached into the room from behind her and pushed upward a protrusion on the wall. Immediately the bathroom was filled with a bright, steady light from a glass globe overhead. This time Abby stifled her gasp and just smiled weakly at him. "Thank you," she said.

She stared at him until he appeared to grow uncomfortable and left the room. She closed the door behind him. Then she put her fingers on the wall protrusion. Pushing it down turned off the light; pushing it back up put it on. Giggling softly, she used the lever several times, wondering in awe what caused the light to come on and to douse so quickly, and without any odor of oil or wood. Whatever the explanation, Mike Danziger was certainly clever to have thought of it.

She looked about the room. It was decorated in cheerful tones of green and yellow wallpaper, with dark green towels hanging on metal racks. There was a large tub like none she had ever seen before. It was pushed tightly against the wall and it had no feet. There was a spout like the end of a watering can hanging at its top. The room also contained a sink, built into a cabinet and with a mirror over it. But there was no exit to the outside, nor any apparent well in here—not even a pitcher. How was she to get water? And Mike had suggested a warm bath or shower, but was he heating water for her at the hearth?

Then there was the object sitting on the floor that she could not figure out at all. When she opened its lid, the contraption resembled a seat with a hole in it, like a privy, but the receptacle was filled with water. Was this the well? Where, then, was the bucket? On one side was a metal pull similar to the lever for the light. Out of curiosity, she pushed it—and with a loud gurgling, the water began to swirl and disappear down a hole.

Abby realized then that the thing resembled a privy for a reason. How handy it was!—just like the lights. And the blessed privacy of this room, after weeks of hiding as best she could on the trail . . . heaven! Were there more surprises here?

She explored the room, looking and touching and moving levers. She discovered separate handles that caused hot and cold water to pour into both sink and tub. Best of all was when she used both together and got comfortably warm water. She ran water into the tub but found that a hole allowed it to escape. Convinced of the cleverness of Mike Danziger, Abby knew there had to be an easy solution. She found a lever beneath the hot and cold controls. When she pushed it, the water remained in the tub.

While the tub filled, Abby pulled towels from under the sink. Then she glanced at herself in the mirror. She looked terrible! Much of her wet hair had fallen from its bun. Her dark eyes looked huge and sunken, her cracked lips drawn in a tight, nervous line—no wonder, after all she had experienced that day. But suddenly she hated how she looked. She wished she could do something to make herself appear attractive to Mike Danziger, for there was something about him that drew her to him like a lodestone. Danziger. Could he be a relative of Arlen's? But how?

She wondered suddenly if he, instead of Arlen, was the Danziger with whom her destiny was intertwined. The thought was both appealing and superbly disquieting. There were too many things happening around her that she could not understand. This cabin had only existed before in a vision. The conveniences here seemed miraculous and incomprehensible. Abby found herself shivering again. Something was wrong, and the only answer she could think of was that she had died when she had made her wish at the fossil site.

But if this was death, it was wonderful! That was what she thought a few minutes later as she lay soaking in the tub of warm water. She had filled it more than she had intended, but she guessed that Mike Danziger would not mind; he would somehow manufacture water here, in the middle of the desert, should he need some. She laughed at herself. Whatever Mike was, she knew from his warmth and strength, his kindness and short temper—and the ready passion he had exuded as they shared that special kiss—that he was a man, not some superhuman creature. A living, vulnerable man. Maybe the terrible pang of danger she had felt was something directed at him, instead of by him.

She washed her hair with the same bar of soap she used on her body. She often scented the soap she made with wild ginger, but this smelled sweeter, reminding her of summertime lemonade.

She did not stay in the tub long, for fear of falling asleep. When she got out, she realized she still had nothing to wear; her dripping clothing, draped over a metal bar, was ruined. Wrapping one towel about her head, another around her body, she opened the door a crack and called, "Mike, do you . . . ?"

A large, fuzzy robe was thrust at her. She grabbed it and closed the door again, then put it on, tying its belt about her waist. She felt warm and comfortable in it, even though it dragged on the floor.

When she came out, her damp hair tumbling about her shoulders, Mike said, "Dinner's ready."

Dinner? It was late enough to be supper, but that did not matter. He showed her into another room. It did not contain a fireplace nor even a wood-burning stove but instead held several large contraptions she did not even try to figure out. It was filled with a pleasant odor of cooked meat, and Abby realized then how hungry she was. Without saying a word, she sat at the place at the table that Mike designated. At least the fork and knife looked familiar.

Mike's dark hair was dry. It hung in thick waves nearly to his shoulders. He had changed into another pair of denim pants and a shirt of that same clingy material that molded tightly to his muscular chest and arms.

He had prepared beefsteaks, and the juicy flavor was delicious. There was wine, and a green salad. Before Abby could consider the consequences, she blurted, "How on earth did you get fresh vegetables on the desert? And isn't it too early in the season for a harvest?"

His dark brows knitted in a scowl. "All right, Abby Wynne. Tell me exactly where you are from."

She knew he thought she had said something foolish and inappropriate. "Pennsylvania," she said, realizing she sounded tentative but waiting for his next angry reaction.

"Pennsylvanians know about salads and electricity, even. . . ." He snapped his fingers. "I've got it! You're Amish, aren't you?"

Abby had heard of the Amish, a devoutly religious group whose members lived mostly in eastern Pennsylvania. She was from a farm in the western part of the state. Why did Mike think her Amish? Perhaps because her dress was somewhat plain.

"No, I'm not Amish." She spoke slowly, hoping his anger would not be incited by her contradicting him.

"Well, then, who are you really? Tell me the truth."

He stared keenly into her face. She tried to remain impassive—which was difficult, for she was enjoying every bite of the fresh vegetables even as her mind swirled with confusion at his words.

"I am," she said, in a hoarse whisper of nervousness.

"Well, if so there's more to the story. Tell me about your family. Where are they now—and don't give me a cockamamie story about a real wagon train."

Abby sighed tremulously. "I don't know. I'd have thought the train—my family—would be here, on this end of the wash where I left them."

Mike rose and loomed over her so that she

68

cringed from the anger he radiated. "Oh, come on. You can come up with something better than that. Why a wagon train? Why not a UFO, if you're so determined not to tell the truth."

She was too terrified to ask what a *UFO* was; the question might inflame him further. When she said nothing, she had the frightening impression that he might grab her and shake her, but she watched as he visibly got his emotions under control. When he sat back down, he said pleasantly, though his eyes flashed with restrained anger, "Pennsylvania? I'm originally from Boston, myself, but I've been in California for a long time. I suppose you'd say you're just moving here. How do you like California?"

She was glad to focus on a conversational topic that seemed almost neutral. They spoke for a while on the relative merits of the weather in all three places, and Abby began to relax. The wine was delightfully pungent, the meat and salad delicious, and Abby found the company of a calmed Mike Danziger enjoyable.

She let herself forget, for a little while, her fear of him and the inexplicable situation in which she found herself.

Abby helped Mike clear the table after dinner. "Sorry I don't have a dishwasher," he said, "but I've heard they're not too good for septic systems."

Abby had no idea what a septic system was, but she said, "We left our servants behind, so we have been cleaning our own dishes, too."

She had done it again. He looked at her as

though she had said something terribly bizarre. Sighing, she started running hot and cold water into the sink as though she had been doing so all her life. He lifted a container of the same strange material as his water bottle from a cabinet and squeezed some liquid from it into the sink. Immediately the water began to fill with tiny sparkling bubbles.

Abby cried, "Oh!" She grabbed a handful of the bubbles and began running them through her fingers. They burst as she touched them, but there were many more to take their places.

Mike did not look at her as he placed the dinnerware they had used into the water, but his narrowed eyes and taut jaw revealed his barely suppressed irritation. He used a brush to wipe the bubble-laden water over the plates, forks, and knives. Everything became spotless nearly immediately. Obviously the frothing fluid was a form of soap, but Abby had never seen liquified soap that bubbled so much and cleaned so quickly and thoroughly. Mike rinsed the dishware, then handed the pieces to her to dry with a small towel.

As soon as they had finished cleaning up, Mike showed her to the bedroom. It was pleasantly furnished with attractively carved masculine pieces. The deep blue coverlet matched the pillows. "You'll sleep here," he said.

"No," she protested. "This is your room."

But he insisted. "The sofa's comfortable."

In the end, she lost the argument. He handed

her a long, loose shirt to sleep in. "Good night," she said.

"Abby . . ." He hesitated. "Look, there's a lot I want to understand, but I'll ask just one thing tonight. How did you know the water was rising like that?"

The vision of the flood had come to her suddenly, as all of her visions generally did—although without the usual dizziness first. In that regard, it was similar to the urgent impression of danger she had felt before. But this man already seemed to regard her as too many others had: either crazy or evil. She certainly could not tell him about her premonitions. "My hearing is very keen," she said, and then she closed the door.

She did not change clothes immediately. Instead she felt drawn outside. Hearing Mike in the bathroom, she slipped out of the cabin.

Her inner voice told her that the stars were in the looser configuration of her vision the night she had believed she saw through another's eyes. She pulled the robe around her against the desert's chill. She was tired; she should go in—but her special sense held her there.

She was unsurprised when Mike joined her. He no longer seemed upset but terribly, terribly sad.

"It's very beautiful here," she said.

"Yes." But he was staring at her in the moonlight, and not at the stars. She felt herself flush.

Both watched the sky for a moment—and Abby suddenly felt as though she had recaptured the vision she had had those nights ago. Now,

71

though, the emotions she sensed in the other person were less lonely, less angry—and more confused.

Mike's emotions.

She glanced up at him and found him looking in puzzlement at her. His storm-gray eyes studied her for a long, immobile moment, but all too soon he pulled away. "Good night, Abby," he said, his voice curt. Then he stomped into the house.

She followed him slowly, feeling wonderment that she had found the man whose thoughts she had shared in her vision—and pain that, if he recognized their connection, he rejected it. As with her visions, if there was a special sharing between them, it must be erratic and uncontrollable, for she certainly had not participated in all his emotions since they had met. That was just as well. She still sensed the darkness in Mike Danziger's soul. Her own feelings were difficult enough; she did not need to take on his trouble as well.

In the bedroom, she changed clothes and nestled into bed thinking of the day's events—and particularly of all the wondrous things she had seen: this cabin; lights and water available in the desert at a touch; the indoor privy; the bubbles. Had she been transported to some magical land as a result of her prayer by the fossil site—or was she dead? She could not believe the latter; the desert, even with all these marvels, was not her idea of heaven.

She wished she had the answers, but most particularly she wanted to know what the special bond between Mike and her meant—and why she had sensed danger upon seeing him.

Before she fell asleep, she thought she heard a low growl from outside. She rose and looked out the window—and saw in the sky the flickering lanterns of a bird like the one in her vision.

Chapter Four

The shimmering waves of heat from the blazing sun made Abby's eyelids flutter. She watched as three small figures searched the distant mountain slope.

"We'll find Abby," Arlen assured Lucy, who clutched his hand.

"I'm here!" Abby cried, but they could not hear her.

They looked exhausted. More than once, Arlen saved Lucy from tripping in her long skirt over a rock or bush. Below, on the desert floor, sat the wagons that oxen had pulled through the gorge.

As the sun dipped lower, Lucy looked up at Arlen, her petite features brave. "You are dear to help, but the others have given up, and I know where your duty lies." She touched the hollow of his cheek as tears spilled from her eyes. "Our entire party will perish if we do not go on and find water."

A cry sounded from below. Hunwet, bent over, motioned to them, and they rushed to join him.

Lucy's voice was full of hope. "Did you find something of Abby's?"

But all he had found were rocks bulging with ancient fossils. "She was lost by magic," he said.

Unwilling to believe, the couple began their search once more. As daylight waned, all three returned to the Wynne wagon, where Lucius could barely lift his head. "Please," he begged, his voice small and weak, "find my daughter."

"Go on," Abby shouted. "Save yourselves." But somehow she knew the distance was too great for them to hear her—or for her to find them.

She sat up—and realized she had been dreaming. Tears streamed down her cheeks. "Papa, Lucy, don't worry about me," she whispered mournfully. Surely her dream had been like that of an ordinary person: born of concern, not vision. After that wonderful, terrible storm, her family could no longer be thirsty—could they?

"Abby?" Mike Danziger's large form in the doorway nearly hid the light from the room behind. "Are you all right?"

She could not answer; she had begun to sob.

Suddenly, strong arms wrapped around her. Large hands gently pressed her face to his bare, firm chest, and she felt the warmth of his body against her. The softness of his chest hair tickled her nose, and she nearly sneezed through her tears, but stopping the involuntary reaction helped her regain control.

"What's wrong?" Mike's voice, though full of concern, was insistent.

"I miss my family." She determined to be as truthful as possible.

She felt him stiffen. "Where are they?"

"I . . . I lost them in the desert."

"You . . . How? Where?"

She pressed her lips tightly together as she slowly shook her head against him. Those were questions she could not answer.

He pulled away, his hands still gripping her upper arms. "All right, don't talk to me. I'll take you to Barstow tomorrow, to the police. Maybe they can help you."

But her special sense told Abby that no one could help find her family.

When Mike left, she made herself recall each detail her mind had shown her. The dream confused her. If it had been a vision, her family might not have experienced the life-giving rain. But if it were a glimpse of reality, the wagons would have been on the far side of the gorge where she had first met Mike. She had not seen them on this side, either—just the cabin that had previously existed only in her visions.

Where were the wagons? All she knew for certain was that she would not find them if she looked merely with her eyes.

Bewildered and tired, her thoughts full of her family—and Mike Danziger—she finally cried herself back to sleep.

* * *

Abby awakened to the sound of rain. No, it was water flowing in the bathroom. Leaving her hair loose about her shoulders, she put the robe on over the shirt she had been wearing and went into the kitchen to cook breakfast. It was the least she could do. Opening cabinet doors, she located plates and glasses and cups—some made of the same odd material as Mike's canteen.

She was startled by the vast array of packaged foods. One cabinet held tin cans with colorful paper wrapped about them that said they were peas, soup, and other food items. In another, paper boxes contained things with odd names she had never heard of: Corn Pops, Minute Rice, granola bars.

Abby explored the rest of the room, including the strange items she had noted last night. The stove was not of black cast iron but of silvery metal. She found no wood to fuel it, which was all right since she saw no matches to light kindling—and after the plumbing wonders she had discovered, she was not surprised to see a flame when she turned a dial on the stove's front.

A second, bigger contraption—a large white cabinet the size of an upright coffin—astounded her. Its door was cool and smooth. Pulling it open by a metal handle, she saw all manner of food inside—meats and cheeses and paper boxes labeled "milk." Most miraculous was that everything was cold—here, on the desert! Obviously this was a form of icebox, but where did Mike get ice?

Linda O. Johnston

"Good morning," came a voice from behind her.

Guiltily Abby slammed the door shut. "I just . . ." She turned. Mike stood there wearing only a towel wrapped about his waist. The long, wavy hair on his head was wet, and she could see the mat of dark, tangled fur on his brawny chest that had been pressed against her cheek the night before. It spread thickly from below his broad shoulders down over sculptured muscles, tapering to a vee at his waist. And below . . . ? The towel hid where her imagination strayed, and she dropped her eyes to the floor in mortification. She had seen bare-chested men now and then, especially in her capacity as a healer, but never before had she entertained such unladylike thoughts.

"I'll get some clothes from the bedroom." There was irony in Mike's voice, as though he read her mind. Though she felt herself flush, she looked up defiantly into his gray eyes. "I thought we'd just have a light breakfast here," he said. "We'll eat lunch in town."

Lunch? That apparently was his name for dinner, and dinner was what he called supper. "That would be fine," she said. "But . . . may I borrow something to wear?"

"Sure, but I doubt I've anything that'll fit."

He took clothing from the room in which she had slept and changed in the bathroom, then helped her select a similar outfit: one of his long, form-hugging shirts over a pair of blue denim pants that he called jeans, rolled up and tied with a rope at the waist. Even though a few women had begun wearing men's trousers on the trail for comfort, Abby felt embarrassed to put on such clothing, but Mike assured her that she looked very fashionable. What fashion? she wondered.

Dressing in privacy in the bathroom, she twisted her pale brown hair atop her head, hoping the few pins she had not lost in the flood the day before would hold its thickness. She stared at her small features in the looking glass. Her dark eyes were wide and frightened, her complexion pale, her full lips still cracked and dry. She found herself absurdly wishing her hated bonnet had not been ruined, for it would hide many of her flaws. Pinching her cheeks for color, she hurried from the room.

They breakfasted on cold milk and sweet grains that Mike poured from one of the boxes Abby had found. He called the food cereal, although it was nothing like oatmeal. Abby picked at the combination, for the milk tasted bland and thin.

They talked of what yesterday's rain would do for the plants and animals on the desert, and their early morning camaraderie gratified Abby. If only her dream had explained what had happened to her and where her family was, she might enjoy being here with this man. She had shared much with him in the brief time of their acquaintance—and even before. Surprisingly, his eyes smiled at her the whole time she ate. She sensed it had been a while since Mike Danziger had smiled at anything.

Linda O. Johnston

When they finished eating, he said, "Let's go buy you some clothes that fit better."

"Thank you," Abby said gratefully. Wishing to repay his hospitality in some small measure, she offered, "Can I help with the horses?"

"What do you mean?"

She had done it again, although by now she was getting used to his anger. "I was joking," she said, while wondering what bothered him about her question.

She found out minutes later, when they left the cabin for the other building she had seen. There was no horse inside. Instead it contained a strange contraption that Abby guessed was a conveyance. It was a large red metal box on wheels. A sign on its side said *Bronco*, but it was most certainly not an untamed horse. She did not want to approach it, but Mike opened a door for her. She had to step up. She felt nervous and confined when he closed the door behind her.

"Sorry," he called out. "I forgot my wallet. Be right back." He left her sitting alone in the metal box named Bronco.

Abby looked around, fingers nervously reaching beneath her chin for bonnet ribbons that were not there. On the panel before her were all sorts of dials and gadgets, but she was afraid to touch them, not knowing what they might do. She noticed a pile of papers on the floor behind the other seat and reached back to pick them up.

They were magazines but looked very different from the *Godey's Ladies Book* she had read back home. The covers were colorful—much brighter than the hand-painted hues *Godey's* sometimes employed. The magazines were named *Handyman* and *Do-It-Yourself*, and on their covers were shiny pictures of houses and furniture and people holding hammers.

And then Abby noticed the dates on the magazines. She stopped breathing. This could not be. The month was correct, she believed, though one lost track on a wagon train. But the year? Impossible! Yet the two magazines said the same thing: 1995.

Suddenly she felt terrified. Her heart hammered erratically as she gulped for breath. Tears sprang to her eyes, and she used her fingers to hurriedly wipe them away as the door opposite her opened.

Mike got in and sat beneath the large wheel. "Fasten your seat belt," he said, then looked at her. "Abby, are you all right?"

No, she was not. Maybe she had died at the fossil site, for that made more sense than that she was in a time more than 130 years in her future.

But she grabbed one arm with the opposite hand and squeezed. She felt solidity and pain. She must be alive. And crazy.

Pasting a smile on her face, she choked back her fear and said brightly, "I . . . I was interested in these magazines."

He shrugged, fighting a grin that gleamed with pride. "My hobby's making things. I built the cabin."

"Really?" She listened while he spoke lovingly of the furniture he constructed, the projects he

81

designed. She reacted with interest, trying not to let her preoccupation show. He lost her completely when he mentioned again his solar panels and electricity, but she gathered that they were what caused the lights to come on so swiftly and brightly. When he stopped speaking, she waited for a moment, then said, "Mike, I'm afraid I've lost track of the date."

He told her what it was—confirming that it was 1995. She stared at him, unsure what to do.

He leaned across her and pulled a strap away from the door. He placed it over her chest and her lap, and she felt trapped—trapped in this box named Bronco, and trapped in her own imagination. For surely that's what it was. She could not be in the future.

But it explained so much—the conveniences she had seen in Mike's cabin. Even this vehicle, for Mike put a key into a slot, turned it, and the thing made a growling sound—not unlike Abby's bird vision. It vibrated beneath her. Mike pulled a lever, and they started forward. Abby grabbed at the panel before her and one on the door.

They went along a gray, solid road that Abby had not noticed before. The speed they attained nearly at once seemed faster than any team of horses at a full gallop. She heard the sound of rushing wind outside, somehow oddly muted, and a soft whooshing from a breeze inside the strange carriage that cast a coolness over her despite the desert outside. Abby rode silently, drinking in all she saw, clutching at the handle on the door.

Her breathing quickened as she realized that what she viewed was the same expanse of desert she had first spotted upon reaching the end of the mountain pass. But instead of a barren stretch of sand and scrub, she saw—well, she was not certain what.

There were great metal skeletons stretching from horizon to horizon, strung together with more wires than any telegraph could ever need.

The gray road led to another, then more, and on each zoomed many other conveyances. Some looked much like the one she rode in, but there were some much smaller and still others that dwarfed it. No matter what their size, they all went at enormous speeds, and each contained people—so many people to be traveling through this barren wilderness! There were no horses, no wagons to be seen.

Farther on, Abby saw signs along the road that spoke of food where there was no inn offering sustenance. Bridges crossed atop their road at places labeled exits, and there were things in the sky—a bird traveling in a straight line much like the one she had visualized in her nighttime imagining, and the one she had seen last night.

Three smaller silvery birds flying beside each other rolled in unison over the desert. "I always enjoy watching Air Force jets practicing formations," Mike said, gesturing toward them, but she did not understand.

She said nothing as she watched everything with awe. The magazines must be correct. She must somehow—through the magic of the ancient fossils, perhaps—have reached the future.

But if she had been in the future during the storm, did that mean the rain had poured down only in this time? Might her dream have been true, and her family still be dying of thirst? She closed her eyes, praying for a vision, yet nothing came—nothing except increased worry.

Now and then she glanced at Mike and found him looking at her, his usual scowl shadowing his handsome face. Each time, she pasted on a smile but said nothing. A terrible—yet wonderful—thought had struck her. She had sensed Mike Danziger through the years. Their connection must transcend time. But what did it mean? She trusted in her special powers. Soon they would let her know. They had to.

Mike lifted one hand from the steering wheel to push his too-long hair off his brow. He was utterly perplexed. Who was Abby Wynne?

Last night, while they were stargazing, he'd had the incredible feeling that she was the other person in his weird hallucination of moving stars and shared emotions. The way she'd looked at him—he had the eerie sense she felt it, too. He should have asked, but he couldn't. He would seem crazy—but, if he sounded sane, he would feel even worse, for his perception might then be true. He had never believed in the supernatural, in ESP or any of that nonsense. He was not about to begin now.

But what was wrong with Abby? She'd seemed bewildered in the kitchen this morning, fiddling with the stove and peering into the refrigerator. She'd asked about some horses and had seemed intimidated about getting into his truck. Now she was looking all around, her dark eyes big and frightened as though she had never seen things as ordinary as cars and road signs and airplanes.

Had she escaped from a mental institution?

What he ought to do was take her to the police and dump her, let them figure out what her problem was.

Yet there was something about her. . . . He found her beautiful, even dressed in his old T-shirt and baggy jeans. Her valor yesterday had touched him—he knew of few women who would have survived an ordeal like the flood, let alone put it behind them without crying about it.

Yet she had cried. She'd had a nightmare last night, and had cried for her family. She claimed to have lost them in the desert. But what had really penetrated his defenses was the way she felt clutched against his chest. She was a tall woman, though still much shorter than he, and her slenderness had felt fragile as he held her. More than that, she seemed to belong there. Despite himself, he felt as though he knew her, as though he understood her sadness, as though he shared it.

No, he couldn't just dump her with the police. Of course, he would not lower his guard with her, for who knew if she had an ulterior motive for her strange behavior? But he'd help her find her family or wherever else she belonged.

And then? Then he would see if he could get her out of his mind.

*   *   *

On the other hand, Mike thought a while later, he at least deserved some answers.

Abby Wynne looked astounded as they reached the outskirts of Barstow. When traces of civilization—gas stations, restaurants, clumps of houses, and house trailers—began to appear in the distance, she leaned forward in her seat and grasped the dashboard as though holding on for dear life.

But she said not a word.

As traffic increased, her eyes grew even larger until she looked like a frightened, forlorn waif. And then there were her reactions after they pulled among the myriad automobiles in the parking lot of the huge, stucco manufacturers' outlet shopping center just outside Barstow. She seemed surprised at the beeping noise his car made when he pushed the button on his key chain. "Just turning on the car alarm," he said.

Her earlier fear seemed to change into delighted astonishment as he walked beside her to the outdoor mall area and began to point out all the stores she might consider for her shopping.

Before she made any decisions he took her hands and said, "What's going on, Abby?"

Those expressive brown eyes clouded over. "I honestly don't know, Mike."

"But . . . Look, maybe I'd better call the police, see if they can help you."

A look of terror flashed over her face, and she shook her head vehemently in the negative. "I am certain," she said, her voice quavering, "that at the appropriate time, I will find my family. May I go shopping now?"

He wanted to insist, but this was not the time or place. He wouldn't force any solution on her; he carried enough guilt over what he had done to a woman. He let her go.

In the space of an hour, Abby had come nearly to accept the incredible; she must be in the future. So much was changed from what she knew. This place was different from any she had ever seen before: so many vehicles similar to Mike's; so many people; so many shops filled with an incredible array of merchandise.

And the people. Women of this time, like men, wore hardly anything in the desert heat—short pants that revealed nearly every inch of their bare legs, tight shirts of the same material as hers, but even more revealing of every curve. Did they all have loose morals? She glanced at Mike, much taller and more handsome than any of the men she saw, but he was not paying attention to any other people. His gray, appraising eyes remained on her.

Flushing, she finally picked a store to walk into. It was as cold inside as the Bronco. And she was astonished. Each ready-made garment had a slip of stiff paper with the price attached, and the cost of one flimsy, sleeveless shirt was enough to feed her family for weeks.

Mike asked, "See anything you like?"

Embarrassed, she shook her head and walked out. She stopped on the sidewalk in front of the store and sat on a bench. She turned away when Mike sat beside her. "What's wrong?" His voice sounded so gentle that she almost began to cry.

"I . . . I have no money, Mike."

"I'll lend you some."

She felt a wave of despair. How could she obtain enough to repay him, even if she bought only essentials? "But I'll never—"

"Look, Abby. I don't like the fact you won't tell me who you are or why you're here. But I found you, and I know you're in trouble. Until I figure out what else to do with you, I'll make sure you're fed and clothed. Got it?"

"Thank you," she said in a tiny voice.

"There's just one thing I want in return."

She swallowed and looked away from him. "What's that?"

His insistent fingers turned her chin until she was staring him in the eye. "Honesty."

Of course she owed him that—but she herself did not know what was happening, except that she now appeared to be more than 130 years in the future. How wonderful it would be if she could trust him, if she could ask him questions about all she saw and experienced. But how could she tell him the truth? He hadn't even believed her when she mentioned the wagon train. If she now explained she had traveled from the past, he would think her insane. Perhaps he would send her away to an asylum.

Certainly, if he put her in the hands of the authorities, as he had suggested earlier, they would commit her to an institution.

She had seen through Mike Danziger's eyes, felt his pain across time. She must be here for a reason—one that had to do with him. So long as she was in this time, she had to stay with him. But how could she give him honesty?

They shopped for an hour, ducking inside cool shops to escape the heat outside. Abby learned much about women's fashions in the 1990s. There were undergarments she would never have imagined—including pretty, lacy things known as *bras* and stockings called *panty hose* that were made of a comfortable, stretchy, sheer material.

How Lucy would have loved them! But Abby tried not to think of Lucy or her father or Arlen— for, whether or not they had found their way across the desert, if her beliefs were true her loved ones were, by now, long dead. And Abby belonged with them . . . didn't she?

But how wonderful it would have been to belong here, where there were such things as instant light and water, fast cars, cold air in the desert, and . . . shopping for frivolous garments with Mike Danziger.

After much searching in several stores, she amassed several pieces of clothing that felt comfortable: long skirts, although their fabrics seemed more frilly than serviceable, and modest cotton blouses. Aghast at the prices, she nevertheless swallowed her pride and allowed Mike to purchase them for her.

He also bought her a pair of the blue jeans he favored, but in her size, plus several other blouses that, although of a more clingy material than she was used to, did not seem overly revealing. He bought her some strange but comfortably cushioned shoes called Nikes, plus a pair of leather shoes as pretty and light as slippers. And he bought her a flowing white nightgown with a high neck and long sleeves.

She wondered at the system of payment. No cash changed hands, but surely the small card Mike handed each shopkeeper, though the color of gold, had no barter value. Besides, it was handed back at each transaction. There certainly was much she did not understand in this time!

When their hands were filled with packages in bags of a thin, strong material she did not recognize, he asked, "Are you hungry?"

She realized she was; shopping and worry had made her famished.

They put their bundles into the Bronco, with its strange beeping sound each time Mike pushed a button. Then they walked a short distance in the desert heat—and Abby felt her jaw drop as she spied the low, pink stucco building with Spanish-style arches, for beside it was a large pink-and-white sign that said *Arlen's Kitchen*. She glanced at Mike. He grinned.

Arlen's Kitchen? Could he also have come here to the year 1995? Abby asked, "What is this place?"

"It's one of my restaurants," Mike said, pride filling his voice. "If you've never eaten in one, you're in for a treat."

"Does Arlen Danziger . . . does he serve food here?"

She enjoyed the way the corners of his eyes crinkled as he laughed, although she did not at first comprehend his humor. "Hardly. Arlen Danziger was an ancestor of mine. He lived sometime in the middle of the last century. He was a cook, and his recipes were passed down through my family."

Abby nearly tripped on the walkway as she swallowed a gasp. Here was a connection! Not only did they share the same last name and similar appearances: Arlen and Mike, despite being separated by several generations, were related.

Might this have something to do with why she was drawn to this time?

"How clever you were to use such an inherited gift," she said, striving to appear no more than politely interested. But her head throbbed as her thoughts spun like a wagon wheel behind a runaway team. How was she to learn her purpose here and how Mike's relationship with Arlen was involved? Especially since she dared not question Mike. Her merest suggestions of her arrival on a wagon train had agitated him.

She must have been successful in hiding her inner turmoil, for as he opened the glass door for her to enter, he continued, "Of course, people in those days didn't worry much about things like high calories or cholesterol. So I modernized the recipes, made them healthier. The idea caught on, and my chain now consists of nearly a hundred restaurants."

Abby walked inside, wondering about the meaning of *calories* and *cholesterol*. Whatever they were, Mike must have dealt with them in a most suitable fashion, for the place looked delightful and smelled heavenly—of spicy meats and warm molasses and good, strong coffee. There were tables all around covered with red-and-white-checked tablecloths. At the front was a counter where young men and women bustled about serving people who carried their food on trays to the tables and ate while sitting on wooden chairs.

Mike took Abby's elbow and led her to the counter. A young girl in a pink shirt and white skirt looked at them expectantly, her fingers poised over a machine similar to some in the clothing shops that tallied purchases. She had blond hair of a pale shade Abby had never seen before pulled back inside a little white cap. She wore enough face paint that Abby thought her father ought to take her home and scrub it off.

Mike asked, "What would you like?"

Before Abby was an expanse of polished metal—the kitchen. A sign describing the menu hung above. There were things like Arlen stews and meat pies and soups. Arlen Danziger had been most helpful to the settlers traveling west, spicing otherwise bland foods cooked hastily over open campfires. Could these really be the same dishes she knew? She decided on a veal stew. She loved the way Arlen had tossed in just a touch of salt pork for flavor.

The girl pushed colored spots on the machine

in front of her as Mike asked for drinks and a barbecue sandwich for himself. Mike paid her; then she grabbed foods from a shelf behind her and placed them on a tray.

When she was done, Mike did not pick up the tray. Instead he said, "The stew bowl's awfully small." He unwrapped the sandwich. "And there's not much meat on here."

The girl shrugged. "Sorry." She put napkins and spoons onto the tray, then smiled brightly. "Have a nice day," she said.

Mike asked, "Where are the johnnycakes?"

Abby smiled. Johnnycakes—the delightful confection Arlen had taught them to make on the trail, composed of cornmeal, water, and molasses—had become one of her favorite foods.

But the girl looked confused. "We stopped serving them a couple months ago, sir."

Mike frowned. "But that was a trademark of Arlen's Kitchens: free johnnycakes with every meal."

"Sorry," the girl said again.

Mike persisted. "Is it just this Arlen's Kitchen, or are none serving them now?"

"None. May I help you?" The girl had turned to the next customer in line.

Mike looked angry as he picked up the tray. "Let's find a seat," he grumbled.

The food was wonderful ! The stew tasted similar to Arlen's but better—richer and thicker, with spices Abby could not identify. She said, "This tastes . . . well, I've sampled similar foods, but the lightness and flavor of this is far superior. It's delicious!"

A pleased expression raised Mike's brows. "The lightness is because we try to be health conscious." He began to explain things Abby did not understand, about cooking in unsaturated fats and using only lean meats like chicken, veal, and turkey.

"Something like dealing with calories and cholesterol," Abby ventured, unsure whether her remark made her sound knowledgeable or brainless. It must have been the former, for he did not react.

Or perhaps that was because he still seemed preoccupied. He wolfed down his sandwich as though hungry, but he might have been eating its paper wrapping, for all the enjoyment he seemed to get.

To move his mind from whatever was bothering him—and to obtain information she needed—Abby asked Mike where water came from on the desert. He began a complicated explanation of reservoirs and aqueducts that Abby could barely follow. None provided a way to help her family if they had not had rain. "But aren't there areas where there's always water, even in a drought?"

He shrugged, and the movement caused a rippling of the dark hair touching his broad shoulders. "There are maps of rivers and lakes. I don't know if they always have water, but . . . if you're really interested, you can go back and see if the bookstore has anything." He soon excused himself. "I have to make a phone call," he said.

Abby nodded, as though she understood what a phone call meant. "I'll meet you in the bookstore," she told him.

"Here's some money." He handed her a piece of paper currency apparently worth 20 dollars. On it was a picture of Andrew Jackson, who had been president of the United States in the 1830s. She felt almost disappointed that the portrait was not of some statesman of the future of whom she had not heard.

After all, as long as she was in this time, why not learn all she could about what was to come?

Mike pulled a phone credit card from his wallet and placed his call. The female voice that answered "Arlen's Kitchens" didn't sound familiar, but she immediately put Mike through to Lowell Quadros, one of Mike's two closest friends and deputies in the running of Arlen's Kitchens.

"Mike, is it really you?"

He assured Lowell it was.

Lowell sounded delighted and relieved to hear from him. Ten years older than Mike, Lowell had been Mike's first employee at his first Arlen's Kitchen—a jack-of-all-trades who ran around as eagerly as Mike, cooking, cleaning, selling food, and fixing the myriad unforeseeable gremlins in every machine. They had grown close in those early days, and Mike had brought Lowell along as the restaurant had grown into two, then a chain. Lowell had little business acumen, but he took direction well and worked hard.

They chatted about one another's health for a few minutes; then Lowell asked, "How are you really, Mike?"

"Not bad—though I'm calling from a Barstow Arlen's Kitchen, and I wasn't pleased about a few things." He described the skimping on food and elimination of the johnnycakes.

There was a pause, and Lowell, his voice a little too bright, said, "Ruth just walked in. Why don't I put her on to explain?"

Mike heard muffled conversation; then Ruth Morgan, his other trusted assistant, said enthusiastically, "Mike! How wonderful to hear from you. Are you okay? When are you coming back?" She paused for an instant. "We miss you."

"Thanks," Mike said with a brief smile. He pictured the petite whirlwind he had hired six years earlier straight out of business school. With Ruth's brains and Lowell's devotedness, he'd no problem leaving Arlen's Kitchens for his desert sabbatical.

Of course, he had also thought he would not mind if they ran it into the ground—but now that he'd seen the changes they'd made, he wasn't so sure.

He exchanged pleasantries with Ruth, then asked about business. Her voice hardly changed, but he heard her hesitation. He mentioned the reduced portions and lack of johnnycakes. "Everything's fine, Mike," she said. "You just feel better and come home soon, okay?"

The anger and frustration he'd felt since arriving at the Arlen's Kitchen boiled over. "Everything's *not* fine! The place is falling apart. Corners being cut, curtness to customers . . . Look, I'll be in the office tomorrow. I'll want to learn exactly what's going on. Make sure Lowell and you are both available." He slammed down the receiver.

Stalking out in a rage, he set out after Abby.

He found her in the bookstore. Her arms were filled with maps, and she was looking at a newspaper with an expression of awe on her face. He was surprised to find his ill temper soften. She was so lovely—yet she acted so strange, like an alien dropped from outer space, if he believed in such things. He wanted answers from her, but he knew better. In his experience, women and the truth went together like sticky-fingered employees and profits.

What would he do with Abby when he returned to L.A.? He should leave her with the Barstow police. But despite his mistrust of her, he would worry about her. Somehow he did not want her just to disappear from his life.

He wondered what she would think of L.A.

He was so distracted by his own thoughts as they reached the Bronco that he failed to turn off the alarm before opening the door. An awful sirenlike sound filled the air till he pushed the right button. "Sorry," he muttered. Abby looked unnerved but said nothing.

She remained quiet on their drive back to the cabin, which was fine with Mike; he had a lot on his mind after his visit to the restaurant.

Still, he kept glancing at her. He enjoyed

watching her profile, the way her soft brow crinkled in concentration as she studied her new maps. He was glad she'd left her hair loose that day. Its golden brown length cascaded long past her shoulders. She was a lovely woman, with a pert nose, well-defined chin, and high cheekbones. Surprisingly she wore no makeup and hadn't asked to buy some. Not that she needed any, but didn't most women feel naked without it?

Her winsome brown eyes were often, illogically, as wonder-filled as a child's at Christmas. But at the moment, the sights outside the window seemed no longer to inspire her awestruck attention.

When he turned on the radio, she jumped beside him, her eyes wide and her lower lip trembling. "The music," she whispered.

"You don't like rock?" He turned on an easy-listening station, shaking his head at her odd reaction.

When they reached the cabin, she seemed preoccupied. "Thank you for everything, Mike," she said in her soft, lilting voice. Her arms were filled with the bags and boxes of things they had bought that day.

"You're welcome." He left her in the cabin while he went out to his workshop behind it. He needed to immerse himself in his latest project instead of dwelling on his thoughts.

Much later, after nearly completing a new table, he emerged. Darkness was falling, and he was pleased that Abby had fixed dinner: chicken salad sandwiches.

She said, "I hope you do not mind, but I heard noises and looked in on you. The work you do is wonderful!"

"It's a hobby," he said self-deprecatingly, though he found himself beaming. She seemed interested as he described other projects he'd undertaken over the years.

After they had jointly cleaned the dinner dishes, he asked, "Would you like a nightcap?"

She looked confused.

"It's a drink before bedtime," he explained patiently.

"Thank you, but no," she said. She excused herself and went off to the bedroom.

He felt deflated to lose her company; the evening had barely begun. He helped himself to a nightcap. A double.

Later he went outside to look at the stars. He felt the weight of responsibility crushing him like the pressure at the bottom of the ocean, and he needed something to lift his spirits.

He needed Abby.

The idea both scared and intrigued him. Last evening, he had felt almost awestruck by a recurrence of that sensation of sharing someone else's emotions; it seemed magnified by Abby's presence. Somehow it seemed to emanate from her, and he had the sense she felt it, too.

Not that he believed in nonphysical connections between people. He left that to the crazy or naive.

But being with Abby in the wash yesterday and staring at the stars last night had somehow left him with the craziness of unwarranted hope, with the naivete of reborn optimism.

That night, though, he watched the stars alone, for she did not join him.

In the morning, when he woke up, he sprang from bed, finding himself unwillingly eager for her company.

But when he went into the bedroom to awaken her for their trip home, she was gone.

Chapter Five

Holding her skirt above the tops of her boots, Abby watched the sky as she hurried along the twisting wash, but no cloud was to be seen. The water had receded, and the ground had dried beneath the baking desert sun except for puddles in pits and ditches.

Making sure Mike was still asleep, she had left his cabin silently half an hour earlier, having chosen from the clothing she'd acquired the garments most similar to those of her own time: a long pastel skirt and cotton blouse. Her hair was bound up in a bun beneath her still-drooping bonnet.

Her new maps in her hands, she hastened toward the fossil site to try to return to her time. The maps told where water might be found. Perhaps she had been sent here to rescue her family and not for any reason connected with Mike Danziger, despite her special sense telling her otherwise. After her bewildering dream two nights ago, she could not be certain the storm had saved her loved ones. And they came first, no matter how sorry she would be never to see Mike again.

Her steps slowed before she got far. She looked up and saw the rock Mike and she had hidden behind during the flood.

Her eyes closed. She sank slowly to her knees. She had a sensation once again of feeling another's emotions—Mike's. He was hurrying after her; he knew where she was going, if not why. And he was upset.

What was more, she wanted to be with him, to soothe his ever-present anger, to tell him she would stay with him. But she had to make certain the emigrants had found water.

Her eyes did not open, but suddenly she saw the ground shift and shimmer. Before her was the wagon train. It was moving, and she heard the squealing of corroded wagon-frame metal against metal, the protests of animals roused from rest. Her family no longer waited for her.

Abby asked her vision, "Did you find water? Will you be all right?"

The wagons continued forward, and Abby saw Lucy driving one with four oxen, her sad eyes anxiously sweeping the trail. As Abby watched, Arlen rode up on horseback and passed her a canteen, and she took a long drink of water.

Water! They had been saved.

She wondered who drove Arlen's team. Lucy and she had often helped when his duties required that he ride ahead, but that was before their father's illness and Abby's disappearance. Abby pursed her lips. Perhaps pushy Emmaline Woolcott was using this way to be noticed by Arlen.

The wagons of her vision passed the spot where Abby stood. In a moment, all she could see was the cloud of sand they had kicked up. The gritty taste lingered in her mouth.

Now she knew her family did not need her. More important, she was suddenly certain that she was not to leave the future until her task here was fulfilled. But first she needed to learn why she had been drawn through the years to this time—to Mike Danziger.

She opened her eyes and smiled as he raced around the bend in the wash she had just passed.

"Abby!" he called, then stopped.

His face had been twisted in a mask resembling anguish, even more gaunt as the hollows in his cheeks deepened, and for just a moment she sensed the vulnerability and loneliness in him that made her want to reach out to him.

But after he saw her, his face changed, lightening for a brief moment, then tightening into a frown of anger. He rushed toward her, storming, "Abby, why the devil did you . . . ?" Only then did he seem to notice that she knelt on the ground. "Are you hurt?" His voice seemed taut with concern as he fell to his knees beside her.

She shook her head while his eyes assessed her as though looking for an injury. She smelled the slightly salty, pleasantly masculine scent of him and noted the perspiration on his brow; he must have run the entire way from his cabin. "I am fine, Mike. I just—"

He grabbed her shoulders with hands as strong as cold iron, and she stopped speaking. Scowling with unchecked fury, he yelled, "Damn it! What do you think you're doing, running off like that?"

Then, quite suddenly, she was in his arms.

He held her tightly against his powerful, tense body, and she felt his chest heave from his prior exertion. He kissed her forehead, her cheek— and then he found her mouth.

A quiver of shock and delight swept through her as, with scant deliberation, she rejected the idea of thrusting him away.

She had no excuse now as she had above the flooded wash, when surely relief and the intensity of the moment had led to his taking such liberties. And to her allowing them—no, participating with such surprising abandon in them.

Now she reveled in the feel of his hot, searching lips against hers. There was no gentleness in his kiss. Pulling the pins from her hair, he buried his hands in the loosened cascade, holding her fast. He seemed to want to punish her for his hurt and fear. With only a fleeting thought for her brazen boldness, she did not hesitate in returning the pressure, reveling in the feel of his tongue thrusting audaciously against hers. She reached up, her fingers catching in the dark waves of the hair at his neck.

Here—for now, at least—was where she belonged.

Mike drew back. He hadn't intended to take Abby into his arms, but he had been inexplicably angry when he realized she was gone, then so relieved to find her that he'd momentarily lost control.

He'd begun by wanting to shake some sense into her, but when he'd touched her, the feel of her lithe body against him had set his libido on fire. She smelled of cinnamon and flowers, here on the plant-sparse desert. She tasted of something sweet, yet enticingly exotic. Her pale brown hair, captured in his hands, was soft, silken fire. He wasn't sure whether he regretted more the fact that he'd kissed her—or that he'd let her go. Was she upset about his embrace, angry that he'd followed her?

So what if she was? She could have died out here alone. She should be grateful he'd bothered to come for her. Ready to shout at her again if she dared to complain, he looked down into Abby's dark, luminous eyes.

Far from seeming angry, they shone with . . . could it be happiness? Then why had she run away? He had to know.

"What's going on, Abby? Why did you leave?" His voice was stern, though he felt a quaver of emotion in it. Rage, of course. He'd sworn off caring for anyone.

"I cannot explain, Mike," she said in a regretful tone. "Not if you want honesty. But I can tell you one thing truthfully."

"What's that?" he growled, even more angry

that she was adding to the list of secrets she refused to tell.

"I want to go back with you now." Her hand slipped into the crook of his arm.

He felt astonished at how compliant he was as he allowed her to lead him back toward his cabin.

Later that morning, they were on the road speeding toward Los Angeles. Abby had kept on her skirt and blouse but had traded her boots for her lighter shoes. Her hair was still comfortably loose about her shoulders.

She had thought she was used to riding on those well-traveled roads Mike referred to as freeways, but the vehicles he'd called cars and trucks multiplied, without reducing speed, as the width of the flat and smooth gray path increased. She tried not to grip the Bronco's door handle, but she had to make a decided effort as other conveyances zoomed by, sometimes seeming to come within inches.

The scenery changed. They passed from open desert into the mountains, and Abby marveled that the Bronco, unlike the horse for which it was named, did not lose power as it sped over rises and curves. What a wonderful way to get from one place to another! She thought of her family on the wagon train and sighed. They might have gotten safely on their way—but certainly their passage was not a modicum as easy as this.

Mike glanced at her, and she gave a bright

smile. His studiously blank expression did not change, and she sighed, wishing she could read his mind at will. At least he acted cordial even if he seldom smiled. Neither mentioned that morning in the wash.

He had changed from his usual T-shirt and jeans into dark trousers and a pale blue shirt whose top buttons were open enough to reveal some of the solid chest that had been so comforting two nights before. Breaking the silence, he said, "We'll be going over the Cajon Pass soon, then bypassing San Bernardino. L.A.'s about an hour beyond that."

A trip of only an hour! By wagon train, it would take days by the same route that Arlen had described in detail to her several weeks—and many decades—earlier. This time in which she found herself was full of miraculous surprises.

"How long have you lived in . . . L.A., Mike?" She hesitated over the initials that she assumed stood for the town of Los Angeles.

"About fifteen years. I came out here for college—UCLA—and stayed, thanks to the scheming of a relative."

He grinned, so Abby knew that the scheming he spoke of did not vex him. He had used more initials. People in this time must consider themselves too busy to speak out full words, she thought. She did not ask what *UCLA* stood for; he had spoken as though everyone would know. She said lightly instead, "And what evil plan was that?"

"My great-aunt Myra was a cunning old soul,"

he said, a fond expression softening his gray
eyes. "She was sweet, but with the sharpness of
broken glass and talons of a falcon. She wove a
spell around me with stories I couldn't forget, so
I never wanted to leave, just as she planned.
While I was in school, I did many a repair on the
old home she lived in with my other great-aunt
Jess."

"Aunt Myra sounds like quite the conniver. Do
you still take care of their house?"

A shadow darkened his face. His voice was
thick with emotion. "Now I pay to have it re-
paired. Poor Jess wouldn't know the difference
between hired fixes and the TLC of someone
who's concerned, and we lost Myra six years
ago."

"I'm sorry," Abby said softly, guessing that
TLC—still more initials!—was something good.
"What stories did she tell that enchanted you so?"

"I don't want to talk about them now." The
darkness had turned into his usual blank un-
readability, and he said nothing more. Still, Abby
sensed a pang of loneliness and regret that could
only have come from deep inside him.

He turned on the machine he called a radio,
and music poured forth. Abby reveled in the delightful sound—and the way people who spoke
between songs seemed as excited as she to discover the wonders of modern cold remedies,
bank loans that made one rich, and something
called *mouthwash* that sounded like a love po-
tion. To think that such miracles should be available to everyone!

As they began their descent on the other side of the mountain, Abby saw a smattering of buildings and houses despite the greenery and walls that created barriers at the sides of the freeway. Roadside placards grew in density, and the number of exits from the freeway also increased. Then there were more buildings and less unoccupied land. Towns much larger than Barstow melted into one another. So many people!

Abby's uneasiness began as a tingling in the small of her back as they passed signs for a town called Colton.

Sometimes she had a similar sensation when about to have a vision, so she closed her eyes and waited. Two in one day? That had never before happened. But no vision came. Instead, teeny, painful pinpricks began to creep up her spine— prickles of anticipation and dread.

The closer the Bronco drew to Los Angeles, the stronger the sensation became.

More than once, Abby had to steady herself to keep from shivering. In the past, she had dreaded her visions. Now she wished for one to relieve the otherwise unmitigated sense of foreboding that filled her. But nothing happened.

Nothing except the growing intensity of her feeling.

She glanced often at Mike. The impassive expression on his well-defined features did not change. He apparently felt nothing, so there must not be a universally disturbing aura about the city. That meant her special sense was alerting her to . . . what? She did not know. Her only certainty was that it involved Mike and the connection that had drawn her to him through the years.

Was he the cause? Abby hated to think so, yet maybe she was here to keep him from committing some horrible act. She had, after all, had a piercing premonition of danger when she first met him. She would have to wait and see.

In any event, without having been there in her life, Abby was already frightened of Los Angeles.

Mike noticed Abby's look of concern when he cut onto the 210 Freeway, even though the sign over the 10 Freeway said *Los Angeles*. "I want to go through Pasadena," he explained. "It's out of the way, but I want to stop at one of my oldest Arlen's Kitchens before we get to the office." She nodded, but he believed he could have gotten the same noncommittal, dazed reaction if he'd said the route was quicker via the moon.

This woman was such an enigma! He recognized her emotions from the expressions on her face without understanding their rationale, and she asked questions without answering any. Why had she run away to the wash that morning, then appeared so happy to see him?

Now she stared wide-eyed at the most mundane things—signs and streetlights, gasoline stations, even graffiti. He could understand her awed reaction to the mushrooming density of traffic; he'd never gotten used to L.A. driving, even after enduring it for years. But how had she made it across the country from her Pennsylvania home without losing her ingenuous wonder at the usual roadside scenery?

She'd claimed she wasn't Amish. But he had come up with no better explanation—unless she was crazy. Or playing a game he had yet to figure out.

A while ago, her wonder had inexplicably seemed to turn to fear as she blinked rapidly and bit her lip. He'd seen nothing to cause her reaction, but nevertheless, since then, he'd been fighting off an unwanted urge to take her into his arms and comfort her.

His shoulders stiffened suddenly. Who was he to comfort anyone?

And why all the mystery with this damsel in distress? She must want something from him. He just wished she'd come out with it.

But he'd play the game her way for now. He wouldn't ask. Just to make conversation, he inquired coolly, "When was the last time you were in L.A.?"

"I've never been there," she said.

He glanced at her in surprise. "What made you decide to move out here?"

"My family heard of opportunities not available in the East."

"But to come without visiting first . . . ?"

"Some friends who had come wrote letters encouraging us. We sold what we could, packed the rest, and started off."

"That's brave," Mike said. Or foolish, he thought. A lot of people hated L.A. at first sight.

She shrugged, an unfathomable smile on her

face. If only he could get her to say what was really on her mind. Better yet, he should toss her out of his life before she wreaked any more havoc with the nice, controlled existence he'd built over the past months.

But he would not do that. Instead he realized he wanted to learn all there was to know about Abby Wynne.

By the time the freeway signs said Arcadia, Mike felt hungry, glad he was heading for another Arlen's Kitchen. He maneuvered toward an exit.

The restaurant was located on Colorado Boulevard, the main street of trendy Old Town Pasadena. Abby stared at the aging buildings much as she had at the Barstow shopping center. Mike sighed quietly in frustration. What the heck was she thinking?

He parked in a space along the street, shaking his head at the way Abby glanced at him when the beep setting the car alarm sounded, and stared with fascination as he fed the parking meter.

This Arlen's Kitchen looked, of course, very much like the one they'd visited the day before. Despite the brick and plaster facade that blended this building with the rest of Old Pasadena, standardization was a key to the restaurant chain's success. Each sported the Arlen's Kitchens logo with its neat, old-fashioned script letters on signs and walls and on paper cups, plates, and bowls; each shared the same color scheme of pink, red, and white.

But there was something about this one. . . . Mike hesitated outside as he recognized the problem. Paper plates and cups strewed the ground outside, and nearly half the homey tables inside were covered with trays and trash.

Abby helped him pick up the worst of the litter and deposit it into a nearly overflowing trash can, then followed him inside as he approached the counter. There was a paper napkin dispenser beside the cash register yawning open and empty, and Mike scowled as he asked for the restaurant's manager.

In a moment, a corpulent middle-aged man in a pink shirt hustled from deep inside the kitchen, a broad smile revealing a set of large, uneven teeth.

"Jose!" Mike stepped forward, pumping the man's damp hand. He was delighted to see a familiar face—albeit with deeper creases at the forehead and mouth than Mike remembered. But he hadn't visited here for months.

Jose had been his first independent manager. Like Lowell, he had gone through many of Arlen's Kitchens' growing pains with Mike. He was loyal and, always before, had been conscientious. "Good to see you, Michael," Jose said, sincerity lowering the normal tenor tone of his voice. "In fact, I can't begin to tell you how good it is that you're back." He paused. "You are back, aren't you?"

Mike hesitated for only a moment. "Yes. But, Jose, what's going on?" Gently he pointed out the dirty tables and missing napkins.

"Oh, dear. A minute, please." He dashed back into the kitchen, emerging with a box of napkins. As he spoke, he refilled the dispenser. "I'm sorry, Mike, but I've had to let a lot of help go in the past months, thanks to the big economy drive at the home office."

"I see," Mike said untruthfully. "Jose, what happened?"

Jose's gaze dropped so that he seemed to study the way his belly hung over his belt. "A disaster. A couple months ago, Lowell and Ruth sent out instructions. All managers were to start a new line of gourmet foods and desserts. Gourmet, in a family fast-food restaurant!"

Mike was astounded. "What? Where did that come from?"

The heavy shoulders lifted in a shrug. "Who knows? But it required extra equipment, and we had to move things around to make room when the home office delivered it. All us managers tried to tell them it wouldn't work. But we were given our orders."

Mike's anger welled up inside. Why on earth would Lowell and Ruth do such a ridiculous thing? "And?"

"It didn't work. Customers stuck with the old favorites. So the equipment was repossessed in only a few weeks. Then there were the cutbacks ordered to pay for the mess."

"Thanks for telling me." Keeping his breathing as even as possible to hide his rage, Mike hesitated. "No johnnycakes at all now?"

Jose's large head shook mournfully. "Too expensive to give away, and customers didn't want to pay for something they once got for free."

Mike gritted his teeth as Jose ran back into the kitchen. No sense killing the messenger.

As Mike ordered from a young girl at the counter, Jose emerged with cleaning equipment and began clearing the tables. When Abby and Mike were served, Mike paid, then stomped with their tray toward an empty table devoid of the usual condiment caddy.

Abby ate in silence, regarding him with a thoughtful expression. Mike's temper itched to explode.

What had happened to the people he'd thought he could trust?

He should have known better, of course. He could trust no one.

Least of all himself.

Abby was pensive—and frightened. She worried about Mike; the constant anger she had sensed in the desert now seemed multiplied a hundredfold. Might he enrage himself into apoplexy? He seemed so empty, except for his rage. So isolated. So alone.

When they returned to the Bronco, she waited for the terrible noise she had heard in Barstow, but there was only a single note. "I remembered to turn off the alarm this time," he muttered with a glance at her. The air here was cooler than in the desert, but it smelled rancid, although Mike seemed not to notice. Soon they were moving again. And immediately her uneasiness grew stronger.

She tried to close her eyes, ignoring the squeezing in her chest. There had been many times after her family began its trek west that she wished they had stayed home; the rigors of life on the trail had sometimes been unbearable. But now she felt a deep nostalgia for the wagon train.

Avoiding Mike's glance, she gasped aloud when she saw how tall some of the buildings were as they got back on the freeway in Pasadena. There were others even higher in the area called Glendale. Nearly all seemed like windowed boxes compared with the opulent splendor of the structures of her time. Did people live in them? Work in them? Maybe they were towns in themselves. And no matter how many buildings, tall and short, they passed, there always were more beyond.

Was this city infinite? At this speed, Mike and she had certainly covered a long distance, yet a seemingly endless expanse of freeway extended before them.

And with each passing mile, each new moment, Abby's anxiety intensified.

If only she could reveal her nervousness to Mike, could trust him and share with him, she would doubtless feel better. But even if there was an inexplicable bond between them, he was incomprehensible. Certainly an eating area should be clean; even on the trail they had made an attempt at neatness. But did clutter justify such rage?

116

After a while, though, he began talking conversationally, confusing her. How had his anger dissipated so quickly?

Or had it?

"The offices are in Beverly Hills," he said, as though certain she knew where that was. "Aunt Myra pushed me into it soon as I'd a little success, though my first space was tiny. Myra thought panache was everything."

Panache? Abby took a guess at what that meant and nodded. "Sometimes an appearance of confidence is as important as truly feeling it." She had learned that as a healer; if she acted certain of a cure, it was more likely to work.

He turned to her, his eyes like hard granite. "I don't give a damn for appearance," he said coldly.

Abby swallowed hard, brushing her unbound hair away from her face; once more she had triggered his irritation and as usual did not know why. Again he became quiet. The thrust of his broad jaw and deepening of the hollows at his cheeks indicated that he had retreated yet again into his disquieting thoughts, and Abby longed to smooth the uneasy wrinkles on his forehead, take away whatever hurt pierced him so cruelly.

She soon understood why the words *Beverly Hills* would have meaning to anyone who knew of it. Buildings and hotels in this area were sometimes 20 or more stories tall. People here strolled self-confidently on sidewalks, many in clothing much like Mike had worn on the desert: both men and women in Levi's and clinging shirts Mike called T-shirts. On some women, the tightness of such clinging material seemed shameless. Abby touched the soft pastel folds at her side. A few women wore skirts, although hardly any of lengths that matched hers; still, there were enough to allow her to hope she did not appear entirely inappropriate to the people in this time.

She stared as they passed stores with windows that had few, but lovely, goods displayed in them. Mike said, "This is Rodeo Drive. You've heard of it, of course."

"Of course," Abby lied, not looking at him.

"It's all true—you can find designer clothes, furniture, even food here, with enormous price tags to match."

Mike hadn't even blinked at the cost of articles in Barstow. For him to comment on these, they must be high indeed!

The Bronco stopped often at street corners. Abby noticed that here, on city avenues, Mike always halted when a red light appeared on a contraption hanging over the road and started when the light was replaced by a green one. She did not understand what the yellow light meant; he alternately slowed, stopped, or raced forward.

Their lack of speed after the previous quickness of this car created a tight ball of tension inside Abby. She reached nervously, as she often did, for the ribbons of her bonnet—which now, of course, was missing. She dropped her hands back to her lap.

She found it impossible to ignore her uneasiness here. She wished she understood its source, but all she could think of was that it involved the tense, angry man beside her. But what danger might lurk in these dignified surroundings?

Mike's office was in a building along a large thoroughfare called Wilshire Boulevard. He directed the Bronco into an opening beneath the building and stopped. From a pile of clothing on the seat behind him, he took a necktie, similar to ones Abby had seen in shops in Barstow. She felt sorry to see him button the top of his shirt, for the hint of chest was no longer visible. He put the band of material about his neck, tying a deft knot without benefit of a looking glass. Then he turned to draw from the stack a jacket that he also put on. Running fingers through his long and thick brown hair as though to comb it, he instead tousled it winsomely.

Giving his key to an attendant, he led Abby to a row of doors. The odor in the air here was even worse than in Pasadena. When Mike pushed a small card into a slot, one door opened into a tiny room. Abby felt terribly confined when the door closed behind them—particularly when Mike pushed a button marked *12* and the room began to move!

Abby had promised herself not to react to anything new in this time—not while with Mike, at least—but could not help clutching in terror at the wall of the moving room.

"You should have told me you get claustrophobic in an elevator." He sounded exasperated.

"An . . . elevator?" Elevate, Abby thought. That

meant to ascend. This room must rise to take people to the top of this high building. She had read in her time of a similar invention to carry equipment in large cities. Perhaps all the tall structures she saw now had similar conveyances. Taking a deep breath, she forced herself to relax, but it was difficult. How high was she? And this room was moving so fast!

For a moment all sound seemed muffled, until somewhere inside her ears, there was a small popping sensation. Afterward the noise of the elevator seemed more intense.

At last the door opened, and Abby found herself looking at a carpeted hallway. Across the way was a large wooden door marked *Arlen's Kitchens* Mike held the elevator door open, then ushered her into the Arlen's Kitchens office.

A bored-looking young lady with short, curly hair sat inside a cubicle filled with gadgetry whose uses Abby could not begin to guess. The young lady said, "May I help you?"

"You're new here," Mike said. "I'm Mike Danziger."

She stood abruptly, obviously flustered. She wore a very short, very colorful dress that contrasted with Abby's long pastel attire. Abby felt a new wave of insecurity flutter through her. Perhaps she did, after all, appear odd to the people of this time.

"Oh, Mr. Danziger," the woman said. "It's wonderful to meet you. I'm the new receptionist, Lydia Jones. Shall I call Mr. Quadros or Ms. Morgan?"

"No need to call Mr. Quadros. Mike!" A short, wiry man walked through a door, hurrying forward to shake Mike's hand. He was middle-aged, with a receding hairline and small spectacles perched on the end of his nose. He wore trousers, a jacket and necktie much like Mike's, and shiny, decorative leather shoes. He maneuvered his spectacles up his nose by a grimace that puffed his cheeks. "So glad you're back. And Ruth will be ecstatic."

"She certainly is!" A small woman perhaps five years older than Abby rushed into Mike's arms. She looked as though she belonged in this place called Beverly Hills, with her white wool dress and flowing scarf and painted nails. Her swaying silver ear ornaments hung below the ends of her short auburn hair that had no strand out of place. When she pulled back, she examined him critically. "Your hair is so long! It looks great." Abby could see a moistness in blue eyes adorned with the face paint used so attractively by women in this time, and she looked at Mike with such emotion that Abby was certain she loved him.

Abby glanced at Mike, but he appeared oblivious of Ruth's emotion. "Great to see you all," he said. He introduced Abby, and she winced from Ruth's curious, antagonistic glare. "Feel free to call anyone you want," he told Abby.

Did he mean call *on*? But she knew no one in this time. "Thank you," she said politely.

He took her aside. "We could contact the L.A. police to try to find your family."

"I believe not," she said, feeling both sorrowful

121

and a trifle panicky. She needed to stay with Mike to determine her purpose here, to find an answer to her uneasiness. Was he about to send her away? She had, in fact, been imposing upon his hospitality. Girding herself for a hurtful response, she lifted her chin and said, "I shall, of course, leave now. You have been most kind, but I cannot—"

"Do you have someplace else to go?" His gray eyes pinned her with a gaze that made her feel he knew all her thoughts, and she tried unsuccessfully to turn away.

Ignoring the frightened lump in her throat, she said, "That does not matter."

"Of course it does. Have Lydia get you some coffee; I won't be long." He turned to his employees. "Now, let's get to work."

Her knees folding beneath her in relief, Abby sat in the reception area with Lydia. Mike was not sending her away! She could remain with him for now. Perhaps even until she discovered and fulfilled her purpose here.

Nevertheless, she realized after a while that, for the moment, he had forgotten her. He was closeted with his employees for quite a long time.

But she had not forgotten him—nor the strong sense of disquiet still churning inside her. Certainly anyone traveling to a new time, particularly with the strain of trying not to reveal where she was from, would feel strange, but this sense went much further. She was sure it emanated from her special powers.

122

Despite her agitation, she hoped that what Mike was learning would calm him, for Mike Danziger was a troubled man.

The receptionist, Lydia, was petite and lively, with sparkling blue eyes. Abby asked her as many questions as she gracefully could about how someone wanting to know about a small item in history—something like a single wagon train— might find all she could about it.

"Try the Beverly Hills Library," Lydia recommended in her high, breathy voice as she placed the tips of her long fingernails pensively on her chin. "The best general library around, though, is the beautiful old downtown branch of the L.A. library. The place nearly burned down a few years back, but it's been rebuilt, though a lot of the books they saved were water damaged." She squinted as though deep in thought. "For info on the Old West, you could talk to a history professor at UCLA"—those initials again!—"or even somebody at the Gene Autry Western Heritage Museum. That's in Griffith Park, near the zoo."

Abby took notes on a pad of paper with a slender, blot-free pen, wondering how she would find these places—and how she would roam this large town by herself. She could not drive Mike's Bronco the way she did a horse, but people here seemed to rely on their cars.

Suddenly there was a loud ringing. Abby looked around, wondering about its source, for she saw no bells.

Lydia lifted a beige object from her desk and held it against her head. "Good morning, Arlen's

Kitchens. Mr. Quadros is in a meeting. Can I take a message?" She wrote something on a piece of pink paper. "Thanks for calling." She put the object down.

Abby searched for a way to learn what the object was without sounding stupid. She pointed to it. "I've never seen one of those quite like that."

Lydia looked startled. "This phone? It's nothing unusual. Can't say much for the quality, but people calling never complain about how I sound."

"Do people 'call' you from outside this office?"

Lydia's brows lowered in a puzzled frown. "Sure, from all over the world."

Abby tried to assimilate this. People used "phones" to call one another, all over the world. Perhaps it was similar to a telegraph, except people could use it to talk to one another. Amazing!

Then there was a large, humming object on Lydia's desk. She called it a *computer*, and it performed remarkable functions, allowing the receptionist to place words upon it that later magically appeared on paper.

Abby chatted with Lydia between calls. She learned about modern fashion and that the use of face paint, called *makeup*, though common, was a matter of choice. She did not, however, grasp the difference between rock, pop, and rap music, nor what the meaning was of something called movies. Still, what a fascinating era she had traveled to!

Mike had been closeted with Ruth and Lowell for over an hour when the outside door opened.

A man a few years younger than Mike stalked in. Dressed in Levi's and T-shirt, he scowled as fiercely as Mike ever did—although the expression on his fleshy face seemed more deranged than sorrowful. Not even glancing at Abby, he asked Lydia, "Is he here?"

Lydia looked confused. "Sorry, sir?"

He said with exaggerated slowness, "I'm Philip Rousseau, Mike's brother-in-law. I heard he was back in town. Is he here?"

Mike's brother-in-law. He was married. Abby's heart sank, though she should not be surprised. Mike was a very appealing man.

Although perhaps this man instead was a brother-in-law because of being married to Mike's sister . . . ? Abby dared to hope.

"He's in a meeting," Lydia said. "Would you care to—"

Philip Rousseau pushed past Abby and into the offices. Knowing the man would cause trouble, Abby followed.

Mike was seated behind a desk in a large office decorated with lots of glass and a silvery metal table, with Lowell and Ruth in chairs facing him. Mike stood as Philip barged in. His face drained of color, and Abby, her mind suddenly filling with Mike's emotions, felt as though she had been struck in the stomach. She grabbed the wall and hung on.

"So you're finally showing your face," Philip snarled. "If you think you're just going to forget my sister's death, pretend you didn't murder her, you're damned wrong."

I'm just damned. Abby did not hear the words but felt them throb through Mike's head. She knew then that Mike had been married to this man's sister, his wife was dead, and this man claimed Mike had murdered her. Could it be true? If so, surely she would sense the evil in him—wouldn't she?

Or had she? Had that been the reason for her stabbing premonition of danger upon first seeing him?

Whatever had happened, Mike was clearly tormented by it. This, perhaps, was the source of his anger, his fear, his terrible loneliness.

The other people in the room approached Philip Rousseau. Lowell's voice was soothing, Ruth's threatening. Philip looked at them both as though they were cockroaches unworthy of notice. But then Mike held part of the phone to his ear and pushed a few buttons. "Security? This is Mike Danziger in the penthouse. We've got a little trouble." He said to Philip, "You have three minutes. Speak your piece or leave."

As furious as he had looked before, Philip Rousseau now appeared murderous. "You killed Dixie, then cheated me out of her money. Well, this isn't over, Danziger," he said. "Not by a long shot."

As Philip swept from the room, Abby heard Mike whisper in a broken voice, "It'll never be over."

Abby turned toward him. He leaned on his desk, his face in his hands, and again she felt his pain. He must have loved his wife very much, she thought. A wave of sadness and longing swept through her, so intense that she swayed on her feet. Mike looked up, his surprised, reddened eyes meeting hers.

Abby flushed. She had forgotten that he might read her emotions, too. She tried to appear sympathetic yet detached. But inside, she wondered at the way this man affected her.

Mike sat behind his desk. Across from him was Abby, ignored by his employees, who spoke in low tones to one another. He leaned his head back and rubbed his eyes. Where was his numbness? He had worked so long at cultivating it, he had thought he could call it up at will. But now he felt suffocated by pain.

He looked at Abby. Her dark brown eyes were soft as they regarded him. Surely his odd sensation of a few moments before was his imagination. He had thought he felt a pang of sadness and need emanating from her. But the feeling passed quickly. Now his agony seemed eased just a little from her lovely, calming presence.

But she couldn't help him. No one could, and the last thing he needed right now was the burden of figuring out the enigma of Abby.

He had thought he no longer cared about Arlen's Kitchens. But, oh, how mistaken he had been. He had sat there listening to Lowell and Ruth try to explain that ridiculous gourmet food idea. Oh, he couldn't completely blame them. He hadn't told them *not* to try something new. But the old way worked just fine.

Then Philip had barged in, reminding Mike of his greatest shame. He had killed Dixie.

"Mr. Danziger?" John Ellenger, head of building security, interrupted Mike's reverie. A beefy man whose muscles bulged beneath his uniform shirt, he stood at Mike's desk looking impatient.

"Thanks for coming," Mike said. He explained who Philip was and that no harm had been done. Then he asked everyone to leave his office—Abby in particular. What was between them? When he looked into her dark eyes, he found his own pain mirrored. And when she ached—how was it that he knew her sorrow as intimately as his own?

Abby waited patiently in the reception area for more than an hour before Mike emerged. He was alone for most of that time. Lowell left the office soon after the guard arrived, clearly upset. Ruth followed shortly after.

Surely it was the miserable scene she had witnessed, embellished by Mike's pain, that caused Abby's disquiet to flare into a sense that something terrible was about to happen. It clawed at her like a live creature, attacking her from the inside out. Was it real? If so, what was the source of the peril?

Abby tried to act normal when Lydia continued their chat between answering phone calls. Finally Mike emerged. "Let's go," he said, barely looking at Abby. He put his card into the slot beside the elevator. With a small smile of farewell to Lydia, Abby turned to follow. She took his arm, wanting to offer him comfort.

But her feeling of frightened anticipation had reached a crescendo. And then there was a sudden vision—of blackness and falling and oblivion. As the elevator door opened and Mike started forward, pulling her with him, she screamed, "Mike!"—just as he stepped toward the void of the empty elevator hole.

Chapter Six

Abby's scream warned Mike. That, plus her frantic tug on his arm, saved him, for he instinctively turned and grabbed the elevator door. One foot dangled before he thrust it back onto the floor. He stood immobile, feeling Abby still clutching him. Then, as if in slow motion, he took a few steps to safety.

He was vaguely aware of Abby's sobs as he sagged against a nice, solid wall, his breath coming in irregular gasps. In a few moments he straightened. His eyes locked on hers. Her dark eyes were rimmed in red, her full lips compressed into a straight line of fear, yet she was still the most beautiful creature he had ever seen. "How did you know?" he managed.

She said nothing. Reaching to wipe the tears from the flawless skin of her cheeks, he checked his movement when she cringed as though expecting a blow. Instead he pulled her tightly into his arms, inhaling her hair's sweet, lemony fragrance, whispering into its softness, "Thank you for saving my life."

Abby felt bereft when, much too soon, Mike drew the strength of his comforting body away, but he said, "I need to get someone to take a look at this."

In minutes, people joined them. Snatches of conversation added to both her knowledge of the moving room called an elevator and to her vocabulary in relation to it. She hung back and watched as the security people, then the elevator repair crew, investigated the incident.

The elevator car was stuck on another floor; its emergency stop button had been pulled. The door shouldn't have opened onto an empty shaft, even with Mike's special card, but it had. John, the head security guard, grumbled about tampering and sent his men to search for evidence but found none. The situation was labeled an accident.

Abby felt uneasy getting into even a different elevator for the ride down to the Bronco, but the uneasiness was born of the mishap, not any supernatural sense. The incident increased the tension between Mike and her; she had never seen his scowl so intense as he watched her. Uncomfortable, she studied the green-carpeted floor of the moving room.

She had not been able to prevent herself from cringing when he'd turned to her when no longer in danger. She had no fear he would strike her but expected a verbal onslaught, accusations of

Linda O. Johnston

witchcraft or worse. His silence did nothing to dispel her worry.

He took her hand as the elevator door opened. Startled, she nearly pulled away. Where was he leading her? A shiver began at her trapped fingers and traveled through her entire body—strangely not entirely of nervousness but from exhilaration at the physical contact.

As they reached the Bronco, he pushed the button to make it beep. "It's time to go home," he said.

Relieved, she felt her insides fall as limp as a lopsided rag doll she had once sewn as a child. Whatever he thought, he was not taking her to the authorities—or abandoning her.

But inside the car, he turned to her. "I'll expect answers later, Abby. I want to know exactly what's going on. And if you're part of some conspiracy . . . well, heaven help you."

She tried to swallow the lump that suddenly rose in her throat. What was he talking about? And with the way his eyes glared so icily, how could she dare to answer anything?

As he drove, she kept her head averted from him, her hand pressed lightly against the cool window of the Bronco as she watched out the window. They passed more stores, tall structures, and even mansions. Were all people in this time wealthy? Beyond the buildings were only a few small, grassy parks. L.A. was a very populous place.

Mike's eyes no longer met hers, but she felt them traveling assessingly over her. A sudden chill made her shiver, not entirely from the cold air blowing inside the Bronco. The silence, except for the usual motor and wind noises, was oppressive. But she did not want music or voices from the device Mike called a radio. Still trembling a little, she grasped for something neutral to ask, finally settling on, "Where do you live, Mike?"

He pointed toward a house- and tree-covered mountain whose base they had nearly reached. "Hollywood Hills." His tone was not unfriendly.

"Is it far?"

"Another fifteen minutes."

Heading up the hill, Mike soon turned onto winding streets so narrow that Abby was not sure the Bronco could pass cars stopped at the sides. A dense forest of houses—of wood and glass and adobe of different colors—lined the hilly roads, their landscaping lush. In contrast, the steepest, starkest slopes wore a mantle of brown, sparse grasses and clumps of cactus.

The higher the Bronco mounted, the fewer the houses, until only a flimsy wooden rail lined a steep drop-off at the side of the road. A few hardy trees clung to the cliff's edge. Holding herself tense, Abby felt as though Mike and she had driven off the earth and into heaven, for the endless city visible below, with its vast checkerboard of streets and buildings, seemed unreal in its blanket of brown haze. Once she said in wonder, "This area is incredible."

"That's why I like it," Mike said without looking at her. "Or used to. It's so inaccessible hardly anyone but residents ever comes up. There aren't many thefts since burglars can't make an easy getaway. The neighbors get terribly peeved when something . . . unusual happens here." His voice oozed irony.

Abby glanced at him, but his face was blank. She asked softly, "What happened, Mike?"

He did not answer, but she suddenly felt the depth of his emotions—despair, anguish, loneliness. She closed her eyes, trying to capture—and understand—his thoughts, but as usual her special powers were not to be controlled. She was suddenly filled with a certainty, though, of the necessity of learning what he had meant.

For only then did she realize that her unrelieved tension, her trembling, were not merely a result of the chill temperature or her nervousness about Mike's reaction.

The incident at the elevator had not been the only danger; her premonition had returned.

At the top the road ended, and Abby wondered if they were going to drive into the blue, cloudless sky. Stopping before a forbidding wrought-iron gate, Mike pushed a button on the flap he had lowered in the desert when the sun beat against his face. Abby was delighted that he lived behind a locked gate; the tall fence might keep the threat she sensed at bay.

Mike's house charmed Abby. High on a rise, it looked like paintings she had seen of Spanish haciendas: arched adobe walls, ornate red roof, decorative tile about the large windows, even a bell tower. Huge and sprawling, it had two stories at the front and a long, low wing on each side.

Mike drove behind the house. When he pushed another button, a door in one of two smaller, matching buildings opened. He pulled the Bronco in beside a tiny car, roofless like an open phaeton. Abby was just beginning to realize that the desert cabin, with all she had considered to be the most modern of amenities, must have seemed primitive to Mike. What else could he achieve here with just a movement of his finger?

As soon as the Bronco was stopped and quiet, Mike turned to her. "We'll talk after dinner."

She tried to smile, but her stomach churned. What did she dare to reveal? And did their bond, which sometimes sent his emotions reeling through her, work in both directions, so he would know if she lied?

She composed herself as he led her into the house. The quiet in the entry hall was disturbed only by the ticking of a grandfather clock. Surprisingly, the place was permeated by the odor of something clean and pinelike, not the mustiness of a dwelling unused for months.

He gave her a brief tour of the house. Three farmhouses like the one her family had left in Pennsylvania would have fit inside. The downstairs front contained a parlor, living room, and dark-paneled office, all lit by wrought-iron chandeliers and matching wall sconces. The tile floor was strewn with colorful rugs. The furniture was of heavy, carved wood—much of which Mike proudly admitted to having created himself.

Each room had large windows framing the view of the sky above and the valley below.

He showed her the vast kitchen and his wood-working room behind the house. Both were filled with contraptions she could not begin to comprehend.

Eventually he took her to an upstairs bedroom. "You'll stay here," he said. Although the spacious room followed the heavy Spanish theme, Abby was delighted with the wooden bed's filmy lace canopy and coverlet that matched the curtains. She looked out a window almost as tall as she onto the greenery of a large courtyard surrounded by the house and its wings.

If her room, as a guest, was so opulent, Abby wondered how plush might be the chamber in which Mike slept. And where was it? In one of the wings, perhaps, for her tour had not taken her there.

A loud gong startled her. Mike scowled. "That's the doorbell."

Abby stood on the balcony above the entry as he opened the door. A short, plump woman in a bright orange dress and odd, tiny white hat threw herself into his arms. "Welcome home, dear, dear Mike," she effused, giving him a great, smacking kiss on the cheek.

Abby swallowed. Who was this? And surely Abby had no right to feel so jealous of someone who so obviously shared Mike's life. She descended the stairs.

The woman regarded Abby intently. Her face was round, her cheeks full, her mouth wide and

colored with an overabundance of red makeup—
some of which remained on Mike's cheek. Abby
tried to be unobtrusive as she studied the
woman. Like a servant, she wore a neat pinafore
and sturdy shoes, but since when did servants
hug and kiss their masters? Abby liked the idea
but could not imagine such a thing happening in
her time. This era was a strange one indeed.

"And who are you?" The woman scurried so
close to Abby that they could have touched. She
smelled of something wildly exotic overlaid with
the pine scent of the house. "Oh, my dear, I sense
you are a Pisces, a fish swimming in two directions. Perhaps we can help you find your way. Or
maybe a Gemini—a twin?"

Abby felt bewildered. She had heard similar
terms at home once from a gypsy fortune-teller
before the seer was made to move on. The words
most certainly seemed out of place here.

The woman placed the back of her hand dramatically against her lightly lined forehead, closing eyelids whose heavy blue coloring evoked a
purplish cast from her cap of starling-black hair.
"Let me see what you are thinking. Oh, poor
dear. You are looking for something."

Abby's eyes opened wide. Was this woman also
able to see things beyond normal human vision?
And had she endangered herself for Abby's sake
by speaking out?

Biting her lip, Abby glanced at Mike, expecting
him to hurl at the woman the usual accusations
Abby experienced when people learned of her
powers. But a ghost of a smile lifted the corners

of his lips. "Knock it off, Hannah. I told you when I called from the office that I was bringing Abby home and that she'd lost her family in the desert."

Abby swallowed in confusion. No one was acting as expected.

Hannah took Abby's arm, standing on tiptoe to speak loudly but conspiratorially in her ear. "Don't mind him, dear. Poor Mike has no imagination. He only sees in shades of black and white—not even much gray, poor boy. But you and I—we see colors, don't we? Marvelous colors." She gave an emphatic wink of one pale hazel eye, then turned back to Mike. "Everything's aired out, and I'll whip up dinner in a jiffy." Again she winked at Abby. "Men are so much more tractable when they're fed, dear."

Pivoting on the tile floor, she sashayed toward the back of the house, the long skirt of her orange dress swishing from side to side. Before disappearing, she turned back. "Abby, dear, things are seldom as bleak as they seem. But though you are wise to be wary, I hope your deep fear will prove unfounded." Then she was gone.

Abby looked quizzically at Mike, who shrugged. "Hannah is as eccentric as they come, but she means well."

"Does she truly know what is on people's minds?" She had, after all, sensed Abby's anxiety.

"So she'd have you believe, but what she says is so broad that she's bound to strike a chord in everyone. Now I'm going to go freshen up."

Wishing to do the same, Abby brought in some

of the clothing she had bought in Barstow, then ascended the stairs once more. She washed her face in a private bathroom off her bedroom. It was charming—full of colorful tile. But she felt distracted. Mike might not believe the talkative Hannah had any true vision, but despite her claims he tolerated her, even liked her.

Might he, after all, continue to tolerate Abby if he knew the truth? Would he simply label her eccentric as well?

She put on a fresh white blouse and dark skirt, then studied her face in the mirror. Perhaps sometime she might try the use of makeup. But only if she learned how not to apply it as garishly as Hannah.

Later, Abby expected that a maid bold enough to kiss her employer would join them for supper, but Hannah did not. Instead she flitted about in the airy dining room, serving them at one end of the narrow table.

Hoping to learn why she was here—and the source of her ever-present anxiety—Abby encouraged Mike to speak. Besides, if he talked, he might forget to question her. She began, "Do you like living in L.A., Mike?"

"Sure." He passed her a basket of bread. "Though it lost a lot of charm after Aunt Myra died."

"I'm sorry." Abby broke off some bread and began nibbling. "She sounds like a wonderful person."

"She was," Mike said. "She changed my life."

"Because she convinced you to stay here after

Linda O. Johnston

you went to UCLA?" Abby was proud that she had recalled the initials. "Or was it the stories you mentioned?"

"Both." He took a sip of red wine from a goblet. "Myra did a lot of genealogical research on the Danzigers. Each night at dinner, she spun another yarn, mostly from childhood recollections of turn-of-the-century Pasadena, but sometimes throwing in more ancient history of the family contributions to L.A."

Hannah bustled in with a platter of steaming chicken mounded with vegetables. The food smelled heavenly. "My own recipe," Hannah said when Abby had taken a bite and remarked on its delightful, fruity taste. "I compete with Arlen's Kitchens or I'd never get to cook for Mike." She gave Abby a broad wink and hurried from the room.

Abby hardly noticed. Hearing of Myra's tales of family history, she felt on the brink of answers she craved. Spearing a Brussels sprout, she ventured, "Mike, you mentioned that Arlen Danziger was your ancestor. How were you related?" She placed the bite in her mouth. Its pleasant tartness in the fruit sauce was wonderful.

Mike shot her a look, perhaps remembering that she once had called him Arlen. "He was my great-great-something-grandfather."

"And you obtained recipes from him to start your restaurant?"

Mike laughed. "Not directly; from Myra. She'd read them as a young wife and updated them. But she never wrote them down. I followed her

140

around the kitchen with pen and paper. Then I had to modify them, too—both to make them more healthy and to work in a commercial kitchen. Just doubling or tripling old Arlen's ingredients didn't always work."

Looking off into the distance, Abby smiled, recalling early, inedible meals on the trail. "I know. When Arlen tried his first batter cakes—" She stopped, her hand flying to her mouth. "I mean, I would imagine your ancestor Arlen . . ."

Her voice trailed off as Mike stared. Fortunately Hannah came in carrying coffee and small dishes of ice cream—a treat Abby loved to make at home, but its texture was never as smooth as the serving before her.

After the housekeeper removed a tray of dirty dishes, Abby tried to change the subject. "How long has Hannah been with you?"

Mike took a sip of coffee. "As long as I've had this house, nine years. When she interviewed with me, she said she was destined to have this housekeeping job, so I hired her. Of course, her mile-long list of glowing references didn't hurt."

He smiled briefly, and Abby relaxed just a little. He found Hannah's special powers amusing, whether or not he believed in them. She remained hopeful that he would simply be amused with her, too.

Still, the better course of action was to keep her silence.

But that was not to be.

As she sampled the deliciously cold and sweet ice cream, Mike leaned toward her. "Okay, Abby.

141

It's time. I want the truth now. Who are you, and why are you here?"

She dropped her spoon into the bowl with a clatter. Finding it hard to breathe, she murmured, "My story is not easily believable."

"Try me."

What choice did she have? She had no lies easier to accept than the truth. She lifted her hands nervously to the bonnet ribbons that were not there. "My name is Abby Wynne. I was born in the year 1836."

"I see," Mike said, not seeing at all. Still, he let her go on.

Soon she was relating the most incredible tale—although one she'd paved the way for ever since he'd found her on the desert.

"My sister Lucy and I did not want to leave our home in Pennsylvania," she was saying, "but my father had what he called itchy feet. I believed he was being kind, that he did not want to tell me that I had scared off suitors for both my sister and me."

He watched her lovely face for a hint of craftiness, but her coffee brown eyes had a dreamy, faraway look as they stared past his shoulder. What was her game? If he let her keep talking, maybe he would learn.

And maybe he would lose the urge to run his fingers through the pale, rich hair that cascaded over the shoulders of her white blouse.

"And how did you scare off, er . . . suitors?" he prompted.

A smile turned up the corners of her full lips

as though she was delighted at his interest. Still, she hesitated, as though formulating what to say next.

"I was a healer," she finally said. "Where most women of my time were content to care for their families, I poked my nose into other people's illnesses, learning matters that many thought did not concern me."

"Such as?"

"Such as cures for all sorts of ailments, mostly gleaned from old wives' tales, and traditional use of herbs and liniments. Our wagon train trip was a giant schoolroom for me, especially thanks to our Indian guide Hunwet, who taught me many healing secrets of his people and other tribes."

Mike leaned back, linking his fingers behind his head. Why on earth was she spinning this yarn? Was it some kind of practical joke on him? Or had she something more sinister in mind?

Since leaving the office, he hadn't been able to shake the suspicion that she was in league with whoever had rigged the elevator. How else could she have known?

And now the nervous way she avoided looking him straight in the eye did nothing to make him think she was serious.

Still, he decided to keep playing along. "Fascinating," he said. "Tell me more."

And so she did—and her capacity for detail was phenomenal, from reaching the "jumping-off place" in Independence, Missouri, in 1858, to buying supplies, packing the wagon, and joining other travelers.

"Once we'd all met and talked, the choice for trail leader was practically unanimous: your ancestor Arlen."

Mike straightened so quickly that he nearly knocked his chair out from under him. Here it was, the reason for her ridiculous fabrication, her "saving" him at the elevator. It had something to do with his business. Maybe she was going to claim a piece of Arlen's Kitchens, thanks to some imaginary link with his ancestor. "So Arlen was the epitome of leadership, was he?" He was unable to keep the sarcasm from his voice.

She glanced at him, pain etching tiny lines at the corners of her eyes. As she did quite often, she raised her slender fingers, seemingly to stroke the taut skin beneath her lovely, narrow jaw. "Arlen was a very nice man," she said quietly. "But he only learned to be a leader from experience."

Mike poured fresh coffee from the pot Hannah had left. He felt disoriented; why didn't Abby just make her claim? Surely she didn't believe her own story. If she were that nuts, wouldn't he see insanity glimmer in her eyes?

He looked into them as he said, "So tell me more about Arlen and this magical journey westward."

"It wasn't magical," Abby contradicted. Those lovely brown eyes glittered, all right, but with anger at his teasing. And still she seemed uneasy meeting his gaze. "It was quite difficult. We even lost Arlen's poor orphaned nephew Jimmy on the way."

He'd humor her to learn her game. "Lost him? Did you use a secret Indian chant and conjure him back the next day?"

Abby drew herself up with dignity. "Poor Jimmy died along the trail."

A tear touched the smooth, flushed skin of her cheek, and Mike, immediately contrite, wanted to wipe it away. Whether she was a lunatic or a damned good actress, he decided to hear her out. "I'm sorry," he said. "Tell me the rest."

As she continued, she met his eyes, earnestness written in the steadfastness of her gaze, the way her body leaned toward him. He wanted to squeeze the slender hand resting on the table to comfort her as she revealed her anguish at her father's illness, her fears for her sister and Arlen and the others.

He might be nuts, too, but he found himself wanting to believe her.

"I have reason to hope that my sister married Arlen; you do not happen to know if his wife's name was Lucy, do you?"

If his great-aunt Myra had ever mentioned the name of Arlen's wife, he couldn't remember. "No, I don't know," he replied, a bit bemused.

Consistent with her incomprehensible comments when he first found her, she claimed that the wagon train was beset by drought upon reaching the desert. "I begged for salvation at the site where you found me," she said. "Our Indian guide had told of the magical quality of such places, where fossilized remains of ancient creatures abound. I suppose the fossils somehow transcended natural barriers, tied our eras, yours and mine together, for I fell unconscious, and when I awoke, you were there, and I was in your time."

She paused, as though waiting for his reaction. Her eyes seemed bright and hopeful, and her lips trembled ever so slightly.

He muttered something noncommittal, and her expression melted into a mask of sorrow. "Well, that is who I am," she finished sadly. "It does not explain why I am here, for that I do not know yet, although I am certain it has to do with my special powers, for—" She drew in her breath. Her hands flew to her mouth, as though to grab back the words that had just spilled out.

"Your special powers?"

Her lips twitched as if trying to smile, to belittle what she was about to say, and again she looked away. "I sometimes see visions, and they tell me of accidents about to befall people."

He thought again of the elevator incident earlier that day. Whether planned or not, she had saved his life. And then there had been the flood she had "heard" in advance in the desert. She'd saved them both there—and that could not have been schemed in advance.

But if this part of her story was true, would she expect him to believe the rest? No matter how much she'd enthralled him, how could any rational man do that?

She must have sensed his denial. "Hannah says she knows things about people. You've accepted that about her."

"I've accepted that she's a good housekeeper," he said.

Her fingers toyed with her coffee cup. He noted again that her hands, although graceful, were callused and dry, as though used to heavy work.

She said, "I wouldn't believe my story myself, except here I am."

"And you're more than a hundred fifty years old? I wouldn't have guessed you a day over a hundred." Again, he did not restrain his sarcasm.

Her gaze flew upward until she stared into his face. Her chocolate-brown eyes glistened with gathering tears, and she appeared as wounded as if he had slapped her. He was immediately ashamed but couldn't help his incredulity. "You can't expect me to accept your story without question," he said.

"I suppose not, but I don't know how to prove it."

He stood. He needed time to think, to sort out Abby's story and what to do with her. "I'm going to finish my coffee in the den."

"I'll see if Hannah needs any help," she said, her voice small and muffled. She ran from the room.

Hannah already had finished the supper dishes, for she was just removing her apron as Abby reached the kitchen.

The housekeeper paused, a stricken expression

147

clouding her face. She pressed three fingers to her brow and closed her eyes. "Oh, my poor, dear Abby." Her voice rumbled dramatically, and Abby froze. Was Hannah having a vision?

"I'm getting vibrations from you of great turmoil," Hannah continued, "and even greater distance. No, time. It's great expanses of time."

Abby gasped. She ran to Hannah at the sink, stopping short of touching her. Perhaps Hannah truly could see beyond normal senses. And oh, how Abby needed a kindred spirit right now.

But Hannah opened her eyes and, grinning lopsidedly, spoke in a normal voice. "I'm really impressed with what you've been through. Traveling through time and all."

Abby felt taken aback; the woman had changed tone so quickly. "You envisioned it?"

"I eavesdropped." Hannah lifted one chubby hand to ward off Abby's dismay. "One does what one must to gain an edge, and when the force isn't quite with you . . . you cheat."

Abby shook her head in confusion.

"One day," Hannah said, "I want to hear all about you and why you've come. A wagon train? Time travel? Wow!" She stroked Abby's arm as if to make sure she was really solid. "I'm tired, now, though, so I'm going home to bed."

She did not offer to remain to chaperon Abby this night. People today must not worry about how such things appeared, Abby thought. Her family would be appalled that she had already spent two nights alone in a cabin with a man, but she had been too overwhelmed then by all that had happened to her in the desert to consider proprieties.

"Say good night to Mike for me," Hannah continued, "and be patient. He has a hard time believing in anything, most of all what's right before that handsome face of his." She paused, her small, hazel eyes boring into Abby. "Trust my ESP for one thing: you'll help him while you're here, but I bet you'll both be hurt in the process."

She hustled out. Abby stood motionless, perplexed. What should she make of Hannah? The woman was shameless, even admitting to listening in on her employer's conversations. But she accepted what Abby had said. And whatever this new abbreviation ESP stood for, Abby sensed it had to do with powers beyond the normal.

But what had Hannah meant about helping and hurting?

Feeling suddenly very alone, Abby decided to find Mike to say good night. Hadn't Hannah asked her to?

Voices led her to the room he had called the den, but he was alone, sipping coffee. The sounds confused Abby, for they seemed to surround Mike as he sat on a divan looking toward a large, carved bookcase on the wall beside the door.

She turned in the direction of his gaze.

He was watching a small box on a shelf that resembled the magical one filled with words that she had seen at his office, but this box was alive—there were people inside!

Mike shook his head as Abby looked at the TV

and gasped. What a good actress! She sounded ingenuously delighted as she said, "This machine has sounds like the radio in your Bronco, and a box like Lydia's computer at your office. What is it?"

"Television, Abby. Everyone in the world knows about TV, even where they're too poor to afford one."

"Everyone in this time, Mike." She sighed, sitting beside him. "Are the people inside that box real? They look so small."

"That's just their picture." He tried to sound patient. "There's a scientific explanation for TV."

"Perhaps there's a scientific explanation for the magic that brought me here." She drew in her breath as though gathering courage, then said, "Please tell me, Mike. You tolerate Hannah's claims of special powers; why do you not tolerate mine?"

She had a good point. And with her sincerity, her seeming lucidity—oh, hell. What was he doing? Surely not accepting her screwy stories. He shrugged. "It's just that—"

"You liked her references. Well, I came to you with the best references of all. You drew me here."

What the devil was she talking about? "What do you mean?"

"The night before I was transported to this time, I stood alone on the desert and watched the stars move into the configuration of today. I felt as though I watched them through someone else's eyes, and I shared that person's feelings of anger, sorrow, and loneliness. I believe they were yours."

Mike gasped. Staring at her, he took a too large swig of coffee and immediately began to choke on the acrid, lukewarm brew. Slamming the cup down, he stood, hunching over, feeling glad as he coughed long, hard, and loud, for he had something else to concentrate on besides Abby's words.

What was she saying? That the bittersweet hallucination that had so shaken him, unrevealed to anyone, had been real? That she had felt it, too—from more than a century away?

As Abby slapped his back, his coughing tapered off. "Mike, do not try to speak, but nod your head. Are you all right?"

He nodded. He turned his head toward her, looking up since he was still folded forward at the middle. She was regarding him with concern and a deep, deep sorrow in those warm brown eyes.

"If you are certain," she said, "I will leave you. Good night."

"Abby," he gasped, unsure what he wanted to say. He only knew he did not want her to leave. Not then. Not until he understood.

But with a last, sorrowful look, she was gone.

She had a bad dream that night. She saw the wagon train roll away without her, leaving her in the desert. Her inner voice filled her with dread, for she was afraid all of them would perish before reaching their destiny.

She woke up shaking and crying. She must have made noise, for Mike was suddenly sitting beside her on the bed, holding her tightly. Again, as on the other night he had held her, his chest was bare, and the hair against her cheeks and nose tickled pleasantly. The smells of soap and something minty nearly, but not quite, masked the wholly masculine aroma of him. The only light in the room spilled through the open door from the hallway outside, and Abby saw that Mike wore only blue, satiny short pants.

This time she only wanted to get closer. She recalled their kiss when he ran to her in the wash. She needed his lips, his body, against hers. As she pressed against him, she knew that was what he wanted, too.

"Hush, Abby," he whispered. "It'll be all right." After a moment, as he still held her tightly, he said, "I'm . . . sorry. All you've said—it's incredible. If only—"

She knew how rare and difficult it must be for Mike Danziger to apologize, most especially if he believed he had done nothing wrong. Warmed by his effort to solace her, she stilled his agonized speech by placing her hand over his firm lips.

At first his hands roving her back atop her long but flimsy white gown were comforting, the way an adult eases a child's fears. But soon they reached the sensitive places at the base of her neck and behind her ears, creating small, sensual shivers each place he touched. His fingers ranged through the loosened mass of her hair, tangling, then releasing it to massage her scalp, and she became aware of how the unevenness of his breathing seemed to direct the irregular cadence of her own.

As the massage crept down Abby's back, and then lower, she stiffened. She wanted him to go on, but she was afraid. Nothing in her upbringing had prepared her for the feelings that inundated her. She had heard hushed whispers of what went on between a man and a woman. Proper ladies waited until marriage, and even then they did not enjoy what went on between husband and wife.

But, oh, the heat and the yearning that coursed through her! Was she odd in this as well? There was a burning inside her that threatened to explode into an uncontrolled conflagration, a throbbing in her most private areas that seemed to generate an unnatural yet quite pleasant moistness.

She pushed closer to Mike, willing him to continue—but he didn't. He ceased all movement. Then, as slowly and deliberately as if the effort caused him untold agony, he pulled away. "I'm sorry," he said once more. "I shouldn't have . . . did I hurt you?"

Abby, her breath still ragged, said softly, "Your touch did not hurt me, Mike."

There was a silence. Then Mike said, "But my words before did."

She said nothing.

"Abby, what do you want from me?" His voice was a sharp cry, his handsome face a mask contorted by agony in the faint light from the doorway, but he gave her no time to answer before he continued slowly, softly, "I've told myself you're crazy. But if so . . . well, I am too. You were right; those visions you described—my hallucinations—no one else knew about them. And if they're true, if we shared them and the supernatural does exist—well, who am I to say you didn't come from a wagon train in the past? I don't know what to believe anymore."

Blindly, she reached out to grasp his hand. Clutching it as though to let it go would be to withdraw from her last shred of hope, she whispered brokenly, "Believe *me*, Mike, please." She drew his hand to her cheek, feeling his harshness against her soft, tear-moistened skin. "Please," she said once more.

He groaned and pulled her close, and all the responses she had felt before, the heat and moistness and need, all rushed back to inundate her in a flood of sensation.

He stroked her again through her gown. Before, the fabric had felt like a protective barrier. But now it seemed like an obstruction, and Abby ached to cast it aside.

Mike's lips found hers, urging a response, searing hers with a fire that could not be quenched, not even by the equally heated moistness of his mouth. Despite everything Abby had ever been taught, everything she had ever believed about an unmarried couple, she was swept along by feelings she had never anticipated—burning and strength and unimagined passion. This simply could not be wrong. After all, had she not scaled a century to be with this man? Did she not share in his emotions?

She found herself shifting to allow him to lift the gown. She wore nothing beneath, and she gasped aloud as his fingers reached around to stroke her breasts. Things were happening so swiftly. She wanted them to increase in speed, to stop. . . . she did not know which.

His mouth left hers, and as she tried to call him back, she felt his teeth gently pull one nipple, then the other. Her breath caught in her throat as his mouth continued its damp, heated exploration.

His fingers traveled lower, and she arched against his strokes. The feeling was like nothing she had experienced before. All of her centered where he touched. He was gentle yet insistent; his fingers generated searing heat that ignited each area he explored like windblown sparks in a dry forest. She writhed and opened to grant him greater access as he continued his exquisite torture. Her breathing grew ragged, punctuated by tiny moans she could not control. Tossing her head from side to side, she began to whisper small, incomplete words that even she could not understand, and he swallowed them as once more he captured her lips. When he boldly plunged his tongue into her mouth, she entwined it with her own.

Her urgency must have been contagious, for her special sense unshuttered, letting her feel Mike's strong emotions, his raging need. He wanted—needed—her reciprocation. Suddenly, despite all she believed about how a woman should react, she wanted to touch him, too. She reached over, feeling his hardness strain at the silky fabric of his shorts. It was his turn to gasp. He moved, and suddenly there was nothing at all between them. She had to know him, to know his masculinity, and so she clutched at his length, feeling herself flush as she curiously pulled and stroked and explored, as gentle and as rough as he continued to be with her.

His control disappeared. He lay her back upon the bed, and she felt him at the very core of her femininity, stiff and prodding and so very welcome.

And then he entered her. She drew in her breath at the initial pain, and he hesitated.

"Please," her voice rasped. "Do not stop."

His eyes, meeting hers, smoldered, then closed as he continued his erotic assault, first gentle and then intense. She found herself moving to meet his thrusts.

The sensual pressure building within her rose to a rapturous intensity—and then, quite suddenly, when she thought she could take no more, the most exquisite sensation of relief washed over her. She cried aloud as Mike groaned, and she knew that whatever she had experienced, he had as well.

Both lay quietly, breathlessly on the bed. After a few moments, Mike said, "You didn't tell me you were a virgin, Abby." Regret filled his voice.

"Did it matter?" She prayed he would not hate her for one more fact withheld.

"Only because I'm afraid I hurt you."

Again, he worried about hurting her. Again, the only hurt she felt was his mistrust.

She burrowed against him, resting her head on his hard, damp chest, reveling in his pleasantly pungent aroma, the feel of his strong arms as they swept around her and held her close.

But she said nothing.

He interpreted the silence for what it was, her recollection of the concern he had expressed earlier. He whispered, "I'd believe you if I could, Abby."

But he could not.

She attempted to sleep, but the effort of keeping her tears from flowing kept her awake for a long time.

Chapter Seven

Eventually Abby must have slept, for dawn was casting tendrils of light through the bedroom curtains when she felt Mike gently pull away. She thought she felt a small kiss atop her head, but she was not certain. He left the bed.

She turned, chilled by the sudden absence of his comforting warmth. She felt herself blush even as she admired the hard masculine contours of his still-bare body.

He smiled briefly, looking a little uncomfortable as he began to search for the shorts he had cast aside the night before. "Sorry I woke you," he said over his shoulder as he pulled them on. "I was going to get you up when I was dressed. Hannah will be coming to make breakfast soon. My room is in another wing of the house."

She wondered how he had heard her cry out in her sleep if his room was not near—by their special connection? It had, after all, called them to one another across years; in comparison, crossing a house was no feat at all.

He looked at her, his handsome features grave. "Look, Abby. I did a lot of thinking before I fell asleep last night. I—"

"Hello!" cried Hannah's voice from downstairs. "I used my key this morning. Breakfast'll be ready in a minute."

"I'll leave so you can get dressed," Mike said, his voice low. "We'll talk downstairs."

Mortified that Hannah must know Mike and she had been together, afraid to think about all that had occurred, Abby studiously kept her mind blank. She showered, wrapped a towel around her, and fixed her hair, leaving it loose about her shoulders, for few women today wore buns or chignons. She wished she had a little modern makeup, settling instead on just pinching her cheeks.

Feeling a kinship with the more daring women of this era, she put on a pair of the jeans Mike had bought her and a loose short-sleeved blouse. Though the temperature here was not nearly as unbearably hot as in the desert, L.A. in July still was warm enough to make Abby envious of the women who flitted everywhere in the skimpiest of outfits. This combination was about as daring as she would get.

She realized she had avoided her thoughts as much as possible. A lot had happened between Mike and her yesterday. He knew most of the truth about her—and, though he seemed regretful, he did not accept it.

159

They had shared an intimate experience last night that she had found wonderful. But he had left her quickly that morning. Had it truly been to protect her reputation with Hannah—or did he now consider her a fallen woman, a seductress, and might he use that as an excuse to banish her?

And—oh, dear lord—what would she do if she were pregnant?

She had to face whatever would happen. Looking in a mirror, she examined herself. Her lips were full and somewhat bruised from Mike's avid kisses the night before. Her dark eyes looked huge, and she appeared frightened. That would never do—even though it was the truth.

Squaring her shoulders, she lifted her chin. There. That was better. She headed downstairs.

She found Mike at a table on a veranda right outside the kitchen that overlooked the greenery-filled courtyard. Ignoring the lush view of the valley below, he studied an expanse of newspaper. His pale blue shirt, of a stretchy fabric, molded tightly to muscles that she had seen bared not long before. Flushing, she tossed him an uncertain smile as he rose to pull out her chair.

The way he squeezed her shoulder seemed reassuring, but he moved away as Hannah bustled out the door. She again wore that silly white cap upon her purple-black hair, but today her pinafore was over a dress of bright green. "Good morning, Abby!" she effused.

Abby swallowed her discomfort. Did Hannah not know Mike had been alone with her in her room? Did she simply not care? Surely Hannah's enthusiastic greeting did not mean that she approved of the situation.

"Good morning," Abby replied, glancing at Mike for guidance, but he was again reading his paper.

Hannah asked, "Would you like coffee? It's vanilla nut decaf."

Abby tried not to look puzzled. Coffee she understood. Even vanilla and nut—but in coffee? And what was decaf? But she did not want to appear stupid. "I'd love some," she said.

Hannah grinned. "I'll bring you a bagel and cream cheese, too." Abby also wondered what they were.

As Hannah left, Abby looked at Mike again. He lowered his newspaper, and Abby wished she knew what he was thinking. "Beautiful day, isn't it?" he said.

How could he speak of the weather when so much was left unsaid between them? But Abby followed his lead. "Is it always so pleasant here in the morning?"

As they continued to discuss the climate, Hannah bustled out once more, a filled tray in her hands. The bagel turned out to be a roll with a hole in the middle. Cream cheese was just as it sounded. And the two together were a delicious combination. The hot, flavored coffee was most pleasing to Abby's nostrils and palate, too. And there was orange juice, tasting as though squeezed fresh from the fruit that was so rare and exotic in her time. Its container was similar to the smooth, flexible material of Mike's water bottle in the desert, and Abby examined it. "What is this made of?" she asked Hannah.

"Plastic," the housekeeper said. She leaned toward Abby and whispered, "I'm not sure when it was invented, but now we can't live without it."

At least Hannah believed her story, Abby thought. She shot a look at Mike, but he was again intent on his paper.

As Abby ate, she watched a squirrel skittering on the lawn. Funny that in all this rich greenness signifying an abundance of water, no flowers grew.

"Anything else you two want?" Hannah asked in a few minutes. "If not, I'll go straighten the bedrooms." She patted Abby's shoulder. "Now, dear, holler if you need anything—or if Mike gives you too hard a time."

That comment finally got Mike's attention. He lowered the newspaper and shot a scowl at Hannah, who went inside.

Nibbling at her bagel, Abby heard a buzzing as a bee flew by. Only then did she note there were a couple more of the insects buzzing around the pitcher of orange juice. Thinking of poor Jimmy, killed by a creature similar to these so many years ago as Abby watched impotently, she sighed, shooing them.

"I didn't mean to ignore you," Mike said.

"I'm fine," she said softly. In fact, she had begun to read the back sheet of the paper he held. It was called the *Los Angeles Times,* and on that page there was a color picture of a strange-looking contraption called a jet. If the article were to be believed, a company called Boeing had just sold a fleet of these jets, apparently flying vehicles for passenger use, to a United States airline.

Those shining birds she had seen in her vision and in the air—people could hire rides on them! How wonderful! She recalled how she'd wished her strange bird could fly the thirsty emigrants from the desert and marveled that her fantasy in the past was true today. She vowed to ride in a jet if the opportunity ever arose.

She took a sip of coffee as Mike began speaking. "Abby, look. About what you told me last night—" Without warning, her heart started to pound. The buzzing in her ears came not from the bees still flying about the table but from somewhere inside her head. The base of her spine began to hurt as though pricked at once by an entire paper of needles.

Surely it was the thought of little Jimmy Danziger that created her reaction, not a premonition of danger here and now. Surely she would have a vision to foretell any peril.

"Damn!" Mike stood suddenly, one hand clutching his opposite forearm. His face was white, his gray eyes wide. She sensed fear, but his voice was calm. "Abby, get Hannah. Tell her to bring the bee sting kit." He slid back into his chair. "Hurry!" He sounded weaker.

Dear Lord! Did Mike have the same kind of reaction to bee stings as his remote relative, little

Jimmy, had had all those years past? No. Mike could not die!

Abby ran into the empty kitchen screaming, "Hannah! Come quickly. Bring the . . . bee sting kit." She prayed that, whatever it was, it would help Mike, for she would be able to do no more for him than she had for Jimmy.

After several long seconds, Hannah appeared. She raced to a corner of the kitchen, pulled open a drawer, and extracted a small orange plastic box. "I've told him not to eat outside. But will he listen?" She ran out to Mike. Abby followed.

His breathing was uneven, as Jimmy's had been, and his face was mottled. He managed a smile as Hannah pulled open the box. "I know. Growing no flowers isn't enough; I shouldn't—"

"Save your breath." Hannah pulled a paper from a clip on the box and began to read. Then, glancing up, she said, "I don't know how to give shots. I ought to make you do this yourself."

"Think of the fun . . . you'll have . . . torturing me." Mike's voice gasped; his breath came in wheezes. So like little Jimmy. Abby, too, felt unable to breathe in her helplessness. Tears spilled down her cheeks.

Hannah thrust the box at Abby. "Push up his sleeve; then unwrap the alcohol swab while I get the syringe ready."

Without understanding all Hannah said, Abby struggled to obey. On Mike's now-bare forearm was an angry red swelling that seemed to grow as she watched.

"Now," Hannah ordered, "wipe the alcohol on

his skin there." She pointed to Mike's upper arm. Hannah unsheathed a needle attached to a vial of liquid, then plunged the point into Mike where Abby had wiped. She soon extracted the needle. "There's another dose if we need it. While I put on the tourniquet, find some pills in the kit and get them down him. There's still juice in his glass."

Mike, his eyes glazed and half closed, was conscious enough to obediently open his mouth. Abby placed the pills on his tongue and lifted the juice to his lips. He swallowed.

"Do you see the stinger?" Hannah asked.

Abby did, a barb in the center of the swelling.

"I'll be right back with tweezers. Then we'll get him to the emergency room."

Abby bit her lip, frightened at being left alone with Mike. What if he stopped breathing?

But Hannah soon reappeared. She bent over Mike's arm, then straightened with an exclamation of triumph, the tweezers holding a tiny, pointed stinger. "Wouldn't think something this small would cause so much trouble, would you?"

The women helped Mike to stand. His breathing sounded less raspy, and his color seemed better. He was improving!

They got him into the Bronco. "Want to drive?" Hannah asked.

Abby shook her head. "I don't know how," she admitted in a small voice. What if that failing caused Mike's death?

Slipping behind the steering wheel, Hannah handed Abby the precious orange box. "Keep a close eye on him, and yell if he gets worse. We'll give him another shot." She shook her head, causing her dark cap of hair to sway. "I knew he had an allergy, but I've never been around when this happened. Nasty, isn't it? Don't worry; he should be fine."

Abby kept repeating that to herself as they sped down the hill and across many roads to a large building identified on the outside as Cedars-Sinai Medical Center, where people who seemed to know what they were about took over Mike's care.

Much later, Mike lay on a narrow white bed in the medical center, dressed in a flimsy gown. He was breathing fine, and his color appeared normal. His eyes were their normal gleaming gray, and he managed a little smile. Abby sat beside him, for he held her hand in a strong grip.

"Thanks for helping to save me," he said. His voice was strong, its usual deep tone sending its familiar pleasant shivers through her.

"I . . . you should thank Hannah. She was the one who knew what to do."

"I'll thank her too, soon as she gets back with the paperwork to check me out of this place." He paused, letting go of her hand. "Abby, we need to talk." His tone was kind. Perhaps too kind. She had noticed police in the hallway downstairs. Maybe he was about to turn her over to them to help find her family. After all, she had frozen, unable to act until he had told her to call for Hannah. He might not forgive her for that. She certainly could not forgive herself.

Did he also revile her as a fallen woman after the way she had behaved with him last night?

She held her breath, hardly noticing that she twisted her fingers in her lap. Quite suddenly the residue of the bagel and cream cheese, orange juice, and coffee all seemed to mold into a large iron cannonball in the pit of her stomach.

She willed her voice, however, to remain calm. "Yes, Mike, I agree that we must talk."

"Abby, you told me some pretty incredible things yesterday, and I don't know how to deal with them. But after your helping me before— and particularly after what we shared last night—I want to give you the benefit of the doubt."

Joy surged through her, but she held it back, unable to accept what she had heard. Letting her breath out slowly, she ventured, "You . . . believe me, then?"

His dubiousness showed in the lopsided twist to his mouth, though when he spoke he sounded regretful. "Not really. How can I accept that a normal woman who is clearly flesh and blood, judging by all I saw and felt last night—"

Abby felt herself turn bright scarlet, and her now-still hands suddenly demanded all her attention.

"—is from more than a hundred years in the past? But I don't know what to make of the fact you claim to have shared my private hallucination. And . . . Abby, how did you really know that the flood was coming? Or that the elevator wasn't there?" He hesitated. "And I saw the expression on your face just before the bee sting. You felt something then, too, didn't you?"

She dared to look up to find his eyes, as hard as the granite of their color, upon her. "Yes, I did. And there is more." She had to tell him, for she could hold it inside no longer. He should know everything before making his decision what to do with her. And perhaps if she shared, he could explain the anxiety that kept her insides churning so in this city, or at least help her find its source.

She glanced away, keeping her gaze partly averted. "I have visions, Mike. No matter what you believe, I felt your emotions across the years, as I think you felt mine over time and now distance. You did sense my crying last night from far away in your bedroom, didn't you?"

"I thought I heard you—but, yes, my room was too far away." His admission was clearly reluctant.

Abby wished she could stop baring herself to him, but she pressed on. "I saw the flood and empty elevator before they happened."

"But—"

She did not let him speak. "And there's more. I have experienced a strange sense of fear ever since we drew near to L.A. I feel danger, but I do not know from where it will come. My inner sense has not ceased tormenting me, so it was not simply a premonition of your bee sting. I believe I journeyed here because you need me, because I can somehow save you from the peril, but—"

He held up his hand. "No more of this Looney Tunes stuff, Abby. I was all set to offer a suggestion to prove or disprove your story, and now you come up with this."

" 'Looney Tunes?' "

"Nutty. Bonkers. Crazy."

She sighed. "I can't help what is, Mike. I wish I could. I've tried but . . . how did you intend to prove or disprove my story?"

"The way you suggested. Finding out if my great-great-great-grandfather Arlen was married to a woman named Lucy . . . what? Wynne?"

"Yes! Oh, Mike, can we do that? I would be so relieved to know that Lucy arrived in L.A. and found happiness with Arlen, and—"

"The only way I know of is to ask my great-aunt Jess, but I doubt she'll remember much. Maybe Myra left notes. And, Abby, even if you're right, unless we prove you couldn't have known Arlen's wife's name any other way, I can't promise I'll suddenly believe this absurd tale of time travel. Or that you're here to save me from danger, for heaven's sake."

Abby lowered her eyes in sorrow. Was there no way to make him trust her? "But if we do learn that it was Lucy, surely you can give my story some credence."

He shrugged those broad, muscular shoulders beneath the flimsy hospital gown. "Certainly more than it has now."

Abby liked the quiet, narrow Pasadena street where Mike's great-aunt Jess lived; it reminded her of neighborhoods in Pennsylvania towns of her time. Jess's gray stone home was set behind a vine-covered brick wall. It was smaller than Mike's house, its feel of wealth more sophisticated.

The bright sun of early afternoon slanted in Abby's eyes as Mike parked in the circular drive. She worried that he had not gone straight home to rest after his mishap that morning, but he claimed to feel fine.

He opened the front door with a key. "Hello," he called. "Anyone home?"

A tall, portly woman in a black dress waddled down the front hall. "Well, Michael Danziger. It's about time you came for a visit. Your aunt asks about you all the time."

Mike introduced Abby to the woman, whose name was Grace. She had dark hair mottled with patches of white, a nose resembling the beak of a talking parrot Abby had once seen in a traveling circus, and a brief, damp handshake.

Mike managed a quick, wry smile. "If I came more often, you'd complain I was a bother," he said.

"Maybe," Grace grumbled. She turned her back. "Come on. She's waiting."

As they followed, Mike whispered, "Don't mind Grace. She used to terrorize me even when I visited here as a kid. For a housekeeper, she thinks she's queen, princess, and first lady all rolled into one."

Grace led them down the long center hall and through a glass-paneled door into a room crammed full of delicate furniture, some of which looked as though it came from Abby's time. On a settee with intricately carved legs sat a tiny woman. A cloud of silver hair framed her face. Her skin had the parched, powdered look of a woman far past her prime, yet, though there were creases in her brow and beside her mouth, her flesh barely sagged. She had a sweetly up-turned nose—and Abby stood in the doorway staring, tears filling her eyes. In her blue flowered dress, Mike's petite great-aunt Jess looked much as Abby would have imagined Lucy to have looked half a century after Abby had last seen her.

"Come in," Jess demanded, her voice strong, if high-pitched. She looked Abby over with myopic, waiflike brown eyes, then patted the brocade up-holstery of the settee beside her. "Dixie, dear, you sit here."

Abby looked quickly at Mike as she took the seat Jess designated, smelling the scent of roses and something harshly medicinal emanating from the elderly woman.

Mike's face was stony as he began to speak, but Grace interrupted. "Now, Jess, you know Mike lost poor Dixie five months back. This is his friend Abby."

"Dixie was my wife," he explained to Abby in an expressionless undertone. "She's . . . de-ceased." Grace and he took seats opposite the set-tee.

Did he not recall the scene in his office with his brother-in-law? Abby had been there. She

171

knew of Dixie and that Mike's wife was dead.

He certainly hadn't killed her, as Philip had claimed—had he? Maybe remorse was the reason for the misery she sensed.

But that could not be. The man who had wooed Abby so gently the night before, who had shown her soaring heights of sensation, who had worried so about hurting her, was surely incapable of killing anyone.

Abby felt a tug of sympathy for Mike. Surely, as unemotional as he sounded, he felt sorrow at his loss.

Grace began, "Jess has been asking about the family, Michael. How is everyone?"

"Fine," he said, but Grace wasn't satisfied with anything less than a description of each person's health. Abby learned that Mike's parents were dead, but that he had a younger brother in a military service called the Air Force. The brother, Ed, with whom Mike did not sound close, was stationed in Ohio. He had a wife and two small daughters.

Abby sat still, not wanting to interrupt, for she was learning more about Mike Danziger in a few minutes here than in the days since arriving in the future.

Finally Mike stopped and said, "Jess, we have a few questions about the Danziger family from way back. You know, things Myra used to research."

The old woman's eyes moistened. "Myra's dead," she whimpered.

Grace patted Jess's hands as they wrung in her

172

lap. "We know, honey." She insinuated herself onto the small seat between Jess and Abby and fussed with Jess's blouse, and Abby saw the genuine kindness in the gruff woman. "Now we need to listen to Mike and his friend. They have some questions maybe you can answer. You'll try, won't you, honey?"

Jess smiled. "Of course. But Myra is the one who can answer. Ask her."

With a sinking feeling, Abby realized how much Jess's mind wandered. She was unlikely to have answers to prove to Mike that Abby was what, and whom, she claimed.

Still, Abby plunged in, explaining that Mike had told her how he began Arlen's Kitchens using recipes that Myra said had come from his ancestor. "I'm interested in Arlen and his family's journey west," she concluded. "Do you have any information about them—Arlen's wife's name, for example? And where did Myra get the recipes?"

"Myra'd want you to tell her," Grace added, patting Jess's shoulder.

Jess laughed, holding up her gnarled fingers as though to stave off the onslaught of questions. "Oh, that Myra. She was something. But I didn't care about all that old stuff, did I?"

She looked at Mike, who shook his head.

"That's how I stayed young, caring about what was new. Well, let me see. Arlen and the wagon train? I remember Myra talking about them."

Biting her lip, Abby asked again if Jess remembered Arlen's wife's name. Jess raised her wrinkled chin toward the ceiling. "Arlen's wife? No . . . but the recipes were in the journals. That's what Myra said. Maybe Arlen's wife is in them, too."

"Journals! You found journals?" Abby's voice came out in a gasp. Her heartbeat surged into a tumultuous cadence, and she held her breath. The journals could be the answer to everything! "Oh, Jess, who wrote them? Could it have been Arlen's wife?"

The old woman's brow knit in confusion. "Those journals—there were three? Four? The handwriting was so pretty. Way back when we were young ladies, Myra read parts to me some evenings. I pretended not to listen; I didn't like old things. But the writing was so interesting."

Abby prompted gently, once more holding back her excitement, "Do you recall who wrote them?"

Jess shook her head sadly. "Who wrote them? I don't . . ." Her voice tapered off.

"Where are they now, Jess?" Mike asked. "Maybe we could take a look."

Jess bit at her bottom lip with teeth too perfect to be her own. "I don't know," she said peevishly. "Ask Myra."

Abby's head drooped, but she could not give up. Not when she knew that journals existed— and that they could be Lucy's.

Looking into Jess's confused, rheumy eyes that somehow hinted at Lucy's gleam, Abby smiled. "I'm sorry, Jess. I didn't mean to upset you, but I'm very interested in those journals. Could I look

around this house, in case Myra left them here?
I promise to keep out of your way."

Grace let out a snort. "You see how riled she
gets just from a little visit. I don't remember seeing those journals for years. Having someone
around tearing things apart, making noise . . . I
don't think it's—"

"Abby will be quiet, and she won't be any trouble," Mike said. His words were placating, but his
forceful tone allowed no contradiction.

Abby glanced at him in gratitude.

"And she won't come till it's convenient," he
continued. "Tomorrow or the next day. You can
schedule the time."

"Well, I suppose—"

"That'll be wonderful!" Abby said. "Thank you
so much, Grace. And most especially, thank you,
Jess. Just imagine how interesting it'll be to read
about the past in those journals."

"But I don't like old things," Jess said petu-
lantly.

As they drove off, Mike practically tasted
Abby's excitement. She seemed almost to bounce
in the seat beside him, even though she dutifully
wore her seat belt, as he'd taught her.

She kept glancing at him, her beautiful dark
eyes sparkling, but at first she said not a word,
as though expecting him to comment.

But he had nothing to say.

Except in his own mind. He kept recalling their
wonderful lovemaking last night, her inexperi-
enced eagerness, her utter sweetness. And her

concern when he had had that god-awful allergic reaction that morning.

But no matter how his libido or any other part of him responded to her, what they had heard from Jess had not convinced him that she was what she said.

Nothing was likely to do that. She had to be crazy, suffering from a delusion.

Or she could be just like Dixie, immersed in some as yet unrevealed plan to con him for all she could get. Well, he'd taken care of Dixie, heaven help him. He clutched the steering wheel so hard his fingers ached. Whatever Abby's intentions, they'd both be better off if she just left him alone.

Unaware of his bitter mood and apparently unable to hold back her effervescence any longer, Abby said, "I know you believe none of this, Mike, but my sister Lucy did keep journals on our westward journey. She had just completed her third volume when I left and was about to begin her fourth. I imagine it would contain recipes learned from Arlen, for surely it would chronicle their engagement and early married life. And that one, too, would tell me how the wagon train fared after my departure."

Now was the chance to throw cold water on her hopes—if they were real. The likelihood of finding any missing journals in that old house was slight. Myra might have put them anywhere. She might even have kept them somewhere away from home—a safe-deposit box overlooked in the disposition of her estate, perhaps. Or she might have donated them to a library. He began, "Look, Abby—"

"Oh, Mike," she interrupted. "To think that I may be so close to finding what happened to my family!"

They were stopped at a red light, and he looked over to see her hands clasped in her lap, a radiant glow in her eyes, a smile on her lovely face. Maybe he should just keep quiet and let her enthusiasm fade when she failed.

He knew well about faded enthusiasm.

"Do you know what's best of all? If we find the journals, I can report to you incidents on the trail that Lucy is likely to have recorded. Grace can be keeper of the journals until you look at them. If I can describe events that Lucy mentioned, you'll believe me then—won't you?"

"Sure," he said with a shrug. But so what if she could describe incidents in the journal? So what if, despite all his skepticism, he had an absurd desire to trust this woman who did marvelous things to his hormones and had an uncanny knack for saving his life? How could he buy her crazy tale even then?

Instead, he'd try to find out how she had pulled off such a scam—and why.

Chapter Eight

As Mike remained quiet in the car beside her, Abby soon realized that her excitement had done nothing to dispel his characteristic gloominess. She felt a momentary pang of uncertainty. Despite their closeness last night, his gratitude to Hannah and her that morning for his rescue, he still seemed disinclined to trust her. In fact she sensed him withdrawing further than ever.

She had to find the journals. They would convince him. They had to.

At least he still seemed to be feeling no ill effects from his ordeal with the bee sting that morning. It was midafternoon, and he insisted on going to work.

Abby accompanied him to Beverly Hills. When she elected not to go upstairs with him to his office, he said, "Here," handing her the small watch he wore on his wrist. "Come back in two hours, though if you're longer, it'll be okay. I have plenty to do."

"I won't be late," she said.

She had a delightful time strolling along the streets, watching the people watch each other, visiting shops full of wonderful goods. She felt right at home, clad in the jeans and white blouse she had donned early that day. Such an outfit appeared nearly to be a uniform of the time in which she now dwelled, and it was certainly comfortable in the sun-laced heat of late afternoon.

She had no money, but that was all right. She could not imagine expending the amounts of money she saw on the tags attached to much of the merchandise she examined.

One store sold vitamins, which she learned were the ingredients in food that imparted their value to the human body. Fortunately she had seen no indication that people were giving up eating in favor of swallowing vitamin pills. Other healing potions were available in the store as well, including medicinal tea and elixirs to encourage sexual potency. She felt her face flush as she read the labels. Mike certainly had no need of such potions.

The shop she enjoyed the most stood on a corner. It was called The Nature Company. A small waterfall in its window caught her attention. Inside, a TV like Mike's showed moving vistas of scenery similar to that she had seen on her wagon trek across the country. There were rows of books, racks of shirts, and all manner of other goods she did not understand. The best items were at the rear of the shop: rocks, both large and small, that were for sale. Embedded in them were fossils much like those she had touched in the place of magic to bring her here. In this time, people must think nothing of being able to purchase such magic! Perhaps they simply did not know the exciting possibilities hidden in fossils.

When the time for her to return to Mike's office neared, she regretfully left this wonder-filled shop.

As she reached the building in which Mike's office was located, she noticed someone familiar pacing back and forth inside the lobby. Philip Rousseau. She walked slowly through the glass door, watching him. His teeth were clenched and his flabby hands were wadded into fists at his sides. He stared at the elevators as though deciding whether to take one upstairs.

A shiver shot up her back. Philip had threatened Mike, and a few minutes later Mike had nearly stepped into an empty elevator shaft. This man, who appeared ferally angry, had to be why Abby still felt a great curl of unease twisted about her insides in this city of L.A. If only she could find out what he had in mind to hurt Mike next, perhaps she could prevent it more easily.

She drew in her breath, then approached him. "Mr. Rousseau?"

The man turned abruptly as though startled. One fist raised as though he would strike her, and Abby stepped back. "Yes?" His small eyes, sunken deep into his fleshy face, widened in recognition. "You're a friend of Danziger's, aren't you? I saw you in his office the other day."

"I was there, yes." She glanced toward the security desk, where the curious guard, a thin man with a receding hairline, watched them. She turned her back to him and said, "My name is Abby Wynne. I wonder if I might speak with you."

"About Danziger? I was getting ready to go after that son of a—" Glancing at Abby, he stopped, then continued, "Thanks to him, I'm being harassed, and my lawyer says . . ." He grew quiet suddenly, as though aware he was talking too much. "What's on your mind?"

"I need to know about Mike Danziger. Personal reasons."

The man's beady eyes looked interested at last.

"Look," Abby continued, "this is not the best place to speak. Perhaps we could—"

"There's a coffee shop next door. I'll buy." He took her elbow and propelled her away from the lobby door. Abby stiffened her arm, bare beneath her blouse's short sleeves. She willed herself not to tear free from the unwelcome touch. An iciness from his cold, reptilelike fingers made her shudder.

The shop to which he led her was small and seemed to have an endless variety of coffees and pastries from which to choose, even the "decaf" that Hannah had offered her at Mike's home. The place smelled delicious, with the dark, warm aroma of coffee laced with the sweetness of baking. Abby asked the Asian woman at the counter for plain coffee and a roll called a croissant. Philip chose something called cappuccino and a basket of chocolate chip cookies. Abby was startled by the loud grinding of the machine that made Philip's frothy drink.

They sat at a small table in a corner. Philip put his food down, then seated himself. He looked at Abby, who took a chair across from him. "So," he said, "what did the bastard do to you?"

Abby tried not to feel discomfited by this man's profanity. She had had a few minutes to think about what to say. "Nothing yet. But you see, I have some money of my own, and he seems attracted to me. You stated in anger that he killed your sister. Were you exaggerating? I must know if he is truly dangerous." She did not believe that of Mike, particularly not from the venomous, irrational Philip. What she really sought was how dangerous the man before her was. Despite his obvious anger that was, for the moment, tempered, her special sense told her nothing—at least not yet. But maybe he himself would reveal what she needed.

"Dangerous? Hell, he's lethal. And talk about hanging on to your money—he's taken all of Dixie's, and it should have come to me. Not only that, my little visit to his office the other day cost me plenty. I've been hounded by the cops ever since. They say I tampered with the elevator. I've had to get my lawyer involved."

"Did you tamper with it?" She broke off a piece of her flaky croissant and put it into her mouth. It tasted delicious and buttery.

Philip set his jaw firmly, causing his thick lips to protrude. "What is this? Are you going to quiz me like the cops?"

Abby held up a hand. "Of course not." But she noticed he hadn't answered the question. She glanced about, suddenly uneasy. At least they were in a restaurant with other people around. She would not want to be alone with this man. Philip's aura of rage was reflected in the flashing fury in his small, dark eyes even now, when he was sitting and sipping a drink.

Though her special sense still sent her no warning, Abby feared this man.

Philip leaned toward her. "You better watch out for Danziger, lady. Before they were married, he forced my sister to sign a prenup."

Abby blinked. "What's that?"

He looked at her as though she were stupid. "A prenuptial agreement. You know, a paper that said she couldn't claim any interest in Arlen's Kitchens if they got divorced, and her heirs—other than any kids they had together, which they didn't—couldn't touch the company if she died. Well, she did die, thanks to him."

Abby tried to ask what had happened to his sister, but he continued without letting her speak.

"That meant Danziger even got to keep her part of the community property. He shouldn't be allowed to profit from killing her. But I was just at my damned lawyer's office, and he says it'd be a waste of his time and my money to contest it.

Danziger's too damned powerful. He should be shot."

Abby drew in her breath. Was this it? Did Philip Rousseau intend to shoot Mike? "That is rather drastic," she said, wishing her voice sounded less hoarse.

"Nothing's too good for Danziger." Philip Rousseau laughed, and Abby cringed at the ugly, bitter sound. "Anyhow, I've warned you. If you know what's good for you, you'll stay away from him."

And you, Abby thought.

Mike glanced at the crystal-and-brass clock on his paper-strewn desk. More than two hours had passed since he had given Abby his watch and sent her out to shop. He shouldn't be worried; she was an adult, and he'd told her not to hurry.

But she seemed so childlike and naive at times. . . .

With a wry quirk of his lips, he put down the ledger he'd been reading. He couldn't concentrate now anyway, not with his mind on Abby. He might as well go find her.

First he invited Lowell and Ruth for dinner and called Hannah to give instructions.

Then he left the office. The elevator reminded him of Abby and how she'd saved his life, more than once. But he didn't know what to make of her strange tale of coming from the past to take care of him. He shook his head. What was her agenda?

She couldn't be for real—could she?

At the security station in the lobby, he told the thin, balding guard on duty, "I wonder if you've seen my guest, Abby Wynne. She's a pretty woman with light brown hair. She's wearing blue jeans, a white shirt, and—"

"The one I saw on your floor the other day when the elevator broke down?"

Mike nodded. "That's the one."

"Yeah. She met some guy here. They went that way." He pointed down the street.

Mike frowned. As far as he knew, Abby didn't know anybody here. "Thanks." He exited the building and walked down the street in the direction the guard had indicated.

The air was heavy and hot, making Mike aware of his own respiration. He recalled the bee sting incident earlier that day: his fear as his throat had constricted and his breathing had grown nearly impossible. He took a deep breath now, simply because he could.

And then he stopped walking abruptly, sucking in his breath. Inside the coffee cafe next door to his building he saw, through the large plate-glass window, Abby Wynne, having an intimate tete-a-tete with Philip Rousseau. Philip, who had been Dixie's brother. Who had threatened Mike just before someone had tampered with the elevator in his building. Who wanted money from Mike, maybe even Arlen's Kitchens.

Abby knew Philip. She'd known Mike's connection to Arlen's Kitchens even out in the desert. And now she was feeding him a ridiculous story about being a time traveler.

Linda O. Johnston

He pivoted on his heel and returned to the building lobby.

"Did you find her?" the guard asked, looking up from the desk.

"No." Mike's voice was abrupt.

"Well, there she is, right behind you."

Mike turned. "Hi," Abby said. She was smiling, as though glad to see him. And why not? She probably saw dollar signs every time she looked at him.

He should send her on her way. But not yet. Not until she'd revealed exactly what she was up to. "Let's go home," he said curtly.

Abby wondered, once they were inside the Bronco, whether she should mention to Mike that she'd met with Philip Rousseau. Probably not. Mike seemed to be in a bad mood, and mentioning his angry, dangerous ex-brother-in-law was not likely to cheer him.

As they drove from the building, Mike said, "I've invited Lowell and Ruth for dinner tonight."

"That should be fun." Abby meant it. Perhaps company would help lighten Mike's mood.

Mike remained quiet on their way home. The deep furrowing of his brow revealed the intensity of his worry—about business? His brush with death that morning? Her? Abby wished she could stroke his cheek, smooth away his cares, but he might resent such a gesture from someone he did not trust.

But his silence gave her too much time to think. Her unease since reaching L.A. had settled

186

to the back of her mind like a bad memory, but suddenly it leapt out. A shudder of dread coursed through her, as though a rodent crept on tiny, clutching feet from her toes to her temples. Was it simply because of her disturbing meeting with Philip?

By the time they reached Mike's home, Abby was quaking from her own inner turmoil. Why did she not simply have a vision so she could know for certain the source of the danger she sensed?

Mike disappeared toward the wing of the house he occupied as Abby joined Hannah in the kitchen. The housekeeper was excited about the dinner party. Serving Abby a cup of cinnamon apple tea, she sat with her at the table to discuss the menu. "Though Mike's in the food business, he doesn't want to be bothered," she said. "Or maybe it's *because* he's in the food business."

They decided on salad, pasta with herbed vegetables, and chocolate mousse for dessert. Rather, Hannah decided. Abby simply agreed, since she was not familiar with most foods Hannah described.

"You'll get the hang of all this," Hannah said kindly, reaching across the table to pat Abby's hand.

Abby looked at the older woman who today wore a bright pink dress beneath her pinafore. "Hannah, are you . . . I mean, do you truly know things others don't?"

Hannah's toothy smile deepened the wrinkles at the sides of her mouth and hazel eyes. "Of course. And what I don't really know, I pretend to. Things get interesting when people think they've no secrets from you."

"But doesn't anyone get angry? Call you a witch, or threaten punishment?"

Hannah frowned sympathetically. "Is that how you've been treated? Poor Abby. No, I'm called eccentric but left alone."

Abby managed a nervous smile. "Do I have any secrets from you?"

"Oh, yes, dear. Many. You're not nearly as readable as most people, since you and I seem to share a bunch of talents. I'd enjoy discussing them, but right now I've got to start dinner."

She stood and bustled away, leaving Abby wishing that she had the nerve to confide in Hannah, to ask for help. Maybe Hannah could give focus to the peril she anticipated.

Despite her uneasiness, Abby came downstairs later prepared for a gala, if intimate, party. She wore her prettiest long, floral dress, and she had pulled her hair back into a neat bun. She had even borrowed a little makeup from Hannah to emphasize her eyes and lips. Finding the effect pleasing herself, she was particularly gratified by Mike's appreciative stare that quickly turned into a scowl. What had she done to anger him?

The dining room had been decorated with flowers. Handsome china and crystal were set out in festive array. But successful parties required convivial people.

Ruth set the tone of the evening when she

failed even to say hello to Abby, who waited at the dining room door to greet Mike's guests. Attractive in a form-hugging black dress adorned only with a pearl necklace, Ruth stood close to Mike, whispering to him as he followed her into the room. She wore matching pearl earrings that dangled even lower than the last pair Abby had seen her wear.

Lowell shook Abby's hand with clammy fingers and murmured in a nervous monotone, "I think this party was a mistake. It can only remind Mike—"

But Mike left Ruth's side to join them then, and Lowell did not finish his sentence, leaving Abby wondering what he had been going to say.

Hannah's cooking was, as usual, wonderful, but Abby did not enjoy supper. Only Mike and Lowell talked, in forced conversation. Lowell was dressed as formally as at the office, from his dark suit to his shiny laced shoes. He punctuated much of what he said by grimacing to push his spectacles back up his nose. More than once, he apologized for the problems at Arlen's Kitchens. "I hope you aren't mad at me, Mike. I just thought we could try a little something different."

"I'm not mad," Mike said each time, but his tone lacked conviction, and Abby understood why Lowell kept seeking reassurance.

Ruth said little, mostly staring at Abby with coldness narrowing her large blue eyes. Abby was certain that Ruth had hoped Mike might turn to her after his wife's death and that she had been bitterly disappointed when he returned from the desert with Abby. Abby kept silent, certain she would seem backward to this modern businesswoman, and she did not want to embarrass Mike.

As Hannah cleared the last of their supper dishes, Ruth finally spoke. "So, Abby, Mike told us that you lost your family on the desert. Have the police been of much help in finding them?"

Abby bit her lip, looking toward Mike for help. But he was engrossed in a conversation with Lowell on a topic that seemed to interest both: something called baseball.

She turned back to Ruth. "I hope to be reunited with my family eventually without involving the authorities."

Ruth's blue eyes narrowed. "I'd have thought you'd be frantic. In fact—"

She was interrupted by the doorbell, followed a moment later by angry voices from outside the dining room. Hannah appeared in the doorway, but before she could speak, Philip Rousseau shouldered her aside. The scowl Mike's brother-in-law wore reminded Abby of the one on his face the first time she'd seen him, at the Arlen's Kitchens office. This night he was dressed informally again, in jeans and a faded T-shirt. There was a slackness to his fleshy face that Abby did not understand until he began speaking.

"Well, isn't this cozy?" His slurred voice oozed sarcasm, and Abby realized he was intoxicated. "A party with a bunch of the same guests as our last one. A few people missing, though, and she's here." He pointed to Abby. "But I wasn't invited. Dixie either. My beautiful sister isn't alive anymore, thanks to her loving husband." He glared at Mike, who had risen to stand. Then, surprisingly fast, he dashed toward Mike.

Philip had told Abby earlier that Mike should be shot. "Be careful, " she cried. "He might have a gun."

"Wish I did," he muttered. He took a swing at Mike.

Mike blocked the punch effortlessly. "You were right, Philip. You weren't invited. And you're drunk." He pulled Philip toward an empty chair and thrust him into it. "Sit down and sober up." The glance he shot at Abby looked almost accusatory, and she cringed. Surely she was mistaken. Why would he direct his anger toward her?

"I'll just bet you'd rather I get in my car and head down that hill, wouldn't you?" Philip continued in his slushy voice. "Especially at a certain little curve."

Abby caught an undercurrent she did not understand from Lowell, Ruth, and Hannah, who all glanced at one another, then at Mike, who towered over the seated man. His hands were clenched at his sides. "You're a bastard, Rousseau," he growled.

Philip's grin was ugly. "And you're a murderer!"

Ruth hurried to Mike's side, placing a restraining hand on his arm. Looking down at the seated man, she said sharply, "That's enough, Philip."

"Get that son of a bitch out of here," Mike said, turning so quickly that he dislodged Ruth's calming touch. He strode across the room to stare out the dining room window. His hands, near his sides, clutched the waist-high windowsill. Abby could see by the rigidity of his stance and the whiteness of his knuckles the effort Mike made not to attack Philip Rousseau.

"Better get him sober first," Lowell admonished.

"I'll rustle up another cup of coffee or six," Hannah said.

"I need to use the john," Philip muttered. He followed Hannah from the room.

Ruth joined Mike at the window. "You need some more mousse to sweeten up this sour evening. Come on, or I'll feed it to you myself." Again taking his arm, she coaxed him to his seat. Pointedly ignoring Abby, she began to talk about the delayed plans to expand Arlen's Kitchens to a new state.

When Philip had not returned after a while, Lowell went after him. A few minutes later, Philip reappeared by himself.

"Here," Ruth said, filling an empty cup with coffee from a carafe Hannah had brought. "Drink this." Surprisingly he obeyed and even downed a few more cups.

Eventually Lowell, too, rejoined the group. Then Ruth, with a dazzling but forced smile for Mike, went to freshen up. Abby hoped that the atmosphere might become more pleasant when everyone was finally reassembled, but that was impossible with Philip's glowering. The party soon broke up.

At the door, Philip turned back. "Getting me sober only makes things clearer. I know that almighty Mike Danziger wants me dead, just like Dixie. Didn't you hear him? And if he doesn't get me, I'll get him!"

Abby was glad to see everyone leave. She hoped for a few moments alone with Mike, to reassure him that surely no one other than his grief-crazed brother-in-law would accuse him of killing his wife.

A certain warmth flowed through her body when she considered being alone with Mike once more in this house. Might they repeat their wonderful encounter of the night before? But he simply excused himself.

Abby went to bed. Her earlier disjointed fear had not abated, and she wished she could either rid herself of the terrible crawly sensation or understand what it meant.

She had a dream that night of being on the desert, surrounded by heat so intense that she thought she might melt. Flames seemed to leap at her from the sun, and she felt unable to breathe in the stifling heat. She called out for relief.

Her own cry woke her. She screamed aloud then, for it had not been a dream after all.

One wall of her bedroom was in flames.

Chapter Nine

Smoke curled from the fiery wall, gagging Abby, as billowing fumes and her own tears blinded her. Along that wall was her closet—and the door into the hallway. She could not get out!

"Mike!" She realized he couldn't hear her—with his ears. "Please, Mike," she whispered, her throat aching. "Help me."

But she knew how unreliable her special powers could be. Worse, she had no idea of the fire's source. Mike might already be injured—or dead.

That could not be! She had to save herself . . . to save him.

Struggling to free herself from her bedclothes, she leapt out of bed away from the fire. All along the wall near the door, flames crackled and roared, licking out like tongues of a myriad frenzied serpents. She had to escape, but how?

The window! In her bare feet, she rushed toward it, throwing it open and gasping as she inhaled the fresh air outside. But the influx of air must have fanned the flames. At the increased crackling behind her, she turned to see the fire charge farther into the room. She tasted soot; a vile, stifling odor filled her nostrils.

Swallowing hard, she turned back. The window was large enough for her to crawl through. But then what? It was high above the ground. If she were injured, she might be unable to help Mike.

Suddenly she heard a noise behind her. Turning, she saw the flames leap away. Someone had opened the door. Mike!

"Mike, be careful!" She screamed, but the sound was a gurgle in her raw throat.

"Abby!" Suddenly there he was, covered head to toe with a sopping blanket as he sprang through the leaping flames. "Come, Abby. Now!"

She rushed toward him. He threw the wet cover around her, too, hugging her close. Then he pulled her through the flames.

In the hall she bent over, gasping at the cool, sweet air. But he did not let her rest. He lifted her into his arms, then ran down the corridor, where he dashed down the steps and out the front door. He hurried to the back of the house, far from the area of the fire. Only then did he set her down as she coughed.

He knocked on the door of Hannah's carriage house. "Hannah!" he cried. "Fire! Call nine-one-one!"

Abby was too relieved they were safe to ask what calling 911 meant. In a minute, Hannah appeared at her door, her round face lightening as she saw them. "Thank God you're both all right!" she exclaimed, hurrying out. "The fire department's on its way. How bad is it?"

"As far as I could see, the fire's just in Abby's bedroom." He wore only jeans and shoes, and streaks of dirt striated his chest and face. His gray eyes were sunken behind a raccoonlike mask of grime. But Abby had never thought him more handsome.

They walked toward the front of the house, where Abby saw smoke curling from its upper story. In minutes a loud, mechanical wail sounded in the distance, its tone fluttering high, then low like the Bronco's noise in Barstow. Then there were two. "Sirens," Hannah said as Abby turned to her questioningly. "The firemen are coming."

Two large red trucks appeared. Men dressed in shining yellow clothing leapt from them, tossing hoods over their heads and masks over their faces. The firemen scattered in all directions. Some dragged long hoses; others carried equipment whose uses Abby could not begin to imagine. Shouting orders, they acted crisply and confidently, as though they had done this many times before.

A young man with freckles and a prominent nose approached the spot where Abby, Mike, and Hannah stood. "Anyone still inside?" He wore a badge that identified him as Montgomery.

"No," Mike said.

Montgomery regarded Mike, then Abby, who,

coughing lightly, realized that her once-white gown was as streaked with smudges as Mike's face, and her feet were still bare, the pavement beneath them cold and rough.

The man asked, "Anyone hurt?"

"She was trapped inside," Mike said, gently thrusting Abby toward Montgomery as she coughed once more. "But fortunately the fire hadn't spread too far into the room."

He cast a questioning glance toward Mike. "You got her out?" Mike nodded.

Abby shied away as Montgomery neared her, but Hannah explained, "He's a paramedic, dear. He'll help you."

Montgomery quickly drew some equipment from a large bag he carried and put a mask over Abby's face. "Breathe," he said.

Still fearful, she nevertheless obeyed. Immediately her lungs and throat seemed clearer and she clutched the mask, inhaling deeply the cleansing air as Montgomery proceeded to check her over.

As they all watched, the black, swirling cloud emanating from the house turned gray, then white. After a while, it vanished.

Still, firemen continued to bustle about. Abby, exhausted but coughing less, sat on the ground, and Mike and Hannah joined her. Throwing her a worried glance, Mike took Abby's chilled feet in his lap and clasped them tightly in his large hands, warming them. She smiled shyly. This was one of the dearest, most tender acts anyone had ever performed for her.

A fireman approached. His badge identified him as Frendz, and he appeared to be in charge. "It was confined to one bedroom," he said. "We'll leave a couple men to watch, but the rest of the place should be all right." He nodded toward Abby, who was coughing lightly. "The guys will run her to the hospital now."

She shook her head vehemently, stopping her cough despite the tickle in her throat. "No. Thank you."

"They'll just check you over, miss. Make sure you're all right."

"I'm fine. Really."

"But . . ."

She looked at Mike, then Hannah. She did not want to leave this place. Most especially she did not want to answer questions strangers might ask, such as who she was and where she was from.

"We'll get her to a doctor if she seems any worse," Hannah said.

Abby held her breath as Mike studied her. What if he used this opportunity to turn her over to someone else?

She closed her eyes briefly in relief as he said to Frendz, "Thanks for your help, but we'll keep an eye on her." The fireman reluctantly agreed and walked away. Then Mike turned to Hannah. "We'll put Abby in the room next to the one I'm in now. We could all use some rest."

"I doubt I'll sleep a wink," Hannah said but nevertheless went inside.

Although she still smelled like smoke, Abby insisted on helping Hannah put on fresh bed linens while Mike stayed out to talk to the firemen. The room was in a separate wing from the one that had burned. It was much smaller than the one she had been in but was decorated with sturdy furniture, possibly built by Mike's loving hands, that reminded her of her own home so far in the past. Abby caught the sheet Hannah shook over the bed. "What did Mike mean that I should take the room next to the one he's in *now*?"

"Till you moved here, he stayed in the master suite to punish himself," Hannah said, shaking her head as she squeezed a fluffy pillow into its case. "That's where you were sleeping."

"I did not mean to displace him," Abby said sadly, then realized, "But it could have been Mike who was trapped!" She remembered with a start how strong had been her sense of crawly uneasiness earlier that day. Her special sense had been warning her of the danger.

Mike soon joined them. He was scowling, his arms crossed. "They think it was arson," he said curtly. "The fire apparently was started in the closet in a pile of clothes where it could smolder for a while."

Abby's teeth caught at her trembling lower lip. She was not surprised, but the idea of someone wanting to hurt Mike that way terrified her as much as the missing elevator.

"Was it someone at the party?" she asked.

"Philip, of course," Hannah said disgustedly.

Mike shrugged. "Probably. But it's possible somebody slipped in to steal something while the gate was open for the guests, like Philip did, then started the fire to cover his tracks. I'll check tomorrow to see if anything's missing."

Hannah said, "But you think it's Philip, don't you?"

"How could I think anything else?" But he looked at Abby, and she had the insight, sadly, that he did indeed think something else: that she had in some manner been involved.

She felt relieved that she was the one who had been endangered by her failure to understand the peril she'd sensed, not Mike. But yet again, as she sank down onto the edge of the freshly made bed, she felt an eerie tickling at the base of her spine. She swallowed a gasp. Despite all that had happened, the danger was not over.

An hour later, she lay in the dark in the strange bed, her hand tucked under her head. Her heart thumped in vague, unfocused fear, and tears puddled in her eyes. At least she was no longer coughing.

After bathing, she had dressed in a gown borrowed from Hannah, who had returned to her carriage house. But Abby could not sleep. She could hardly rest.

Mike was still in danger. She knew it, but there was nothing she could do.

She was angry with her special power. What good was it?

Reason told her that, despite Mike's suggestion of an anonymous thief, the source of the peril must be his brother-in-law Philip. He had been there the day of the empty elevator shaft. He had burst in last evening, and the fire had occurred soon after. Both times Abby had sensed something wrong. She should be able to predict the next threat emanating from the angry man, particularly after she had made a point of questioning him.

But she could not predict a thing.

Again she recalled little Jimmy Danziger, dead on the trail west so many years ago because she could not foretell his reaction to the bee sting. Had she come forward all these years to protect Mike, only to find she could not save him either?

"Abby?"

The familiar deep voice from the doorway startled her, and she sat up, clutching the sheet to her. "Come in, Mike."

He turned on the light, entered the room, and sat on the bed beside her. She smelled the clean scent of soap; he, too, had showered. His damp hair, the color of rich coffee, was mussed over his forehead and hung to his shoulders. A short, silky blue robe was tied about his waist, and his lean and muscular legs were bare.

"You can't sleep either," he said. It was a statement, not a question.

"No." She hesitated. "Mike, why—?"

"Why am I here?" His voice sounded confused. His eyes were shadowed as they bored into hers. "Because you called me. Just as you called me with your crying last night and from the fire tonight. As you claim to have called to me from . . . how many years ago?" He paused. "This can't be real. What the hell are you doing to me?"

Feeling his torment, she reached out to him, and suddenly she was pressed tightly against his chest. And then his mouth came down on hers.

She responded quickly and ardently, loving the way his lips were harsh without hurting, the way his tongue plunged inside her mouth to explore without invading. He tasted of the herbs and spices used at dinner, overlaid with fresh mint and the unique flavor of him.

His hands moved up to grasp her hair, not gently but without hurting, holding her head immobile as he deepened their kiss. "Abby." His voice was a murmur against her lips, a single word that sounded at once of pain and reproach, sensuality and surrender.

Her hands reached up his back, stroking the cool smoothness of his robe and hating the way it interfered with her touching his skin. He moved abruptly, at once laying Abby down and stripping off his impeding garment.

He was bare underneath except for his abbreviated male underclothing, and as he stretched out atop her, pushing her nightgown up, Abby could feel the hot engorgement of his manhood against her thigh, straining to be free. She whimpered as he stroked her sensitive skin, her sides, her stomach, and finally barely touched the curve beneath her breasts. Teased, tortured, she shifted so that his hot, searching hand covered one eager mound. She gasped as he brushed, then squeezed her nipple.

She wanted more. She wanted to feel nothing

between them. She wanted to experience again the delicious, forbidden union that they had achieved before. In an uneven voice, she whispered, "Mike, I—"

His mouth did not let her finish, but she did not have to. He knew what she wanted. She did not know if he read her mind through their unique connection or whether he acted for his own need, but suddenly he rolled away, dragged off her gown and his own underwear, and pulled her tightly to him.

His firm skin was a sweet conflagration against hers. The wavy mat of his chest hair scraped her sensitive breasts like soft wire. She felt his hands inquisitively probing her thighs, and instinctively she parted her legs.

He stroked the most intimate part of her with his fingers, while she moaned softly. She had to touch him in return—the muscular breadth of his chest, his tight, firm buttocks. She heard his quick intake of breath as she wrapped her fingers about the searing length of him. "Abby," he murmured. His mouth captured hers once more as he pulled his body away for an instant.

And then he was inside her. It did not matter that the lights were turned on, for her eyes were tightly closed, the better to concentrate on the enormity and ecstasy of tactile sensation.

Fleetingly she recalled once again her own society's prohibition against such activity without benefit of marriage, the assumption that a woman could not feel any enjoyment even then, but the thought was overwhelmed by the exquisite pleasure that grew as he began to rock, first softly, then more fervently, as she moved to meet his thrusts. She could not keep any part of herself still. Her hands roved his back, pressing him insistently to her. Her mouth kissed his neck, bit his shoulder, tasted the surprising, salty essence of heated masculine skin.

As before, her release came, a delicious starburst of sensation that made her feel as though dying or reborn, she was not certain which. Its delight escalated as she heard Mike's concurrent crow of satisfaction, felt, through their bond, that he was as pleased as she.

As she lay there afterward, enveloped in strong arms against his hard, warm body, listening to his breathing grow even and feeling his heartbeat slow, she wondered if he had shared the sensations she felt. He must. He had come to her because she called without speaking. Surely he also experienced her intense feelings as they made love, just as she enjoyed his.

But, oh, his terrible loneliness! Even now, after the magnificence of their joining, she felt his sudden emotional withdrawal to that realm of solitary suffering, and it pained her, too.

He remained quiet for so long that Abby believed he had fallen asleep. She felt a modicum of comfort that, despite the way his thoughts flayed him inside, he was soothed enough to remain in her embrace. She savored the moment, for how many others might there be like it?

Whatever the reason for their connection, whatever the purpose for which she had been drawn across a century, she now was certain of only one wonderful, agonizing fact: she had fallen deeply, irrevocably, impossibly in love with Mike Danziger.

She smiled sadly to herself and nestled closer. From the darkness his deep and dear voice whispered, "Abby, are you awake?"

She responded by tightening her embrace.

"You're not conspiring with Philip to steal Arlen's Kitchens from me." He spoke a statement, not a question, yet he did not sound convinced.

"No!" The cocoon of safety and warmth in which Abby had been furled crumbled about her. "How could you imagine such a thing?" She tried to pull away, but his strong arms still held her close.

"You knew about Arlen's Kitchens on the desert." His voice was muffled against her hair.

"I knew about Arlen. You look like him."

He gave a small, disbelieving snort. "And . . ."

She felt his hesitation through the tensing of his body. "What?"

"I saw you with Philip yesterday."

A new wave of Mike's emotion plunged through her, a piercing sense of betrayal. But it was not a current pain. She knew he was reliving the way he had felt when he had first seen her with Philip. Tears welled in her eyes, and she burrowed closer to him, holding him tightly, soothing him. She inhaled his pleasant masculine aroma, tinged with soap and heat and salt.

She began to explain. "I saw Philip outside your office when I returned." Her soft voice wavered. "I wanted to talk to him, to see if I could learn how he next planned to attack you. But I was unable."

Mike remained silent.

"Oh, Mike. You must have believed I told him of your dinner party, but I did not know of it then. You informed me about it afterward."

"You could have called him." She drew herself taut to protest, but he spoke again before she could. "But I know you didn't." His arms tightened about her. His hands began to rub her back. "If you'd been conspiring with him, you'd have told him that you were sleeping in my bedroom. The fire would have been set to hurt me, not you."

She let her breath out in a quick sigh of relief. He believed her. She wished, however, that he had been convinced not by circumstances, but by the trust of her that she craved.

He continued slowly, a forcefulness in his tone despite his hesitancy. "I . . . Abby, I don't know what's happening between us. I don't want to believe you're for real. I don't even know who you are. But I hear you when I'm far out of earshot, I'm drawn to you when . . . Look, why don't you go to Jess's tomorrow? See if you can find those journals. I still can't promise they'll turn me into a believer, but I want—"

Warmed, thrilled at the step he was taking toward overcoming his incredulity, she silenced the words that were so difficult for him with an ardent kiss.

* * *

"The arson investigators are here now," Mike told Abby the next morning at the kitchen table over toast and coffee. The place still smelled of smoke and chemicals, and water had dripped downstairs from the dousing of the bedroom. Fortunately, though, only the front of the house was damaged. "And the insurance adjuster should be here in a while. After I talk to them I'll be going to the office. So I'm leaving you in Hannah's capable hands. She'll take you shopping and to Jess's."

Abby smiled. Perhaps he was as eager as she for the journals to be located, for Abby to prove she was what she said. She was once again clad in a too large T-shirt and jeans of Mike's, for those of her new clothes that had survived the flames nevertheless had been ruined by smoke and water. Hannah had lent her a headband to hold back her hair.

There were several strange men about the place when Abby and Hannah left a short while later—the arson and insurance people, Abby assumed. So far Mike had found nothing missing.

Hannah drove the small, open-roofed car that usually sat beside the Bronco in the outbuilding Mike called the garage. Abby enjoyed the feel of the sun on her face, the breeze rippling her hair behind its headband. Before they went far along the twisting descent, Hannah slowed the car at a sharp curve and stopped, pointing to one of several large, gnarled trees clutching the shoulder of the road beyond a new-looking metal railing. Beyond, the land sloped gradually for a few feet, then dropped off into a void. "There's where it was," she said. "Feel the vibrations?"

Abby's neck did, indeed, tingle inexplicably. She recalled Mike's intimation the first time he had driven her up here that something had occurred to shake up his neighbors, and she'd sensed his own disturbance, too. "What happened?"

"That's where Mike's wife, Dixie, died."

Abby sat still for a long moment, aware her heartbeat had sped up in anticipation. She was about to learn the source of a giant's share of Mike's sorrow. "Tell me about it."

"This is Dixie's car." Hannah's voice was a monotone as she touched the steering wheel of the small vehicle in which the women sat. "One night last winter, Mike was driving his Mercedes down the hill. This is as far as they got. The car slammed full force into this tree, killing Dixie. Mike was injured, but more in mind than body, I think."

Looking at the emptiness of the drop-off near the trees, Abby clasped her hands in her lap and said in a small voice, "They both could have been killed." She shuddered.

"Mike wishes they both had been."

Abby, shocked, turned to Hannah. The older woman was studying her, as though Abby's reaction was very important. Abby whispered, "He loved her so much that he wanted to die with her?"

Hannah shrugged. "He blames himself."

Abby thought of Philip's accusations. "But . . .

it was an accident, wasn't it?"

Hannah started the car once more. "Sure," she said. "But Mike won't believe it."

"What do you mean?"

"You'd better ask him." Hannah pulled a lever, and the car began to move down the hill.

Abby thought of Mike's bleak loneliness. Now she understood its source: grief . . . and guilt. But she was puzzled. There was more here than Hannah had explained. "Hannah, why—"

Hannah held up one hand. "Sorry, Abby. Yes, there's more to the story, but no, I don't think I should be the one to tell you."

Abby felt shaky as they continued toward their destination. She wanted to be with Mike, to comfort him . . . to learn what Hannah had not revealed. She thought of their wonderful nights together, and sorrow welled up inside her. Was she simply an inadequate substitute for the wife Mike missed so terribly?

Hannah stopped the car in the parking lot of a large structure she called a shopping mall. Though also filled with stores, it was different from the single-story group of shops Mike had taken Abby to in Barstow. They made their purchases in a large department store, where Abby replaced the clothing she had lost with similar blouses and long skirts and, of course, this time's ubiquitous T-shirts and jeans. She also bought replacement shoes and a small leather purse.

Hannah explained credit cards when she tendered a small plastic card to pay for the purchases as Mike had done; its use was not dissimilar to the grocer's keeping a running account for Abby at home.

"This card's Mike's," Hannah said. "He lets me charge things for him."

They resumed their drive. In a few minutes Hannah parked the car before several small stores. "Be right back," she promised. She slipped inside a shop whose sign proclaimed *Psychic*.

Sitting in the car alone, Abby tried not to think of Mike's guilt and the way he must miss his beloved wife, but she could not help it. Perhaps she could find a way to save him from the physical danger she sensed, but what could she ever do to salve his unbearably painful conscience—or soothe away the hurt of having lost someone dear to him?

A few minutes later Hannah emerged, dropping a magazine called *Los Angeles Psychic* on Abby's lap. "You might be interested in seeing this," she said.

Thumbing through it, Abby asked, "What does 'psychic' mean?"

"A psychic sees things other people don't." Hannah again started the car. "This one's a mind reader. Some are fortune-tellers. Some even help the police solve crimes."

Abby's hand rose involuntarily to her mouth. "Do . . . do they see visions?"

"That's what some say. Others feel things or see them in tarot cards. Some are astrologers. It depends on the particular power."

"And people today just accept that? They really

don't think it's witchcraft? Or evil?"

While the car was stopped at a light, Hannah looked at Abby. Her smile was kind, etching a starburst of wrinkles at the corner of her eyes. "Like Mike, most people don't believe such things are true, so they ignore people who do or shrug them off as harmless nuts. But there are plenty of believers, too, who revere people with such power."

Abby's mind spun. Of all the wonders of this age, this was the most remarkable. If anyone learned of her visions, most wouldn't revile her. Some might think her crazy, as Mike did—but others might actually honor her. That was too wonderful to imagine.

She said to Hannah, "You are a psychic, too, no matter what Mike thinks. How else could you have known that I am one? I did not mention my visions to you."

Hannah grinned mischievously. "Sure, I play the kook around Mike since he won't see farther than what's in front of his face. But I actually have a little paranormal power. Not nearly as much as I sense in you, though." Her expression sobered as she glanced at Abby, then back toward the road. "I wish I could have foretold that accident and saved Mike all that grief. But one thing I do know is that I'm glad you're here, for his sake."

When they reached Aunt Jess's gray stone house, Abby stared at it, hopelessness creating a heaviness in her chest. She touched her chin, reaching for missing bonnet ribbons. The three-story edifice appeared huge. How was she to locate four small—but oh, so essential—items within its thick walls?

Jess's housekeeper Grace met them at the door. She wore a black dress similar to the one she'd had on when Abby first met her. The frown she wore beneath her parrot's-beak nose was even less welcoming than the one she'd turned on Abby on her prior visit. "I knew this wasn't a good idea," Grace whined. "Jess has been fussing all morning waiting for you. And you promised not to be a bother."

Abby squeezed Hannah's arm as she opened her mouth to protest. "I'm sorry," Abby said gently. "We'll convey our greetings, then go off to look, if that's all right."

Grace sniffed. "As long as you're quiet."

Jess waited on the settee in the antique-crammed parlor where she had been on Abby's prior visit. Once again Abby drew in her breath as she saw Jess, with her bewildered expression on a face so much like an aged Lucy's. Abby hurried across the room and took the ancient, dry hands from the elderly woman's lap, squeezing them gently. "I'm so glad to see you again, Jess."

The puckered mouth curved into a heartbreakingly sweet smile as again Abby smelled roses amid medicine. "Happy you could come, Dixie." She peered up myopically, then shook her head as though to clear it. "You're not Dixie. You're Abby, and you're here to look for the journals."

Thrilled at her sudden lucidity, Abby said

softly, "Where did Myra keep the journals?"

"In the box under her bed, of course. When we were young she took them out lots of evenings to read to us."

Abby's breath quickened. "Where was her bedroom?"

"The hallway upstairs, first room on the right," Grace said. "But don't get excited. That room's been cleaned many a time since Myra's been gone. There's nothing under that bed now except the dustballs that've accumulated since the last time our cleaning girl swept."

Abby refused to let her spirits plummet. "Where might the box have been put, Jess?"

But the aged, cloudy eyes had shuttered over once more. "I'm sleepy, Grace," the soft voice managed. "Is it time for my nap yet?"

"Of course, Jessie." Grace shot an angry look toward Abby, then rushed to help her charge turn to lie comfortably on her settee.

"We'll start upstairs," Abby murmured, motioning to Hannah to follow.

The room that had apparently once been Myra's was nearly empty, except for an antique bed and matching dresser. The journals were not, of course, on the bare wood floor under the bed. They were not in this room.

Nor were they in any of the other unoccupied rooms on that floor. Abby went downstairs for permission to search Jess's and Grace's rooms, but Hannah and she found no journals in either.

They began sifting through the attic, a large, single room that spanned the entire top floor of the house. It was filled with dusty old boxes, many of which contained books. By the time the two women were ready to leave for the day, they had completed their search in only half the boxes.

They returned the next day with no further success. The day after that, Jess had a doctor's appointment, and Grace grumbled about leaving them there alone, so Abby reluctantly agreed to stay away. Concerned she might never find the journals, she began to use the research suggestions given to her by Lydia; Hannah and she visited two libraries and the Gene Autry Western Heritage Museum.

She found, in one old volume, the sketchiest reference to the Danziger train and the fact that it split apart in the Mojave Desert. Many members of the defecting group perished—as did several of the remaining party. But no names were given.

She held back tears as she realized she still did not know what had happened to her family. Nor did she have any way of proving to Mike who she was.

That evening Abby tried very hard to act normal with Mike, though she felt too depressed for light conversation. She ached for him, and for herself. She sorrowed over his grief and guilt. She worried about her family. And, she acknowledged to herself, her illogical hurt from learning how deeply Mike had cared for his deceased wife seemed to increase as she spent more time with him.

The following day, Hannah and she returned to Jess's house. At the end of a week, they had searched through every room, from the attic to the garage and an old tool shed in the garden. Abby felt uncomfortable in the half-basement, particularly when Hannah nonchalantly explained that the metal poles here and there must have been supports added to shore up the house after one earthquake or another, but she examined the empty shelves along its walls nonetheless.

Still, there was no sign of the journals.

Abby had run out of places to look.

And her sense of foreboding was growing stronger once more.

Chapter Ten

On the evening of the last day of Abby's search, Mike sped home, as he did each night. After wrestling all day with ledgers, invoices, and bottom lines that were seemingly unable to sink much lower, he considered his house a haven, despite all the postfire reconstruction work now going on.

The fact that Abby waited for him certainly had nothing to do with his eagerness.

That evening, as usual, she greeted him at the door with a smile on her lovely face. She wore a plain white cotton dress, and her hair, held back from her face by matching wooden barrettes that set off the shade of her light brown hair, revealed all the more clearly her excellent bone structure.

But the sadness in her eyes told him immediately that, once more, she hadn't found the journals.

Not that she was ever anything less than cheerful.

"Guess what Hannah's made us for dinner," she said.

"Arlen stew," he guessed, as he did each night, earning an exasperated shake of the head.

"No, pasta with seafood pesto."

Each night there was a different dish, a veritable encyclopedia of healthful culinary delights: savory chicken casseroles; bean stews; pastas and rice with amazing and creative toppings.

Hannah was outdoing herself, with Abby's help in the kitchen. But Mike knew that Hannah was trying to keep Abby occupied after each day's fruitless search. The more downcast Abby's mood, the more intricate the gourmet meal.

But the only place her depression ever showed was in the dimming of the brilliance of her dark eyes, more each day.

That evening he sat down at the dining room table set with everyday dishes dressed up by candlelight. After a moment Abby joined him.

"Here you are." Hannah placed a plate before each of them.

But Mike hardly tasted the first bite of pasta as he noticed Abby just twirling the noodles around her fork.

"Give it up, Abby," he growled, shaking his head. Nothing was worth her becoming so despondent.

"Give up what?"

"Your search for those damned journals."

"Oh." She seemed to mull that over. Then her

217

listless gaze rose to fix on him. "I can't, Mike. Will you trust me if I don't find them?"

"What I think doesn't matter. What's important is—"

"Your trust is the only thing that matters," she said, her hair sweeping partway forward behind the confinement of her barrettes as her head dropped again. Once more she toyed with her food. "How else can I save you?"

Suddenly furious, he slammed his fork down on his plate, the clatter reverberating through the room. "Just leave me alone, Abby. I don't need saving, and I don't need my thoughts revered like some kind of god's. I'm just a very human bastard who's had enough."

Ignoring the tears that suddenly filled her eyes, he strode from the room and down the hall toward the den. She was a kook—or a wily schemer whose purpose he could not guess. She claimed only to want him to believe her incredible story. Her sole way to convince him was by the alleged contents of the missing journals.

Very convenient.

And then he stopped. Bastard was right. She had done nothing to merit his rage except to talk to Philip. And she claimed she'd done that for him, to try to reach inside his brother-in-law and read his mind.

There *was* something about her that was—different. Magnetic. Even frightening.

She knew of his hallucinations. She had saved his life twice and had lived through a fire meant for him. A fire he now blamed on himself. He'd found nothing missing from the house. That meant the arsonist was someone who'd been in the house that evening: Philip. Philip had been a hothead before Mike killed his sister. Her death must have driven him insane—one more thing that Mike could blame on himself. Or, more likely, Philip had hopes he'd inherit something on Mike's death, since he hadn't gotten much on Dixie's. But so far the police hadn't found enough evidence to arrest Philip. At least Mike no longer believed Abby had conspired with him, not when she'd been the one trapped by the fire.

Mike heard fleet footsteps behind him. He turned in time to see Abby enter the hall.

"I want you to know I understand, Mike," she said. Reaching him, she looked up wistfully. "You can't force yourself to believe something that sounds crazy. The last thing I wanted was to add to your feeling of guilt."

What did she think she was—an amateur pre-Sigmund Freud shrink? "My guilt is my own concern," he said childishly, stomping away.

He had gotten into the habit of watching TV with Abby after dinner, but now he headed for his workshop, his evening haven for years. He tried to lose himself in lathing an intricate chair leg but gave up after half an hour, before he ruined any more wood for lack of concentration.

He read in his room until quite late. Eventually he heard Abby enter the bedroom next door. He felt nearly crazy, imagining her undressing, hearing her shower run, knowing she was so near.

He'd visited her in her room nearly every night

over the past week. He now planned ahead enough to use protection against pregnancy. Still, their joining had been nearly spiritual. Somehow she always sensed what he needed: slow sweetness or fast careening. Or was he sensing her needs?

He was beginning to think like her, damn it! He'd had enough. She wasn't going to find those journals, and even if she did, they couldn't serve the purpose she wanted. So why didn't she just cut it out?

He turned out the light around midnight, but sleep didn't come. There was no noise from next door. How could she sleep with him lying there so miserable? So much for the myth of her sensing what he felt. If she did, she would know—

He saw the faint glow of light from the hall as his door opened. It closed. The edge of the bed sagged a little with Abby's slight weight, and then he felt her warmth just inches away. She smelled of cinnamon and potpourri.

"Mike?" Her whisper was hardly louder than a breath. "Are you awake?"

With a low growl, he pulled her to him. For the first time he failed to be gentle, but her eager response, the way she moaned aloud and raked her nails down his back, told him that she wanted nothing different. She bucked beneath him when he entered her, and the intensity of the sensations centered in the place of their joining soon made her gasp with pleasure. The sound, coupled with the feeling of her throbbing release, sent him spinning into his own crescendo.

A while later, utterly spent, he cradled her close. She had rattled him. Too often she seemed to see right through him.

Guilt. Maybe he did carry too much, but he didn't want to feel guilty for the way he treated Abby. He could help her find answers—even if they weren't the ones she was looking for. And then he could let her go.

He hoped.

He kept his voice low, even though the light unevenness of her breathing indicated she must be awake. "Abby?"

She responded immediately, her voice a golden caress against his chest. "I apologize for before, Mike. Hannah told me how your wife died. I suppose you can't help feeling guilty, though you weren't. You must have loved her very much, and I should not criticize the way you grieve."

"Grieve?" He snorted. "Hardly. I'm thrilled!"

She pulled away, as he expected. Wasn't every bereaved husband supposed to revere his dead wife?

But her inevitable shock at his reaction did not send her running from the room. Instead she found his hand and held it tightly. "Tell me, Mike," she urged, nestling against him once more.

He hesitated. His inclination was to tell her to mind her own business. But maybe it was time to uncork his emotions—and why not to someone who sensed them anyway? Abby would surely stop worrying about him once she understood what a son of a bitch he really was. Nice guys didn't do away with their wives.

Feeling his eyes narrow in steely resolve, he began, "Dear Dixie was a beautiful woman with charm no man could resist. I certainly couldn't, when she set her sights on me. Apparently she thought it would be amusing to marry a restaurant chain." He tried to keep the pain from his voice, but he must not have succeeded, for Abby pushed even closer. He didn't want her sympathy. His tone hardened. "I bored her—particularly when I made it clear that my profits were not earmarked for her personal amusement. There was a limit to how many designer outfits, jewels, and people she could buy."

The room was utterly silent for a moment. Then Abby said softly, "I see." Her soft hand released his to caress his cheek, but he grabbed it, thrusting it away.

"No, you don't. We fought all the time. And then she had the gall to have an affair and flaunt it."

"How awful for you," Abby whispered, again reaching for his hand, now balled into a fist.

The memory still had the power to torture him. Just wounded pride, of course. He'd no longer cared about the witch by then—she'd long since destroyed any affection he'd felt for her. He'd never loved her. But she certainly had fascinated him—when it suited her interests.

He went on in a monotone, "She laughed when I said I wanted out; I'd have to buy my freedom, and it wouldn't come cheap. That last night, we had a pretheater dinner party. She made a scene in front of my friends and employees. I wanted to strangle her. I was so upset that I argued about everything, even which car to take to the theater. Finally I insisted on driving mine, but I was so angry. . . . "

He had to stop for a moment as the recollections overwhelmed him: the yelling in the car, the cloying miasma of her expensive perfume, his rage so great that he couldn't function, couldn't get the brakes to work—

"Mike?" Abby's sweet voice brought him back to the present.

He didn't want to go into detail. He said simply, "I lost control on the way down the hill."

"Oh, Mike."

The sympathy in her voice unnerved him; he had to show it was unmerited. He pulled away from her, sitting straight in the bed. "I laughed, Abby. As we hurtled toward the cliff, I laughed. I remember thinking how ironic it was; neither of us would live to throw away my money."

"But you survived." Abby found him again in the dark, caressing his tense jaw with her fingertips.

"Yeah. Lucky me. Do you know the most ironic part of all? Right then, I didn't just want her out of my life; I wanted her dead. She died. I killed her."

"It was an accident, Mike."

"Sure," he spat. He waited for the usual wave of self-blame to drown him as it did each time he let himself remember the crash.

223

But somehow, now that he'd revealed the truth to Abby, it didn't hurt as much.

He'd caused Abby pain, though. Maybe he should give her the benefit of the doubt, the way she did with him. Yet—

He blurted out before he could change his mind, "Tomorrow, we're going to find those damned journals." He felt, rather than heard, her sharp intake of breath. "Look, maybe I've been too—" He never finished the thought as his mouth became too busy to say more.

Once again, Abby walked through the glass-paneled door into Aunt Jess's antique-jammed parlor, this time following Grace and Mike.

Jess sat on her favorite settee, knees primly together beneath the long, sky blue skirt tucked about them. Her silvery hair billowed around ancient features, so like Lucy's, that always made Abby want to weep with homesickness.

"Now don't upset her," Grace scolded before Mike began to speak.

Wearing dark trousers and a crisp yellow shirt, he moved his large frame with pantherlike suppleness that reminded Abby of their wonderful, secret nights together. Like last night. She never had imagined that lovemaking could steal all sense of propriety. Or perhaps it was the fact that she made love with Mike that transported her to such amazing heights. She would not need a ride on one of those soaring jets, so long as she could remain with him.

She wished she did not feel so relieved that

guilt alone, and not grieving over the loss of a beloved wife, caused his sorrows. Yet the fact that he hadn't loved Dixie perversely lessened Abby's despair. His coming here to help her brightened her mood even further. Now if they found the journals, she would be the happiest woman in this time!

Jess turned to Mike. "So good of you to come." Her voice was shrill but strong.

"I've brought Abby, too, Jess."

Abby approached the elderly woman with a smile.

"No journals yet, dear?"

"Not yet," Abby said, excited that this was one of Jess's more lucid days. Surely, with Mike here, they would find the journals. "We'd really appreciate your assistance."

"Oh, dear."

Concern knitted Jess's brow, and Grace scowled at Mike and Abby. "It's all right, Jess," she said. "If you don't want to think about the journals today, we'll just send Mike and his friend along."

"Now, Grace, don't fuss," Jess scolded. "Abby, sit there." She pointed to a chair near the settee. "Mike, come closer, and let's think like Myra."

Mike laughed. "Sure, Jess." He led her into a reminiscence about his college days when he lived with Jess and her sister. After a few minutes, he tried to nudge his aunt into a suggestion where to find the journals. "Remember when Myra first said I had to move here to be successful?"

"Certainly, dear. She considered California the land of opportunity. That was why our ancestor Arlen came here, according to the journals."

Abby leaned forward, but Mike motioned to her to wait.

"Where did Myra put papers that showed how important her home in California was?" Mike's face remained impassive, but his body tensed as he waited for an answer.

"In the box under her bed, of course," Jess replied.

"I didn't find boxes or anything else in her room," Abby told him in a low voice.

He nodded, then continued, "You don't suppose she put the journals in a safe-deposit box, do you?"

Jess waved her small, wizened hand in a gesture indicating Mike's foolishness. "Heavens, no. Oh, she kept some old jewelry at the bank, since our lawyer Mr. Peebles insisted, but we looked in that box after . . . when she left us. There wasn't anything but the jewelry. Remember?"

Mike nodded. "Did she have more than one box?"

"Of course not."

The discussion continued, and Abby was caught up in it despite her unfulfilled wish to focus on the journals. According to Jess, Mike had been quite a rapscallion while here, frequently getting into scrapes from which his great-aunts took enormous pleasure from extracting him. "Why, there was that time when you had promised two young ladies a night on the town—the same night." Jess giggled. "Myra told them both you'd suddenly been taken ill, and you joined your friend Peter at the Dodger game."

"Which time was that?" Mike asked, his face red but smug.

Jess's smile was fond. "That kind of thing happened a lot, didn't it?"

As everyone but Grace laughed, Abby wished she had known Mike in his carefree, mischievous days. Had the responsibility of a business changed him? Or perhaps Dixie was to blame.

Grace rose, her thin lips pursed. "You're never going to track down those journals this way. I'll go make some tea."

"Tea? And the journals." Jess suddenly tried to rise but sank down again on the settee. Her wrinkled face had gone white. "That's right," she murmured. "Myra kept the journals under the bed when we were young to read from them, but after the burglary we had back in 1979, she put them with the tea set."

Abby met Mike's glance. Her heart was beating wildly, for here was a clue. But the only tea set she had seen in her search was one in the sideboard in the dining room. It had contained no journals.

"What tea set?" Mike queried gently.

"Arlen's, of course. The pretty silver one he carried on the wagon train west."

Abby felt her excitement ebb. "Arlen had no tea set," she whispered despondently. She had sometimes driven his wagon when he had to be on horseback, and she had seen inside it. He'd stuffed in kettles, pans, and other cooking utensils in abundance, but no silver tea set.

Unless . . . Abby stood and pulled Mike to the corner of the room. She kept her voice steady despite the thrill coursing through her. "Mike, *we* had a silver tea set. It had been our mother's, and when we lost her it belonged to Lucy. If Lucy married Arlen—oh, Mike, it was as dear to her as her journals. Perhaps they were passed along together."

He glanced at her, his face an impassive mask. Nothing less than the journals would convince him.

Abby approached Mike's great-aunt. "Jess, what did the tea set look like? Might it have had an embossed pattern of tiny violets set in a nest of swirling leaves?"

Jess's cloudy eyes opened wide. "Why, yes, I believe it did."

"And was there a matching teapot, tea caddy, sugar, and creamer?"

Jess clapped her hands together in delight. "Then you found it? How wonderful! It's been years. May I see it?"

Abby glanced at Mike for help, but he apparently waited to see how she reacted to Jess's request.

She could not tell them where these items were. Would they assume she had found them, studied them, then hidden them once more?

Even worse, if they did not turn up, might Jess think her a thief? Oh, dear lord, might Mike believe that of her, too? He already mistrusted her.

"I didn't find it," she said quietly. "I'm sorry. I'd better go."

She tried to muster her dignity as she stepped toward the door, but tears blinded her, and she nearly tripped on the edge of the rug. Strong arms caught her. Large, warm hands grasped her elbows and led her back to her chair. "Abby just made a lucky guess," Mike said to Jess. "Let's see if we can figure out where the tea set is."

Abby had never loved Mike more than at that moment. He supported her, whether or not he believed her.

For the next several minutes, they discussed where the tea set might be—but Abby and Hannah had examined all the suggested locations and had not found it.

Grace came in, carrying a plastic tray with a metal teapot and four unmatched cups. "Here," she said, placing everything on the low table near the settee. "Herb tea. No caffeine."

Abby inhaled the refreshing scent of warm apples and spice as Grace poured. The tea tasted as delicious as it smelled, but it failed to soothe Abby.

Grace resumed her seat, and Mike explained they had been talking about a missing silver tea service. "Do you know where to find it? It has . . ." He glanced at Abby, then continued. "It's embossed with violets and leaves. Five pieces."

"Of course I don't," Grace snapped. Then she hesitated. "Only . . . there are a few old boxes of junk down in the coal cellar. We had it made into a separate room when the place was brought up to earthquake standards after the shaking in 1971."

"That was before I got here," Mike said. "I used to fix a lot of crumbling patio walls and shorted light fixtures, but I don't remember hearing about the sealing off of any rooms."

"It's accessible," Grace said. "Just hard to get to." She paused, then looked at Abby, her usual scowl mellowed into an expression of apology. "I'm sorry I didn't think of that room before, but it's a mess, just junk inside. I can't imagine Myra leaving anything of importance there."

"We were robbed back in seventy-nine," Jess said. "Someone broke in and took all the jewelry we had about. Thank heavens for Mr. Peebles; all our good pieces were in that bank box."

Mike nodded. "Poor Myra," he said, his head shaking nostalgically. "That was the year before I arrived, and she still felt violated. I'm not surprised if she hid things of value. And what better place than somewhere no one would think to look?"

"But she told me she wanted you to have the tea set," Jess said, shaking her head. "That Myra. I never will understand why she set such store in old things."

When Abby looked at the empty metal shelves in the small cellar, she had not imagined they concealed the half-height door into the old coal cellar. The framework was on wheels that had corroded over time, so Mike had to lift it away.

Carrying a cylindrical portable light he called

a flashlight, Mike went first into the coal cellar. Abby followed. There was no other illumination in the small, dingy room that still smelled of coal dust. Abby tried to hold her breath as her eyes followed the beam of Mike's light around the room.

There were several boxes on the floor. "I'll carry them out," Mike said. "You go first."

He toted the boxes one at a time up the steps and through the cellar door to the landscaped backyard, where he deposited them beside the steps to the kitchen. Seated on the stairs, Abby pored through the boxes.

The first two contained old papers that were stuck together, ruined, for the coal cellar must have been flooded at some time. She nevertheless went through them as well as she could. Fortunately the journals were not in this damaged clump of pages.

The third box was filled with silver so blackened with age that it appeared covered with carbon. Abby picked out the pieces one at a time. There was a water pitcher, a serving platter—and beneath them, a tea service. Everything smelled musty from mildew, and even the cardboard of the box began to disintegrate from being touched. Abby took her finger and rubbed the surface of the teapot. It was the same shape as her mother's and—yes! Beneath the layer of tarnish was the familiar embossed pattern: violets and swirling leaves!

Abby hugged the filthy pot, ignoring what she was doing to her shirt. This was a piece of home!

As Mike brought up another box, he looked at her questioningly. She knew she must look a sight. And she had not taken the most important step of all. She reached inside the large tea caddy first.

"Mike, look!" she screamed in excitement as she lifted one small bound book, then a second and a third. All seemed in fairly good condition.

Mike stared at her, his gray eyes narrowing as though he could not accept what they were telling him. Oh, he had to believe her now!

"Only three?" she asked aloud, continuing to look.

From the bottom of the box, she pulled a fourth journal. But it had not fared as well as the others. Its cover was nearly off, and its pages were stuck together.

Abby glanced at the dates at the front of each journal. "Mike." Her voice was raw with emotion. "Please give these three"—she handed him the volumes from the tea caddy—"to Grace to hold. I'll tell you some of their contents. But this one—" She held up the moldering fourth. "I want to borrow it. It will tell me what happened to my family."

Abby checked to make certain there were no more than four journals in the box. Before Mike and she left, they got Grace's promise to read the journals so she could tell Mike their contents the next day.

232

In the Bronco, Abby felt jubilant. "You see," she said, "I'm not so 'looney songs' as you thought."

He tried to hide his brief smile. "The expression is 'Looney Tunes,' and I was never convinced you were crazy. Not totally, anyway. But you have to admit this entire episode is . . . well, incredible."

It was more than an "episode" to her. It was a volume whose ending had not yet been written—unlike the journal she had placed inside the waistband of her jeans with care so as not to damage it further. Tenderly she reached down and patted it. She would read it that night.

"What's happened between us is not something people could anticipate, Mike," she agreed.

As they drove up the hill, Abby glanced at the tree where Dixie had been killed. Mike had not loved her. Might he now begin again to trust others? He surely would learn from what was in the journals that he could trust Abby.

And she might yet save him from whatever caused her burgeoning fear, for not even finding the journals that day had lightened her anxiety.

Abby helped Hannah prepare supper. "You must eat with us," she insisted. "I have so many stories to tell. . . ."

As she chopped vegetables for a salad, Abby said, "I thought you told me Mike loved Dixie."

"I let you draw your own conclusion. Did he tell you the whole story?"

"Enough," Abby said sadly. "Poor Mike."

"Yep. Thanks to her conniving and his hormones, he went through four years of hell—that's how long they were married. Me, too."

"Married?"

"No, hell. She fired me every other week, but I'd been with him for years, and he said only he could let me go. That didn't encourage her to be nice."

"Why did you stay?"

"Damned if I'd let her get the better of me! Besides, Mike needed an ally. At least he finally saw the light and asked for a divorce. I just wish for his sake she'd gotten out of his life the easy way instead of dying on him. This way he keeps on suffering."

Abby sighed. If only she could help him with that. But first she had to save him from the peril she sensed. And to do that, she had to make him believe her.

As they finished cooking, Abby had Hannah add pencil and paper to the table settings. "You should take notes," she said. "That way you'll be sure if I'm telling the truth when Grace confirms the stories."

As they ate, Abby regaled Mike and Hannah with the tribulations of the wagon train during the months on the trail. She described her father's illness in the desert. Sorrowfully she told them of the death of the trail leader's orphaned nephew Jimmy. She hesitated over the story of how she had foretold little Mary Woolcott's near-crushing by a wagon wheel, how her parents

Cora and Jem blamed Abby, how Jem's sister Emmaline had set her cap for Lucy's beau—trail boss Arlen Danziger.

Abby saw Mike hesitate as he raised a bite of fish to his mouth, his gray eyes capturing hers. He said, "So my ancestor not only made a mean stew, he was a ladies' man, too."

Abby smiled briefly. "Not really. He is—was— very nice, and everyone, man and woman, recognized it. I will bet that the fourth journal tells of his marriage to my sister, but that I do not know. I can't usually choose my prognostications." She flushed. "But I stand by my belief that something bad awaits you, Mike. I feel . . . frightened." She glared at him boldly, then looked down at the broiled chicken on her plate.

When no one else spoke, she continued her story. She described how the usually calm Daniel Flagg led the defectors from the wagon train while Arlen and the Indian guide Hunwet searched for water.

When she was through, Hannah asked Mike, "You were with Abby when she found the journals?"

"Yes."

"And you don't think she had a chance to read what was in them?" Hannah continued her catechism.

Mike shook his head. "No. And if what you're driving at is that, if her stories are there, then I have no choice but to believe her—well, I suppose you're right!" He threw down his napkin and stalked from the room.

"He's afraid," Hannah said, running fingers through her black cap of hair. "He figured me for a harmless eccentric, but he won't be able to shrug off the unexplainable anymore. And that means he's going to have to take your warning seriously."

Abby ached for him. She loved him so much. Would his being forced to take her seriously let him care for her, too?

Or would it drive them even farther apart?

Abby excused herself after helping Hannah with the supper dishes. She wondered how Mike was after his explosive departure, but she had tortured herself enough. She retired to her room to learn what had happened to her family.

The last journal, from the bottom of the box, had fared even worse than she'd feared. She could not pry most of the stuck pages apart, and the ink on those that she could separate had run. There were only a few pages she could read the entire way through.

But in just touching the volume, she felt connected with the past. "Poor Lucy," Abby sighed as she gathered from the first pages of the journal how Lucy and their father had suffered when Abby disappeared without a trace. "Papa, I'm sorry!"

She skipped a clump of stuck pages, reading what she could. "Oh, Lucy, I'm so glad!" she said after learning Arlen had finally asked Lucy to be his wife. But what had led up to it? She wanted all the romantic details.

Carefully she pulled some of the sticking pages apart. Except for the last few, they were impossible to separate.

What she was finally able to read made her gasp. "No!" she said. It could not be true!

According to Lucy's journal, her missing and presumed dead sister caught up with them after several days, and she saved Arlen's life when he was stung by a bee. The end of the journal indicated that Abby remained in the past long afterward.

She had no choice. If Arlen Danziger died on the trail, his descendant Mike would never be born.

Abby had to go back.

And she could not tell if she ever returned.

Chapter Eleven

Mike felt confused. He was a normal man, used to believing in what he could see and hear and touch.

The crazy things he had experienced with Abby—fortune-telling, her sharing of his hallucination—had not really happened. They couldn't have.

Yet everything he had ever believed in was about to turn upside down. How could it be otherwise if the tales she had told were repeated in those old journals? She couldn't have falsified them, then hidden them in a room long forgotten in his own aunt's house.

So far she'd made no claims on his business, had made no demands at all. So what kind of scam could this be?

He considered running back to the desert to escape Abby and his unnerving thoughts. But his thoughts would come along. And so, therefore, would Abby.

By running out of the room earlier, he'd hurt her. Like it or not, he could feel her sorrow as if it were his own. And her unhappiness was his fault.

Dixie had deserved to be hurt for the pain she'd inflicted. But she hadn't deserved to die.

And Abby? No matter what the truth about her, he did not want her to suffer because of him.

And so he did the only thing he could. In the dead of night he crept into her room. "Abby?" he called softly.

There was no answer. The room was dark, and it smelled of her fragrance of cinnamon and spices. The sorrow that was not his permeated the place. He hurried to the bed.

She lay crying silently, her body shaking. He touched her, and suddenly she was in his arms, sobbing as though her heart were breaking.

His heart shattered in response. "I'm sorry, Abby," he said, his voice low, from deep in his gut. "I never meant to hurt you. I . . . I believe in you, no matter what's in those damned journals."

She hugged him tighter, but her weeping did not stop.

"Oh, God, Abby," he groaned, raining kisses on her damp cheeks, tasting the saltiness of her tears. He buried his face in the unbound cloud of her soft, sweet-smelling hair. "I love you."

Abby did not want to return to Jess's the next day. She knew what would happen, and she only wanted to pretend it was not so.

But of course they went. When they arrived, Grace was more animated than Abby had ever seen her. "Those journals were amazing," she said, walking with Abby and Mike to the parlor. "I've told Jess she should have them transcribed, send them off to a publisher. She'll make a fortune." She stopped in the doorway, her familiar glare back, trained on Abby. "Of course, we don't know the end of the story. Not till we see that last journal."

"It's in terrible condition," Abby said. Her voice reflected her growing sorrow. She sat in a chair opposite Jess, who was, as usual, on her settee; Abby did not want to be too near Mike or his great-aunt. "The journal is mostly unreadable." She had to keep it, of course. She did not want Mike to see it. After his declaration the night before, he might try to stop her from fulfilling her destiny. And if she failed to return to save Arlen, there would be no Mike.

No, she would keep her secret buried deep inside. But she wondered what would happen to this time if the past were changed. Was there a possibility of her coming back quickly despite what the journal said? But why would she stay as long as the volume indicated if she had a choice?

"Ready, Abby?" Mike said gently.

"Of course." She tried unsuccessfully to sound enthused. She should have felt thrilled that her love for Mike was returned. Last night, when he proclaimed his feelings, she had responded with tenderness. He did not need to be burdened with her fears.

But his feelings were simply an additional complication. She loved him, and so she would go back when she was finished here. If she could. But she felt certain that the magic that brought her here would see her home. Hadn't Lucy's journal said so?

It also said she'd stay there, without Mike, for a long time. And then the journal ended.

She had to come back here. How could she go on if she thought otherwise?

Maybe the threat she sensed to Mike was not really imminent. Maybe she could remain here for a long time, waiting to save him, savoring their moments together.

She knew, though, that her special power was telling her otherwise. Mike was in trouble now. She would help him first. And then she would leave.

"Okay," Mike said to Grace. "Let me tell you a little about what you read."

The aging housekeeper looked startled. "Well, I don't—"

"Let Myra read the journals," Jess demanded, her tone grumpy. Abby glanced with sympathy at the elderly woman who looked so like Lucy. This was one of her off days. If only she had not been so lucid the day before . . . but no. What was to be would be, and Abby was better off knowing, to be prepared.

"Myra's not here now," Mike told his great-aunt gently. He turned back to Grace. "The journals were written by a Lucy Wynne, right?"

She nodded. "Quite an interesting tale. See, she and her—"

"Father and sister Abby were traveling west on a wagon train," Mike interrupted. "The wagon master was my ancestor Arlen Danziger, and there was an Indian guide named"—he turned to Abby—"Hanwet?"

"Hunwet," she corrected.

Mike went on to describe the incidents that Abby had related the night before. Grace appeared more and more disgruntled, as though the wind were being swept right out of her sails. "Well, if you knew all this," she grumbled when Mike was through, "why did you insist that I read these dratted journals right away?"

"For corroboration," he said. "Did I describe events mentioned in the books?"

"Well, yes. Though there were a lot more interesting things that went on. Like the time—"

"I'd love to hear all of them, but not now," Mike said. "I've shed any doubts. Really."

He looked at Abby. His eyes had lost their former storminess; the gray in them now was the softness of kittens, the caress of a dove's wing. Her heart melted. Certainly she would leave him when she had to. But for now they could be together. They *had* to be together so she could protect him from whatever triggered her anxiety.

With a tremulous smile, she walked across the room and into the haven of his strong, waiting arms.

* * *

242

At Abby's request, Mike left her back home when he went to his office. She had something important to do.

She had been unable to save little Jimmy from the affliction that followed Danziger men through the centuries. At least now she was armed with knowledge. She knew she would be successful when Arlen was stung by a bee.

But she had to be prepared.

She found Hannah in the kitchen scrubbing the sink. That day the dress beneath her pinafore was bright purple. The sides of her raven black cap of hair were plastered against her head with metal clips that Abby had learned were called bobby pins. The style emphasized the moonlike roundness of her cheeks.

Abby inhaled the familiar, pleasant pine scent of the cleaning materials. She would miss that smell. She'd miss a lot from this time.

But she would come back. And she was not leaving yet—though she believed it would be soon. Her unfocused disquiet was no longer a sleepy ogre; since that morning at Jess's, it had begun to stretch and rumble and terrify her. She still did not know from where the danger would come, or when.

But she did not believe it would be that day. So for now she would wait, but not idly. She had preparations to make.

Standing next to Hannah at the counter, she began, "I am curious. After that terrible time Mike was stung by the bee, I wonder if he keeps many of those lifesaving kits about."

"Of course." Hannah turned toward her, a sponge in her hand. "Anyone that allergic had better be prepared. He's got a couple of kits in that drawer." She pointed a dripping hand toward the one from which she had extracted the box that saved Mike's life. "There're some in the garage near the stand with the rake and pruning shears, though he's hired a gardener to do the outside work. He should have one in his car, one at the office—I don't know. All I'm sure of is that he has me call his allergy doctor now and then for prescription refills."

"Prescription refills?" Abby did not know what that meant.

"That's right. The kits aren't available over the counter."

"Over what counter?"

"In the drugstore." Hannah laughed. "I guess this is all foreign to you. See, there are certain medications people can get only if a doctor prescribes them. They're too dangerous to be used by someone who doesn't need them. These kits are among them. The others, the things easy to obtain, are called 'over the counter.'"

"I see. So it's difficult for most people to obtain these kits unless they have a doctor who will . . . prescribe them?"

"Exactly."

Abby's heart sank. How was she to obtain a kit to take with her? She would have to take one of Mike's—but only if he had a sufficient number that she would not endanger him. She thought quickly. "I'm worried about Mike after that frightening experience," she began.

"Who isn't?"

"If you can call the doctor for additional kits, will you do so now? I would like to see one in every room in the house."

Hannah tilted her head, smiling kindly. "You have it bad for him, don't you?"

Abby felt heat spread from the base of her neck up her face.

Hannah did not wait for an answer. Putting her wet hand atop Abby's on the counter, she said, "I hope he appreciates you, dear, but our Mike is not an easy person. He's had a lot of heartache—some brought on himself, I admit. But he deserves caring. And love. Sure, I'll call the doctor today and get a bunch more of those kits. You can even carry one in your purse to keep handy."

Abby felt as though a yoke had been lifted from her neck. Not attempting to hide her relief, for Hannah would misunderstand its source, she said, "That's a wonderful idea! Oh, Hannah, thank you."

The drugstore was like no apothecary shop Abby had ever seen. It was nearly as huge as the supermarkets where she'd gone with Hannah to shop for food. It, too, contained food, although not perishable items. And there was so much more!

While Hannah shopped, Abby walked up and down the aisles. Though she had seen such items in the market, she was particularly enthralled by the variety of first-aid equipment: sterile bandages of every shape and size, antiseptic liquids, salves, and ointments. She had long believed that cleanliness was a major factor in healing a wound. People in this day apparently agreed.

And then there were the medicines—so many of them, readily available to take home. Remedies for colds and coughs, stomach upsets, and every kind of pain.

Oh, if she only had unlimited funds, imagine the good she could do by bringing with her to the past an assortment of these! But she had no right to toy with fate. What mischief might she create should she change the past beyond what she was meant to do?

Still, she intended to come back early. . . .

She rejoined Hannah at a counter just as the housekeeper was handed a bag by a woman in a white jacket whose name tag indicated she was the pharmacist. Abby had already been pleased to learn that in these days women were not restricted by their sex from entering any profession—although Hannah had told her they still had to work harder, often for less pay.

"Here's Mike's prescription," Hannah said, placing it in a plastic basket that she slipped over her arm.

How strange things were in this time! The medicines that Abby had understood to be "over the counter" were freely available for purchase from shelves, yet the ones subject to prescription were handed to patrons over a counter.

They walked to the front of the store, where

Hannah paid with a credit card. The young man at the cash register put everything in a filmy plastic bag. As they left the store, Hannah reached inside the bag and extracted a familiar-looking orange box, handing it to Abby. "Here. Keep this one in your purse."

"Thank you," Abby said, feeling tears rush to her eyes. She looked away. She felt joyous that she now was prepared to do what was needed, but her tears were not entirely from happiness.

She was one step closer to leaving Mike.

A short while later, Hannah drove Abby to the street in front of Mike's office. Before getting out of the car, Abby asked, "May I borrow the credit card?"

"Sure," Hannah said, her curiosity obvious in her hazel eyes as she took the card from her wallet and handed it to Abby.

But Abby did not explain. She had an errand to run. She walked a few blocks to the store called The Nature Company, where she made a purchase.

Then, returning to Mike's building, she greeted the now-familiar guard behind the desk. Swallowing the fearful lump in her throat, she used the elevator to go upstairs.

Lydia was on the phone. "I understand, Mr. Rousseau," she said, shaking her head so that her short curls bobbed about the petite features of her face. Her blue eyes appeared quite irritated. "But like I said, Mr. Danziger is in a meeting. He's not taking calls."

Philip Rousseau. His presence on the other end of the phone was surely why Abby's sense of disquiet made her heart somersault in her chest.

Even from across the desk, Abby could hear the angry roar from the other end of the phone, followed by a loud noise. Lydia flinched, putting down the receiver. "It's bad enough the s.o.b. has to call and yell," Lydia complained, "but it's not fair that he has the fun of hanging up first."

Another abbreviation—one Abby had yet to learn. But the meaning was not as important as another question. She managed a smile. "Does he call or come here often?"

"Too often, if you ask me." Lydia snorted. "Now he's threatening again to sue Mike for killing his sister. I think it's a good idea, myself. Bringing the thing to court would get the facts in the open, show that Mike didn't do anything wrong to cause the accident."

"Really?" Abby was thrilled. Maybe, once and for all, Mike could be cleansed of the guilt that plagued him about Dixie's death.

Lydia shrugged. "Well, that's my opinion. But who knows what the dratted lawyers would dig up? There'd be all sorts of dirt thrown all over the place, and no matter what, Mike might look bad." Reaching again for the phone, she announced Abby's arrival to Mike.

In less than a minute, he was in the reception area. There was a broad smile on his face, though furrows of apparent pain were etched on his brow. "Come in, Abby," he said, his deep voice tired. "Boy, do I have a headache."

He seemed to need to talk, since for the next minutes he explained his activities of the morning. As he sat at his desk, she stood behind him, gently massaging his temples. She reveled in the small contact, wishing she could smooth away all his hurt—now, and that to come when she left.

"I've struck deals with the equipment creditors on that gourmet food fiasco. The stuff depreciated on delivery, so even when they repossessed it, they claimed they were still owed money. There wasn't cash to spare, since the perishable supplies still had to be paid for, so I worked a deal to give the creditors a share of a couple new Arlen's Kitchens I have on the drawing board."

"Drawing board?"

He laughed. "Give me a while and I'll have you speaking the idioms of this time like a native."

Pleased that he now took her arrival from the past for granted, Abby wanted to tell him that they didn't have a while. Instead she caressed his soft, wavy hair, now slightly shorter than when they met on the desert, yet still longer than most men's she had seen in this time. Oh, if only she could be with him long enough to learn all he wanted to teach, to teach him, in turn, how very wonderful he was.

She would come back. There would be plenty of time then.

He picked up the phone and called Ruth and Lowell to join them. Abby, not wanting to intrude, stood behind him near a window. The others took seats across the desk.

"I've got everything worked out now," he said to his assistants.

Lowell frowned from behind the glasses perched at the end of his nose. "What do you mean?"

Mike explained his agreements with the creditors.

Ruth's blue eyes moistened, her small hands folded carefully atop her finely woven skirt. Unpursing her red lips, she said, "Mike, I want you to know we—I . . . the idea was a mistake, and the fault's mine. Lowell suggested we needed a change, some oomph, and I had to agree, because—"

"I'm sure you both meant well," Mike interrupted, "but next time check with me before doing anything drastic."

Lowell seemed unable to stay quiet any longer. Grimacing to push his glasses higher, he said, "We didn't have enough time. We were still ironing out the bugs in the system. In another month—"

"In another month there'd have been no system left." Mike glared at his subordinate.

At first Lowell stared back, but his eyes dropped quickly. "Sorry, Mike," he mumbled.

"Forget it," Mike said, dismissing them both.

That afternoon, while Mike finished in his office, Abby exercised the marvel called a computer to do research on nineteenth-century history, thanks to some on-line services that Lydia showed her how to use. How breathtakingly exciting this era was in which to live!

Later Mike drove them both home. After eating the delicious supper Hannah had waiting for them, they adjourned to the parlor, where Abby no longer felt startled by the moving, lifelike pictures on the television. But even after relaxing with Mike before this machine on other occasions, she remained awed by the ability to know instantly what was happening anywhere in the world—and was fearful of the atrocities and mayhem that seemed to pervade this age. Many frightening attacks occurred on people right here in Los Angeles.

Beside her on the sofa, his arm around her shoulder, Mike seemed to sense her thoughts. "It all sounds horrible, doesn't it?"

She nodded, nestling closer.

"Believe it or not, there are lots of nice people who aren't killing one another. The news concentrates on the most awful situations."

"Why?"

He shrugged. "That's what people want to watch. TV networks and stations measure success by ratings—the number of people watching."

"Do you mean more people watch if terrible things are shown?"

Mike nodded but pushed a button. A new picture appeared, one in which a woman performed amazing kicks to overpower a man with a gun.

"Is that real?" Abby asked in amazement.

"Well, some women today learn self-defense techniques. Men, too. But that's just a stunt-woman in an adventure show." He smiled at her,

251

amusement and love softening the expression in his silver-gray eyes. Abby smiled back tremulously as his mouth dropped to hers. "I think it's bedtime, Abby," he murmured against her lips. She nodded.

They reached her room first. For a moment, common sense took over. She should not invite him in. She should tell him she was tired, that she felt ill. She should say anything but the truth: that they should do nothing to bring them closer together. Not now. Not till she knew she would not hurt him by failing to return.

But he did not wait for an invitation. He shut the door behind them, pulling her close and covering her mouth with his, no longer gentle. His hands ranged over her back, scorching her everywhere he touched. She met with urgent desire each increasingly feverish kiss, each tantalizing thrust of his tongue. He tasted of the garlic and spices of supper and of his own special, savory flavor.

Her nobler thoughts evaporated, swept away by his heated caresses, his irresistible kisses. Endearingly, his fingers trembled as they unfastened her clothing. Her body quivered in response, moistening, demanding more.

She tried to help him remove his clothes. She managed his shirt and the T-shirt beneath, then stopped to run her fingers through the thick, silken mat of dark brown chest hair. His chest was hard, deeply muscled.

As her hands continued their delighted exploration of hot flesh beneath soft hair, he grew impatient. She was not certain whether the remainder of his clothing disappeared before or after he laid her on the bed, but soon they were together, skin to burning skin. She smelled the pungent, enticing aroma of their urgency, and it stimulated her need. His mouth nibbled at her chin, then moved down to fasten on one pebbling nipple as his fingers found the other, and she gasped at the doubly exciting sensation.

He pulled away for a moment, sheathing himself in the fascinating skintight covering she had learned was for birth control and other protection.

Then his hand eased her legs apart. His touch was like feathery fire; his increasingly bold stroking caused her to arch to avoid—no, to meet—his erotic touch.

Feeling his swollen hardness against her stomach, unable to wait any longer, she whimpered, "Mike, please."

And then he was on top of her, inside her, thrusting and burning, and she rose to meet each delightfully torturous stroke.

She cried aloud as she reached her pinnacle, and heard at the same time his groan of release. While her heart still pounded beneath her ribs, before his breathing had calmed, she heard him whisper raggedly, "I love you, Abby."

She said what she had to, because it was the truth—even though it would hurt him more, in the long run, when she had to leave. "I love you, too, Mike."

* * *

They ate breakfast together the next morning, and Mike invited her to join him at his office. As before, Abby spent the day working on the computer, learning all she could about this time she would soon be leaving, about the time to which she would soon return, and everything in between. She would have to be careful to keep her counsel once back in the past; knowing the future then would only heighten her reputation as a witch.

Mike and she returned home together after a long day, and Abby found their evening similar to the one before, as, to her delight, was their night.

In fact, the next days and nights formed a pattern, one filled with peaceful days of sharing, marvelous nights of passion.

They grew ever closer. The distant, cool Mike Danziger seemed to have disappeared, replaced by a man who joked and laughed and made love with abandon.

But as their closeness increased, so did Abby's anxiety. The prickling at her spine had become a near constant stabbing of fear. She could hardly eat or drink, for her throat was constricted and her stomach seemed heavy and bloated with her unspecified terror. Still, she tried to keep it from Mike. Most of the time she was successful.

One morning, though, as she picked at her breakfast, he said, "Spill it, Abby. You've been keeping something back. I'm the one whom you claim felt your sadness from more than a century away, remember."

"I *claim*?"

He laughed. "I guess it's true. But don't change the subject." He leaned toward her over the table, his gray eyes dark with concern. Touching her chin with his fingertip, he asked, "What's wrong?"

His tenderness was almost too much to bear. She sighed. Maybe he was right. He had accepted all the rest; perhaps now he would believe in her unfocused premonition. "Remember I told you I've felt afraid of something ever since arriving in L.A.?"

He nodded. "And since then you've saved me from the elevator and a bee sting, and you nearly roasted to death yourself. I'd say any feeling you've had of danger was justified."

"Mike, it's getting worse. Something terrible is going to happen."

"Well, as soon as you figure out what, sweetheart, tell me what to avoid. But right now I've got to get to work. Are you coming with me?"

"Of course."

Late that afternoon he called her into his office. "I've got to work late," he said. "No sense your waiting. The phone system's out; as part of my economy drive, we're putting in a cheaper one, and I'm going to take advantage of the peace and quiet. I've called Hannah to pick you up; she'll take you to a movie."

The idea of seeing on a huge screen one of those wonderful moving pictures she had seen on TV certainly intrigued her. Still, with her fear for him so intense . . . "You come too, Mike."

"I can't. But I promise, just a few more days of intensive stuff. Then I'll have time to show you all there is to enjoy in this time. Movies, museums, plays, travel—you name it!"

"Then I'll stay, too."

He shook his head. "Hannah's already on her way. There'll be nothing for you to do here."

"I don't mind. Really."

He stood and took her into his arms. "Stop worrying so much. I'll be fine. But I'll get more done on my own."

She did not want to leave, not with her anxiety so intense. But it had been growing steadily. She had no reason to think anything would occur that evening. And Mike was insistent.

And so when Hannah arrived, Abby went with her.

But when they reached the place Hannah called the movie theater, Abby was unable to get out of the car. Her neck prickled, then throbbed with pain. Huddling against the seat, she watched inside her mind as a black shadow slithered up a wall behind Mike, holding something long and threatening—a knife, a gun; she could not tell which, but it was aiming at Mike. It was going to hurt Mike. To kill him!

"Oh, God, Hannah!" she finally managed to scream. "It's tonight! It's now! Mike! Oh, Mike, dear lord, behind you!"

Chapter Twelve

Mike was exhausted. He'd been staring at the same ledger page for the last ten minutes. The only light in the office was from the fixtures overhead; it was after nine o'clock.

But he had accounts to finish, taxes to tabulate. Then he would be done. He could go home to Abby.

Abby. She was beautiful. She had saved his life twice, had foreseen the fire that almost took hers. She had told him she had special powers, and clearly she did. Hadn't she shared his hallucination? They had both seen through the other's eyes, felt what the other felt.

And if she also told him she had been born 159 years ago, that she had trekked across country on a wagon train with his ancestors, that she had tasted the recipes he used to start Arlen's Kitchens more than a century before he was born, well, then she had, journals or not.

She had taught him to trust again.

The hell with this! He slammed the ledgers onto his desk. He was going to the theater. He wanted to be with Abby.

And then he heard a scream in his head. It was Abby's voice. "Mike! Oh, Mike, dear lord, behind you!"

Ducking, he turned—in time to see a raised arm come crashing down. He felt a burst of pain at the back of his head—then nothing.

"This is ridiculous, Abby," Hannah barked, wheeling the sports car around a Beverly Hills corner so fast that the tires shrieked. "Even if you're right and Mike's in trouble, what can you do?"

"I have to be with him," Abby said. She would know what to do when the time came.

"Of all times for Mike's phone system to be out. Look, at least let me stop next time we pass a pay phone. I'll call the cops."

"Take me to him first," Abby insisted. "The police might not believe you."

They reached Mike's building. A light was on in the empty lobby, and windows on most floors were lit. But counting upward, Abby saw no illumination on the twelfth story.

"Don't they have a security guard at this hour?" Hannah demanded.

"Let me out," Abby said. "I'll look for the guard. Then I'll help Mike."

"I don't know about this." Hannah shook her head. In the dim green light from the numbers on the car's dashboard, she looked pasty, frightened.

Abby shuddered as her entire body pulsed with fear. "Can you feel it?" she whispered.

Hannah seemed ready to cry. "Abby, about my powers . . ."

"Have faith in yourself," Abby said, opening the car door.

"Hey, wait. Take this." Hannah removed a flashlight from a compartment in the dashboard. "Push this button forward for light." She demonstrated. "And if necessary, it's hard enough to do someone's head some damage."

Abby sucked in her breath. "Thank you. Now please find help." With that, she ran from the car.

The glass door to the building was unlocked. Abby pushed it and walked in toward the front desk. She, too, had thought that a building security guard would be on duty at night. But no one was there now.

She looked about. A computer behind the desk was turned on, indicating someone had been there. Her heart thudded in the ominous silence. Something had happened to the guard. She, and she alone, had to help Mike.

She knew for certain now that many of the terrible things that had happened since her arrival in this time had not been accidents. She had seen someone attack Mike. That same person intended to kill him. Tonight. Now.

But who was it?

Philip Rousseau, of course. Was he here this night? Would he murder Mike?

Not if Abby could stop him.

Taking a deep breath, she pushed the button for the elevators. The middle one rumbled in its shaft. She looked up to see the lit numbers track its downward path: 12, 11, 10. Would it stop here? Perhaps Mike was on it. It had started off on his floor.

Its descent continued: 9, 8, 7, all the way down to 1, where Abby waited. But the doors did not open. Instead, the elevator continued to the below-ground parking area.

Abby pushed the button again, but the other elevators seemed not to be functioning.

Mike had been on the elevator. She was certain now; their special bond told her so. He was hurt. She had to get to him. But how?

She looked about. There was a door marked *Stairs* beside the elevator.

Quickly Abby entered the stairwell. It was dimly lit and smelled of old cigarettes and stale food. She stood still and listened. Her ears heard no sounds. Neither, now, did her mind.

Oh, surely Mike was not badly hurt! But if not, should she not be able to sense his emotions in his time of peril?

She descended the narrow concrete stairs quickly, trying to remain quiet. Reaching the bottom, she slowly pushed open the door to the garage floor, then stopped. She would be a target, for the only illumination came from behind her.

She whispered, "Mike?"

She heard nothing. Saw nothing. Sensed nothing.

Feeling braver, she threw open the door and thrust herself through, staying low to the floor.

Still nothing.

How was she to see with no lights? If she used the flashlight, she would be easy prey. But how could Philip see without light? Perhaps if she stood still, he would reveal himself.

Pulling herself tightly against the wall, she waited.

She did not have to wait long.

Suddenly all the lights went on, momentarily blinding her. She ducked, looking around, feeling vulnerable. She gripped the flashlight as a shadowy form hurtled toward her. Then she was thrown to the floor.

Mike heard a soft moaning. Jerking awake, he realized he was the source.

His head hurt. God, did it ever! He rubbed it gingerly.

He looked around. He was lying on a cold concrete floor beside the Bronco. How had he gotten here? Last he recalled, he had been in his office thinking about Abby.

And then he'd heard her voice in his head. He'd turned—and the blow that had probably been meant to kill him had only knocked him unconscious.

But why had he been brought here?

Suddenly a pair of dark-clad legs appeared before him. "So you're awake," said an angry voice as brittle as untempered glass. Gloved hands gripped his arm, dragging him to his feet. He considered lunging sideways, but before he could stir, something hard was shoved into his side. "This is a .357 Magnum. If I were you, I'd get up nice and easy."

Although disguised, the voice was vaguely familiar. Philip Rousseau's? Mike knew no one else crazy enough to pull such a stunt. He turned his head slowly but saw only a ski mask—and the gun now pressed to his temple. "Got a good look? Good. Now maybe you won't try anything else."

There was a quaver in the voice. Maybe whoever it was felt as scared as he did. Philip? Mike wasn't sure.

At least there was only himself to worry about. Thank God he'd only imagined he'd heard Abby calling. He didn't know what he'd do if she were there, too.

And then, turning slightly to assess his chances of escape, he saw her—a small bundle on the ground beside the car. She was in one of her long skirts. Her lovely pale brown hair spilled about her face, and she was not moving.

Without thinking, he lunged toward her, only to be brought up sharply as his captor shoved him against the Bronco.

"What did you do to her?" he snarled, frightened beyond belief. She was as still as death. He could not see her face beneath her hair.

"She tried to play hero," their captor said. "I didn't want to hurt a woman. I never wanted to hurt a woman, but sometimes . . ." The voice lost its low, masked growl and rose in hysteria. Mike was not sure what was more frightening—a cold, calculating thug or a lunatic out of control. He believed now he faced the latter.

"Let me go to her," he cajoled. "I'll make sure she's all right; then you can let her go. You won't have to hurt a woman any more."

"Forget it." The voice was hard-edged once more. Mike moved only his eyes to look at the man. He was shorter than Mike, and slighter but wiry. He wore all black: long-sleeved T-shirt, pants, socks, and—wing-tipped shoes! That seemed incongruous. Why not boots or athletic shoes? A gun-toting executive?

And then Mike knew exactly who it was.

Abby's head hurt. She tried to stay very still, for moving made it ache all the more. What had happened?

And then she recalled. A man in black, a dark mask over his face and hair, had pushed her to the floor, and she'd hit her head.

She remembered no more—except that she had to help Mike.

Mike! She heard his voice. He was alive!

Slowly she opened her eyes, then closed them again as pain shot through her head. She could not pamper herself. Mike needed her.

Through her lashes, she saw him beside his Bronco, one of the few vehicles in the garage at this late hour. The shorter man in black held a gun, and it was aimed at Mike's head.

She had to do something.

Mike seemed calm. "Let us both go," he said conversationally. "We don't know who you are, and you haven't really hurt us."

"I intend to, though," the man said, sounding angry. "I always meant to kill you."

Mike's eyes closed for a moment, and the shaking of his head looked almost sympathetic. "Why, Lowell?" he asked.

The man gasped, his hand holding the gun beginning to shake. "You know?"

"I do now."

Lowell removed the tight-fitting black mask from his face. He looked old and scared to Abby, who remained still.

"I helped you start Arlen's Kitchens, but you treated me like a trained seal. 'Order this, Lowell.' 'Use this recipe.' 'Open this bank account and close this one.' 'Go fix the grill.' But did you ever ask for my advice? Listen when I gave it?" Holding the gun in his right hand, he awkwardly used the left to pull his glasses from a pocket and put them on.

"I'm sorry, Lowell. I never realized—"

"And then when I finally got my big opportunity, you came back from the desert too soon. Another few weeks and my gourmet idea would have taken off."

"Of course it would, Lowell." Mike's voice sounded soothing.

"Don't patronize me!" The gun hand jerked, and Abby gasped despite herself. Surely he wasn't about to shoot Mike.

He turned toward her, grimacing to let his cheeks push his glasses up on his nose. "Oh, you're awake. I didn't mean to hurt you, you know."

"I know," Abby said, trying to sound as calm as Mike. "I'll bet if you let us go, Mike will listen to your ideas, won't you, Mike?"

"Of course. And—"

"I told you not to patronize me!" The gun swung wildly around from Mike's stomach to Abby's and back again. "Get up, Abby. Get over here where I can keep an eye on you both."

She tried to rise, but the movement made her throbbing head swim.

"Get up!" he demanded.

She forced herself to sit, then kneel, ignoring her dizziness. Slowly she drew herself to her feet.

She heard a voice inside her head. "Abby, run."

She glanced at Mike. He stared at her, a look of intense concentration on his face. His fists were clenched; obviously he was preparing to spring, to create a distraction if she bolted as he wished.

But she wasn't able to move very fast. Nor would she abandon Mike to this pathetic madman.

She made her way to Mike's side. He glared at her fiercely, but she gave a gentle smile of reassurance.

"Good," Lowell said. "You've certainly been an elusive target," he told Mike. "I hoped Philip would do the job for me. That's why I kept him informed about your whereabouts. But the wimp was all talk." He sighed, shaking his head. "At least I learned a lot about mechanical things, being your flunky. I tampered with cars and elevators, even set up an incendiary device to start a fire in what I thought was still your bedroom—and you always got away."

Abby swallowed at the fury that narrowed Mike's eyes as he asked, "You tampered with what car?"

Lowell gave a crazy little laugh. "Yours, of course, the night of that fancy little pretheater party of yours last winter. You were talking about all your plans for Arlen's Kitchens—things I never heard about—without even getting my opinion, let alone my ideas. I didn't mean for Dixie to get hurt, but it was okay. When she was gone, when you were so depressed and had no one else, I figured you'd kill yourself and leave the chain to Ruth and me. And Ruth I can manage."

Abby heard Mike's uneven breathing. He was growing so angry that he was liable to try anything. Facing a madman, that could be fatal.

But at least any guilt Mike might have harbored for causing Dixie's death must surely now have evaporated, cast into oblivion by Lowell's confession.

"But you're like a cat with nine lives," Lowell whined, this time using the fingers of his free hand to scoot his glasses up to the bridge of his nose. "You escaped all my traps. I could have cried when you told us at the office about your little episode with the bee sting. Had I known, maybe I could have gotten rid of your medical kit or put something else in the container. I finally decided to be direct. And you were so helpful, working late when the phones were out so even if you heard me upstairs you couldn't call for help. No way will you survive gunshots to the heart. When you're gone, I'll take your wallet. It was hard work dragging you down here unconscious, but it was worth it. When the police find you in the garage, they'll figure this was a random robbery gone wrong."

Abby drew in her breath. He must have seen her move, for he turned to her. "Didn't really mean to get you involved, Abby, but maybe it's better. Mike's not likely to try anything if he thinks you'll get hurt. Besides," he said, his voice plaintive, "he's fallen for you. He may have seen to it that you'd get the restaurants if you survive him. I can't take that chance."

She hazarded a glance at Mike. She had never seen him so furious. His lower jaw jutted, and his gray eyes blazed like lightning in a thunderstorm. But he remained still.

What could they do? If either moved, one would get shot. The other might be able to grab the gun before Lowell took another shot—but maybe not. And in any event, it might be too late for whomever was hit. If only she had the kicking skills of the stuntwoman she had seen on TV! And the flashlight Hannah had given her—she must have dropped it when she was attacked, and she did not see it now.

How long would it be before Lowell made his move? Abby felt like crying. Her powers had failed her, as they had so many times before—

sometimes neglecting to warn her of a danger, other times, like now, warning her when she had no ability to change events.

Could nothing in this age of miracles save them?

And then she remembered—the Bronco.

"You know, Lowell," she began, "it won't be long until the police arrive."

She felt Mike shoot her a warning look. He wanted her to keep quiet. But concentrating, she looked hard at him, willing him to hear her thoughts. Calmly she turned back to Lowell.

"Hannah drove me here. I knew there was something wrong, so I sent her to call the police. I think I already hear their sirens. Don't you?"

Mike must have understood. His hand crept toward his pocket. He reached his key holder, for suddenly an awful noise erupted from the Bronco.

Immediately Abby threw herself toward Mike, who grabbed her, shielding her unwilling body with his. Both tried to dash behind the car.

Up and down went the earsplitting tones from the Bronco's alarm, magnified in the enclosed garage. As she ran, Abby risked a look back. Lowell glared at them, raising the gun, pointing it, just as other sirens sounded in the distance.

"Damn you!" Lowell shouted. And then he fired.

Chapter Thirteen

The pain! It was so intense that Abby could have shrieked aloud. The skin of her upper body felt aflame; her insides heaved in agony.

She concentrated on breathing. Tears filled her eyes. She tried to focus on the source of the fiery torment: shoulder? Chest? Heart?

Surely it couldn't be serious. Mike had to live. But his mind reached out in his suffering, and she shared every iota of his pain.

Abby leaned on one of the many pillars that held up the low ceiling of the garage, ignoring Hannah's inquisitive stare. She did not recognize any of the paramedics. None of them had come to Mike's house during the fire. But the men and women who bent over Mike looked equally efficient.

She had tried to leap behind him, to be the one whom Lowell shot. But Mike, faster and stronger, had thrust her out of the way.

And now he lay on the hard pavement of the garage, bloodied, surrounded by strangers and in the excruciating pain that radiated from his mind, enveloping her. At least she knew he was alive—for now.

"Come, dear." Hannah stood beside her, her face chalky, her hand trembling as she took Abby's arm. "Let's sit down. We're in the way."

In the way. What a terrible twist of fate it would be if Abby had ventured through time to warn Mike and had simply wound up in the way. She now understood his feeling of guilt about Dixie's death more than ever. The difference was that he had wanted Dixie out of his life—and she, perhaps impossibly, wanted him in hers.

Shivering, and not entirely from the chilliness of the garage, she allowed herself to be led to a small stairway nearby, where Hannah and she sat on a hard step.

Abby had already been questioned by a kindly police officer who checked her for wounds, then seemed entirely befuddled by her gasping, pain-racked responses. Gritting her teeth, she had carefully related all that had happened that night—everything except her knowledge that something had been about to happen to Mike, and her later sharing of his torture.

There were police cars all over. Lowell sat in the back of one near the Bronco. They had not yet taken him away. Abby glanced toward him. He sat erect, staring straight ahead over the top of his glasses, which had slid to the tip of his nose. Was he glad? Remorseful? She could not tell. She had never felt any of his emotion ricocheting about this underground chamber.

Suddenly she felt nothing from Mike. She gasped aloud, the tears she had been holding back coursing down her cheeks.

"He'll be all right," Hannah said from beside her. "I sense it. Don't you?" She looked hopefully at Abby.

But would he? Or was he already gone?

The paramedics had not ceased their ministrations. That gave Abby some comfort. Perhaps Mike had merely lost consciousness.

Abby glanced back at Hannah, who looked haggard and frail, for all her chubbiness. Abby swallowed. She was not the only one who needed comforting. Hannah had known Mike much longer than she. "Of course I feel it," Abby lied, taking Hannah's icy hands in hers.

Abby sat beside Hannah for many long minutes, not quite hearing the words of the paramedics treating Mike only a few yards away. The police had found the security guard, also unconscious in the garage, and another team of paramedics was seeing to him. Abby thought that, in years to come, no matter where she was, she would always recall the smell here: the lingering stench of gunpowder, the dank mustiness, the medicines.

The circle of paramedics around Mike broke. Abby could see the body on the floor being held down by strong arms.

"Wait, sir," a voice commanded.

"I'm all right," a faint but irritated voice protested. Abby was suddenly overcome with feelings that were not hers: frustration, irritation, weakness. But only an aching; the terrible pain was dulled.

Feeling her moist eyes glow with relief and joy, Abby smiled at Hannah. Mike would be fine.

Abby rode with Mike in the vehicle called an ambulance through the streets of L.A., siren blaring. He was taken once more to the medical center named Cedars-Sinai. Again he was rushed into the emergency area and removed from Abby's presence.

Much later he was taken to a room where she was permitted to join him. It was small and sterile, with a faint odor resembling the alcohol she had used on Mike's skin while treating the bee sting.

The wound had been in his shoulder: painful but not permanently damaging. "Thank God," Mike said, his voice still weak, when the tall, authoritative man who identified himself as Dr. Shreve came in. "This shouldn't affect my ability to do woodworking, should it?"

Abby held her breath for a moment, knowing how much his hobby meant to him.

The doctor pulled off his spectacles and folded them about the stethoscope around his neck. "As far as I can tell," he said, "you should make a full recovery."

Abby's breath whooshed out in relief as Mike

smiled. She was pleased to see that his color had returned. He glanced at her with a sparkle in his marvelous gray eyes, though their lids drooped in exhaustion. The hollows in his cheeks had deepened.

When the doctor left, Abby sat on the bed, her head nestled against Mike's uninjured shoulder, his good arm holding her close.

"I'm sorry, Mike," she said against his chest. "If only I could have prevented this, but I—"

His laugh was weak but hearty, rumbling through him and gently bouncing her head. "You sound like me. I thought I should've been able to prevent Dixie from dying, that I had no right to take someone else's life even if that person frustrated the hell out of me. After she was killed, I dragged that thick chain around my neck no matter where I went, when common sense told me her death wasn't my fault."

"It wasn't," Abby stated, sitting up to look him directly in the eye. "Even if it had been an accident instead of Lowell's treachery."

"You're right, of course," he agreed. "And so I told myself—as I let myself sink deeper into the morass of guilt. So don't you do that. I'm all right, thanks to you. If you hadn't come, Lowell would have shot me there in the garage, maybe before I'd even regained consciousness. He was setting it up to look like a random robbery."

"But you were shot nonetheless. Had I devised a better plan—"

She was abruptly and thoroughly silenced by

a kiss that, while lacking in strength, made up for it in tenderness.

"Oh, Abby," he murmured as their mouths separated. "My little wagon train traveler. How I love you."

And then he pulled her close once more.

Soon his breathing grew more even; he was asleep. Abby slowly drew away so as not to awaken him.

That night, kind nurses overlooked the rules to permit Abby to stay with him. By the following afternoon, the hospital was ready to release him. Hannah came, and together Abby and she brought Mike home.

They installed Mike back in his bedroom. The trip home had exhausted him. He didn't even protest much when the women did not let him go upstairs to see the progress on the fire repairs but instead promised to nap before dinner.

First, though, he insisted that Abby sit beside him as he lay in bed on top of the covers, still dressed in the clothes Hannah had brought him to wear home: blue jeans and a black, clinging T-shirt that revealed his contours—including the bulge of the bandage at his shoulder.

His large hand held Abby's, and she clasped it tightly, absorbing its warmth, memorizing the comforting grasp of his fingers, the roughness of callused palms.

He smiled up at her, his gray eyes alluring in their sleepy, seductive droop. "You know what worried me more than anything?"

Bending, her face just inches from his, Abby made her voice a gentle sigh. "What's that?"

He met her mouth with a kiss as soft as butterfly wings. She kept her eyes closed for a long moment after he withdrew his lips, placing her cheek against his. A nurse at the hospital had shaved him that morning, so his beard's growth, though scratchy, was normal for late afternoon.

"I was afraid," he said finally into her ear, "when I first regained consciousness after being shot, that I'd been hallucinating, that you were as unreal as I'd decided my vision of the shifting stars on the desert was. But when you were there, insisting on climbing into the ambulance with me, I felt whole again. No matter how serious my wound, I was determined to survive so we could be together."

With effort, Abby prevented her tears from falling, but the lump in her throat lent a huskiness to her voice. If only they *could* stay together.

She would come back. She had to.

"Whatever gave you the will to fight, I'm glad," she said. "Now get some sleep."

He turned, this time letting his mouth rove searchingly over hers. "That's just a sample of what's to come."

Straightening, she looked at him reprovingly. "Get your strength back."

He winked. "Give me a little incentive."

With a mischievous smile, she bent over him again, initiating a most torrid, yet exquisitely gentle, kiss. "Sleep well," she whispered, caressing his cheek with her fingers. And then she left his side.

It was over. Abby's mission here had been accomplished. Mike was saved, his peril vanquished. She felt no more anxiety.

She had to go home.

She returned to the bedroom adjoining Mike's to pore through the fourth journal—what was legible of it—trying to find a way to stay. But Lucy's words left no room for compromise:

> Despite the fact that we are traveling forward, I had to steal the time to write, for I must record the most extraordinary events that occurred this day. My dear sister Abby rejoined the wagon train today. She was most reticent, claiming she did not recall where she had been for nearly two weeks, or how she had caught up with us here, nearly at the summit of a mountain pass, when she had been lost in the middle of the desert. I, of course, did not believe her, for over the years I have shared many of the secrets she keeps from others. But this time she will not even confide in me.
>
> Still, thank our dear Lord, she returned at the most opportune time, for my wonderful Arlen was stricken as he tried to quiet a rearing horse, much as his poor nephew

Jimmy was taken many weeks ago, stung by a bee.

Abby insisted that she be left alone to treat him while I went for water and assistance. I was near hysteria. All I saw was that Abby reached into an unfamiliar bag she carried, but I could not see what she extracted. Yet by the time I returned in mere minutes, Arlen, though weak, was better.

Dearest Abby had been most distraught that she had had no visions to warn of Jimmy's malady and that she could do nothing for him. She would not reveal what she learned in the interim to help Arlen, but I give thanks to God that she learned it.

Abby was fearful that she had already missed the opportunity to save Arlen. The journal stated she had been lost for nearly two weeks, but nearly a month had passed in this time. But the two need not coincide. Surely she would return to the right time to save Arlen. Didn't the journal say so?

She examined it further, hoping to discover that she had somehow disappeared once more. That would signify that she had been able to return to this time. But most of the remaining journal pages were stuck together and the few that weren't were water-smeared and illegible. Yet at the very end, she'd been able to separate a few pages. On one of the last were the telling words:

Our new home is finally complete, after many months of hard work by my dear husband Arlen. It feels so good no longer to live in and about our wagon!

Father is out in the garden with Abby. He seems to be thriving. Despite all of our tribulations, I am certain now that our voyage westward was the best thing for our family.

Abby had to return, for if she failed to save Arlen, there would never be a Mike. She apparently remained for the long weeks to complete the journey and beyond—time for Lucy and Arlen to marry, to settle in Los Angeles, to spend months building a home.

But why would she stay so long in a time where her powers were not accepted? Where she was not accepted?

In a time without Mike?

The obvious answer pounded at her hopes, turning them to dust. She would not be able to return to this time.

But she would try. By all that was within her power, she would try.

Perhaps she should tarry here during Mike's convalescence. After all, he might go into a decline without her.

But that was simply an excuse. He would recover, whether or not she remained. She should leave soon, for her heartbreak would grow greater the longer she stayed.

At least she had learned, to her relief, that she was not pregnant; the first times Mike and she had made love, they had used no protection. Hannah introduced her to the very convenient methods of this time to deal with feminine hygiene, yet another thing to miss.

She pulled from a drawer the maps she had purchased and began to compare them with Mike's paleontology books and references in Lucy's journal to the area where Abby had rejoined the wagon train. She packed the maps in a canvas tote bag she had acquired and placed the journal on top of the bureau.

When Mike awakened hungry, she kept up an animated conversation at supper. His color was good, and she basked in the warmth of his glances.

That night she slept in bed with him. Rather, she slept little, afraid of turning the wrong way and hurting him. Mostly she snuggled close, letting her fingers rove over his sleeping form so that, in days to come, she might recall as much as possible. She memorized the texture of his skin, with its light smattering of dark hair; the silken hair on his head; the hardness of his muscular chest and biceps; his pleasingly masculine aroma.

The next morning, Mike called Ruth to come out that day to discuss business, for she would have to run Arlen's Kitchens, with his guidance, in the week that the doctor ordered that he stay home. He would be closeted with her for hours, Abby thought—an opportune time.

Still, a pang of jealousy shot through her; Ruth might yet get her wish and capture Mike's attention, for soon Abby would not be about to distract him. If only—

No. Dreams must not dissuade her from the inevitable.

While Mike read the newspaper, Abby went into the kitchen where Hannah was doing the breakfast dishes. "I must ask a favor of you," she said, choking back her tears.

"I don't like this," Hannah said, shaking her head ominously as she drove the sports car up the Cajon Pass through the San Bernardino Mountains. "I had a terrible dream last night that you went to the desert and didn't come back."

"I am not returning to the desert," Abby said. "There is something I must do at a historic site in this mountain pass."

She sighed, watching the road zip by as the car climbed. She might never again travel so fast. She glanced upward, seeing a glint of silver in the brilliant blue sky, and bit back yet another sigh. She had never had an opportunity to ride on a jet.

But she squared her chin and looked forward. She had something better—the chance to save a very important life.

While Hannah had gone to get her purse from her room that morning, Abby had finished packing her tote bag. She had selected clothing similar to the dress she had been wearing when she arrived in this time and located at the back of her closet her old bonnet and boots. She left her makeup, T-shirts, and jeans behind.

"There," she said, spotting the correct freeway exit. Although it might not have the ancient sea life fossils of the desert, she hoped that the pre-historic Indian site would provide appropriately magical surroundings. In fact she felt certain that they would; had Lucy's journal not recorded her return to the wagon train somewhere around here?

Hannah followed her instructions, then stopped the car where Abby designated along a railroad track. When Abby got out of the car, the straps of her canvas bag over her arm, Hannah began to follow.

"No," Abby said, barring her way out of the open car door. "You must leave me here and return to Mike."

Hannah's pale hazel eyes widened in shock. "What do you mean, leave you here?"

Abby said nothing, but this time she could not hold back the tears that trickled down her cheeks.

"Hey," Hannah said in a wondering voice. "Except for the desert, my dream was true!" She beamed for a moment until her face crumpled. Sniffling, she embraced Abby in a tight, comforting hug. "I'll miss you. We all will." She pulled back, biting her bright red lips. Almost to herself, she said, "What the devil can I tell Mike?"

"Tell him . . . tell him I love him," Abby said. "Tell him I'll be—" She stopped herself from saying she would return. That she could not know. She did not want to hurt him further by giving him false hopes. Her own hopes were fragile enough.

She had one consolation, though. She would see her family again.

"Tell Mike I'll be thinking of him." She gave Hannah a final squeeze, then ran off down the path.

Wading across a shallow stream, she soon located the ancient Indian campsite, now little more than indentations on the ground. From her bag she pulled out her maps so she could reach a fist-sized rock covered with small, fossilized sea creatures. She had bought it to keep with her for just this occasion when she last visited The Nature Company a couple of weeks earlier.

She sat in the middle of one of the circles, touching its sides and clutching the fossils. Would she still have the shamanlike power that had let her travel to this time? "Please," she said aloud. "People where I come from need my help. Let me return."

Her mind reached out for the ancient Indian magic of this site and her fossilized rock. As once before, her skin began to tingle. The ground seemed to move; the earth beneath her fingers grew hot.

Her mind began to spin, its circling mirroring the swirling wind that blew about her, whipping up dirt and leaves until she could see nothing.

She slipped sideways to the ground, unconscious.

Chapter Fourteen

1858

Abby heard the wagon train and its echoes in the canyons before she saw it: the squeals of aging axles against wheels and frames against beds; the chaotic thudding of the feet of cattle and the hurried animals' protests; men's calls to one another.

Since awakening at the ancient Indian site, she had walked for hours along the twisting dirt path that hugged the side of a folding, weathered mountain. Her special sense had been her guide.

Hoisting the strap of the tote bag to the crook of her elbow, she lifted her awkward beige skirt and began to run. She soon saw the rear of the last wagon, its tattered canvas cover flapping as it rolled forward, its light breeze swaying the low trailside bushes along the edge of the mountain.

Smiling, Abby quickly passed the rumbling prairie schooner. She waved with only a brief hello to the travelers walking beside it, ignoring their amazed cries, for she thought she spotted the rear of her family's wagon rounding a bend ahead. In a moment, she was sure; a familiar figure in a blue flowered dress trudged alongside. "Lucy!" Abby shouted.

Lucy stopped and stiffened. She pivoted, eyes wide in shock. Despite the shadow cast over her face by her bonnet, Abby could see her mouth form the word "Abby!"

In moments they were in each other's arms, laughing and crying and talking at once. Lucy pulled away first, her brown eyes sparkling. "I thought I would never see you again." She looked Abby up and down. "You look fine. A mite peaked, perhaps, but very well for someone lost in the desert for almost two weeks."

Or in the future for nearly a month, Abby thought. But Lucy's journal had been accurate despite the disparity in time, which was yet another inexplicable aspect of her adventure.

Single file along the turning trail, the two hastened to catch up to the rolling wagon. Abby's long skirts swished beside her feet. She missed the easy freedom of blue jeans, but now that she had returned to a time in which she was too uncomfortably often the subject of gossip, she wanted to invite no more by daring to wear men's clothing. Her head seemed heavy and confined beneath the bun tucked inside her bonnet.

Her sister asked, "Where have you been, Abby?"

Abby knew that she must not say. Lucy would

try to accept her story, but even her sister, so trusting of Abby's oddities, would find this one difficult to believe. Plus she would have the additional strain of keeping it to herself, for if she told anyone, she would brand Abby as a lunatic or a witch—and herself, too, should she profess to believe it.

Looking into Lucy's dear face with its up-turned nose so like Mike's great-aunt Jess's, Abby lied, "I . . . I must have hit my head. I woke up all hazy, and now I can't remember."

As Lucy's eyes narrowed skeptically, others in the party joined them, calling, "Halt the wagons!" The cry, from the rear to the front of the caravan, echoed among the mountains.

As the train slowed, a grumpy voice shouted from the driver's bench of the four-oxen Wynne wagon, "What's happening? Why are we stopping?"

Lifting her skirt, Abby ran to the front of the wagon. The irritated expression on the wizened face of Lucius Wynne dissolved immediately. "Daughter!"

Abby climbed up and hugged her father. He seemed thinner yet stronger than when she had left. "Papa, I'm so glad to see you," she said.

Others on the train massed about, clogging the narrow path, and Abby climbed down for their greetings. She would have a difficult time getting used to seeing, as well as wearing, the clothing of this time: the men in wrinkled woven shirts, pants with suspenders, vests, heavy boots, and bandannas; the women in long dresses, bonnets, and laced boots. Milling together, the group exuded the pungent odor of sweat on unwashed bodies. Abby had barely noticed before, but after enjoying twentieth-century hygiene, she had to rub the base of her nose to keep from wrinkling it in distaste.

Nearly everyone was cordial, even the previously unkind Jem and Cora Woolcott. However, Emmaline Woolcott, her wide, flirty eyes now suspicious and cool, asked questions all must have been thinking. "How on earth did you catch up with us? We thought you were lost way back in the desert."

Abby shook her head. "I wish I knew. I was injured."

She smiled in relief as Hunwet slid through the milling crowd, his coal black eyes grave yet welcoming. The Indian guide was dressed, as always, like the other men in the party. His dark, straight hair was longer than Mike's had been in the future. "It does not matter how you returned, Abby. We are pleased you succeeded."

As with Hannah in the future, she knew she would find a sympathetic ear in Hunwet. But at this moment, her anguish about all she had lost was too raw to share. Perhaps she could never share it.

For now she would merely keep her eye on Arlen.

Arlen! She had been so excited about seeing her family that she had not looked for the man who was the reason for her return. Dread suddenly shot icy tendrils through her. Keeping her voice level, she asked, "Where's Arlen?" Surely she was not too late.

"He's ahead," Jem Woolcott said. "There's a horse acting a mite skittish, like it had a burr under its saddle, and—"

Abby did not wait for the rest. Clutching the strap of her tote bag, she lifted her skirts and pushed her way on the thin, treacherous path, around people, past wagons, and oxen teams. Breathing heavily, she inhaled the almost forgotten stench of sweat and other livestock excretions in the otherwise sweet, pure air of this time. She tried hard not to trip along the uneven trail as she increased her speed. She had to reach him.

She was vaguely aware of slower footsteps behind her, her sister's cry, "Abby?"

She found Arlen near the front of the wagons, trying to quiet a rearing roan on the narrow dirt trail. "Abby!" he shouted with a delighted smile.

His appearance made her hesitate. His face was fuller than Mike's, his chin not quite so firm, his eyes deeper set and more pale. He was shorter, his body more slender yet muscular. His clothing consisted of wrinkled but sturdy trail garb. But he still resembled Mike enough that Abby nearly cried.

Arlen turned quickly away as the nervous horse demanded his attention. He tethered it to a sturdy bush then approached, his arms outstretched. "We were all worried, Abby." He pulled her close in a brief hug, then released her. "Where were you? How did you find us?"

She forestalled further questions by confusedly rubbing her moist brow with the back of her hand. "I can't explain what happened, Arlen, for I truly do not understand. But I'm happy to find you well."

"I'm never otherwise, but no thanks to old Jack, here." His glower when he turned toward the prancing, neighing horse reminded Abby so of Mike that she closed her eyes. "He usually hasn't this much pep, especially after all the exercise he's had on our big jump west. I wonder what's ailing him."

"Bee sting, I expect," Abby said. "And that's why you should get away—"

But even as she spoke, Abby saw the small, striped form of another of the insidious creatures land on Arlen's arm atop the sleeve of his faded blue shirt. "Don't move," she whispered, reaching forward just as Lucy joined them.

"Abby, what is the matter?" she cried.

Before Abby could brush the insect away, Arlen cried, "Ouch! Damned little critter stung me—pardon my language."

"Oh, no!" Abby cried. "Arlen, you must stay quite still."

"Surely he will not have the same reaction as little Jimmy," Lucy whispered.

"Surely he will," Abby replied grimly. Nearly immediately Arlen clutched his throat as his breathing turned to wheezing gasps. His color heightened and became mottled. He slid to the ground, nearly unconscious.

Lucy screamed. "Oh, dear Lord, no! Please do not take my Arlen." She joined him on the ground, weeping hysterically.

She would be of no assistance. Besides, Abby did not wish for her to know how she would attempt to save Arlen. "Go back to the wagons quickly, Lucy, and bring me a filled canteen. I will require water to save Arlen's life."

"Can you?" her sister cried through her tears.

"Only if you hurry."

Without a further word, Lucy rose and, holding her full skirt, ran toward the wagons.

Abby got busy. Reaching into her bag beneath the fossil rock, she pulled out the small, orange plastic box. She scanned the instructions, although she felt certain she recalled what to do. She swabbed Arlen's skin, gave him an injection, put a tourniquet about his arm. She placed the pills into her hand and thrust the entire box back into the bag as Lucy returned.

"Here," she said, thrusting the canteen at Abby.

Abby placed the pills into Arlen's mouth with water, then forced him to swallow. For want of tweezers, she used her short fingernails to pinch out the stinger. Then she sat on the ground to wait.

Arlen gasped for breath. Oh, what Abby would do for an ambulance full of paramedics! But there were only she and the small box she had brought.

As quickly as the attack started, it was over. Reminiscent of Mike all those years in the future, yet several weeks ago to Abby, Arlen began to breathe more easily. His color improved. Still, he continued to wheeze more than Mike had, and his pallor did not totally disappear.

"He's going to be all right, isn't he, Abby?" Lucy clutched her sister's arm.

"Yes," Abby said, her eyes narrowed in determination. "He is."

The two sisters were soon joined by others in the party. They helped Arlen back to his wagon and into his bedroll, where he fell asleep.

Abby volunteered to drive Arlen's wagon so she could check on him continuously. Lucy rode with them, her journal on her lap. Abby wished she could have rushed Arlen to a hospital emergency room, but of course that was impossible.

"How did you save him, Abby?" Lucy demanded, shouting over the sound of the wagon's progress. But Abby, jouncing about on the driver's bench, did not explain.

Lucy put her hand on her sister's shoulder. "I know you are keeping much from me, Abby. I'll respect your privacy. But thank you for what you did for Arlen." She kissed Abby's cheek.

Glancing inside the wagon at Arlen, Abby was not sure that he was, as yet, saved. He looked pale and weak; he certainly did not recuperate as quickly as Mike. She had one more shot she could give him, but should she have brought more than one kit?

Maybe she should have carried a supply to leave here if—when—she returned to the future. Maybe her destiny was to remain here to save Arlen from future attacks, and she had already failed by neglecting to bring extra lifesaving kits.

No. What she had done was enough. Lucy's

journal had mentioned Arlen alive in the future. But Abby could not help sighing. She had harbored a hope that she would treat Arlen, then defy the journal and disappear once more, heading for the place of magic that had brought her here. Heading back to Mike.

But she could not think of leaving this time until she was certain of Arlen's recovery. And that meant going forward with the wagon train, leaving behind the magic site.

Hearing a sound from inside the wagon, Abby turned. Arlen was gasping for breath. "Here!" Abby handed the oxen team's reins to Lucy and reached inside her tote bag, just as Arlen turned over and began to breathe more quietly.

"Is he okay?" Lucy's voice was anxious.

"He's fine," Abby assured her. Still, her fingertips rested for comfort on the precious plastic box.

Before she withdrew her hand from the bag, she reached around for her other items of comfort.

The fossil rock was there, but she did not feel her maps.

Stifling a gasp, she glanced inside. She did not see them. With her fingers, she rooted about the bag's contents.

They weren't there. She must have dropped them as she'd whirled back through time. She turned her head away from Lucy's curious stare, blinking rapidly as worry flooded her. If she did not have the maps, could she find the ancient Indian site again? Without Mike's books, she could not hope to locate another potentially magic location.

She breathed deeply until her panic was under control. After all, she could not be certain how useful the maps would have been. Many potential routes shown on them to the Indian site would not yet exist. She would find it again somehow if she needed to.

More important, she still had her precious fossil rock. When she was ready to go back to Mike's time, surely, with it, she could make her own magic.

The wagons reached a clearing in a gully where they settled for the night. Abby made certain that Arlen was comfortable. Lucy promised to stay with him and call Abby if there was any change.

Later Abby knelt uncomfortably in her long skirt at the campfire, the ribbons of her bonnet irritating the sensitive skin beneath her chin as she perspired.

She stirred a pot of Arlen's stew—the precursor to the culinary delight that would help Mike found Arlen's Kitchens. Tasting it, she found it more greasy, less appetizing than the Arlen's Kitchens' stew.

After only hours, she already missed more than the food from the future: comfortable clothing; the fast, smooth-moving Bronco; bathroom facilities that eliminated the need to hide in underbrush for privacy.

Mike.

She learned over supper of an accident on a particularly treacherous path that had claimed two lives in their party. That was why she'd read in the future of casualties among those who stayed with Arlen in the desert.

She also heard of the unexpected storm that had save the travelers' lives. It had blown up about the time of Abby's disappearance, making their intense search for her all the more difficult, for the wash flooded.

They'd collected all the water they needed in barrels and canteens. After waiting till the temporary river receded, they saw no sign that the storm had struck anywhere but in the vicinity of the wagon train. Again they'd searched for Abby but finally had to go on.

When all had finished eating, Abby helped the other women clean up in cold stream water and without a dishwasher. Finally she felt free to escape for a while. She told her sister the direction in which she would walk, then grabbed her shawl from the wagon and threw it about her shoulders. Carrying a flickering candle in one hand and holding her skirt with the other, she picked her way along a path in the cool, crisp mountain air. She found a rock-filled clearing, a former stream bed, where she could look up and see the myriad stars.

"Oh, Mike," she whispered brokenly to the heavens. "I miss you already."

She waited for the stars to shift, for her mind to be transported to that time yet to come, to feelings that were not her own.

Nothing happened.

Shivering more from emotion than from cold,

she put the candle on the ground and pulled the shawl more closely about her. She refused to acknowledge the wetness in her eyes; crying would solve no problems.

She looked up again—and then, through the blur of her tears, it happened, just as it had before.

At first she was not certain whether her tears caused the shifting of the stars. But then the humming of a jet—she had a name for it now—sounded in her ears as its lights blinked overhead: not lanterns held by a soaring bird, as she had once, in her naivete, believed.

Immediately Abby wished she had not brought this vision on herself. Pain racked her—not her body, but her very soul. Mike's loneliness that she had shared before was nothing compared with this terrible isolation that resembled, but was not, her own. She heard his deep voice, hollow with grief, ringing as though from inside her own head. "Abby, why did you leave? I believe in you now, damn it."

He paused as though waiting for an answer. She tried carefully to make her thoughts coherent as she explained that she'd had to return, that it would not be forever, just until she was able to rejoin him.

But as always, her powers were fallible. Despite her ability to sense his thoughts, not just his emotions, he must not have understood hers. This time, when he spoke again inside her mind, his anguish seemed overshadowed by excitement. "I feel you. Abby, where are you?"

Once more she tried to send him a message. But he grew impatient. "Are you playing with me, Abby?"

"No!" She had never wanted to hurt him, to cause him to lose his newfound trust in people, so arduously won.

For long minutes, Abby stood staring at the stars, willing them not to return to their usual places in her sky. She sensed the transition of Mike's mood as she had so often while with him. In despair, she tried to send calming, loving thoughts, but she began to receive a jumble of emotions until, finally, he yelled through his thoughts, "Stop this, Abby. Forget the games and come back."

"I will," her mind cried. "As soon as I can."

But he did not hear. "Damn you!" he shouted, that beloved, hurtful voice inside her head. "Why did I ever think I could trust you?"

Abby dropped to the ground in grief. As the stars shifted to their usual position for her time, she bowed her head to sob.

Eventually her tears stopped flowing, but her pain did not. Lucy's journal had been accurate so far. Abby had returned to the wagon train. She had saved Arlen's life. She wanted desperately to return to Mike and his time right away. But the journal said she stayed.

She would do all she could to make that part of the journal false. But she did not know if she would succeed. Ever.

And Mike was furious. He was hurt. Perhaps it would be better for him just to forget her.

Yet how painful for her.

She would go back to him as soon as possible.

But she would not search for him again in the nighttime sky.

Chapter Fifteen

Despite her own sorrows, Abby celebrated the wedding of Lucy and Arlen with joy. Arlen, jolted into greater awareness of the fragility of life, had proposed to Lucy soon after his incident with the bee sting, and she accepted.

The wagon train stopped for an entire day in the small town of El Monte, a willow-laden enclave along the San Gabriel River within the old La Puente rancho. The townsfolk, of Spanish descent, seemed suspicious at first of the settlers from the East, but their reserve thawed when they understood there was to be a wedding. Throwing themselves into the spirit of the festivities, they lent Lucy a lovely, sweeping lace gown and mantilla for her wedding attire and Arlen a snug-fitting black suit and white, frilled shirt.

In a chapel formed by the trees along the riverbank, an English-speaking priest performed the ceremony before the excited travelers and townspeople. The fragrance of flowers filled the fresh air. Abby laughed and cried to see her sister so radiant on the arm of her handsome, adoring new husband—so like his descendant whom she loved.

Hunwet, the Indian guide, was dressed in a loose white shirt gathered at the sleeves and tied at the neck, a braided leather thong holding his straight black hair from his face. He offered his own blessing on the marriage, which he later translated as "Many days, many children, many acorns." Acorns, the main foodstuff of his Cahuilla tribe, were the seeds of life.

That night, only Abby and her snoring father slept beneath the Wynne wagon. Arlen and Lucy had crept off, of course, to be alone.

The remaining few days of the wagons' journey blended together. Abby had decided to defer her return to the future until she was certain Arlen had fully recuperated. Besides, she wanted to see for herself that her family was settled and happy in their new location, for when she left the next time, she would never come back. But she would spend only a few weeks here, in her own time— not the months or years of Lucy's journal. She would return to Mike much more quickly than that.

Beyond the San Gabriel Mission, the voyagers passed greater numbers of ranches, but the increased density of the population still seemed sparse to Abby. She clutched her canvas bag often, reaching inside for the fossil rock, the hard plastic of the bee sting kit. Only by these tangible reminders could she convince herself that her experience—and Mike—had been real. Her sojourn in the future already felt like a figment of her overactive imagination, a vision that outdid all others.

Lucy now took her place in Arlen's wagon. She rode beside her new husband or drove the oxen for short periods while Arlen, though tiring easily, finished his duties on horseback as trail leader. Abby took turns walking beside the Danziger and Wynne wagons, delighted their father was able to drive.

Only a few days after the wedding, Hunwet, riding his horse swiftly, stopped near Abby. "We see the buildings of the town in the distance." They were on a plain. The grand San Gabriel Mountains rose to the north.

In a few hours the wagon train halted. They had reached Los Angeles.

But, oh, Abby thought, what a tiny, primitive place compared with the L.A. she had known and lost. There were a few squat buildings, and no indication that this would be the location many years from now of busy freeways filled with cars and towering skyscrapers filled with people.

Yet there was an unwelcome similarity that reminded Abby of evenings with Mike when she watched with dismay as news events unfolded on his television. Residents in this time, coming to greet the travelers, were quick to remind them of warnings they had heard even before beginning their journey: with all its many opportunities, this town was a violent place, where shootings were plentiful.

Abby did not know the cause of the brutality in the Los Angeles of the future, although people seemed fascinated by watching even fictional versions on television. Here the disturbances resulted from clashes between gold-seekers from the East and their Mexican counterparts. To avoid having to deal with the violence, or even think much about it, most respectable families settled some distance from town. Others took precautions for safety.

The voyagers made their farewells, assuring one another they would meet often.

Hunwet approached Abby. A wry lift to his full lips underscored the prominence of his cheekbones and breadth of his nose. He looked too kind to be the "bear" of his Indian name. "We are to part ways now, Abby," he said.

She nodded, feeling a lump as bitter as mesquite-flour cake, to which Hunwet had introduced her in the desert, rise in her throat. "I'll miss you," she managed. She was separating from many people important to her these days.

"We have never spoken of your disappearance, but I know it was the magic."

Abby nodded and looked down, afraid she would cry. "Where will you go now?"

"To my people first. I must make certain they have water. And then I will find a new journey as guide to other people, although I do not believe any will be as fine as you."

Impulsively Abby hugged the Indian. "Thank

you for accepting me," she said.

"I thank you for the same," he said, holding her tightly. Then, releasing her, he walked away.

While they decided where to go and how to begin their new life, the combined Danziger-Wynne family found a place to camp in an area where other transients gathered, some also looking for new homes, others preparing to head for the gold fields.

Although it was already late September, the air was hot and dry; there was no nip of fall in the air as there would be in the East that the travelers had left behind. Nor was there the choking smog that Abby had come to detest in the L.A. of the future. That, at least, was a blessing.

One day became two, then a week. Abby reached longingly for her fossil rock several times a day, but she was not yet ready to leave. Although Arlen had improved greatly, Lucius seemed to have expended too much energy at the end of the wagon train trip. Now the small, wizened man slept a lot. Abby would wait until she knew he would be all right.

Arlen located a job as a cook at one of the town's three hotels. Then one day he galloped his horse into their camp. "I've found it!" he cried to Lucy.

He led all of them to the homesite he had picked out. It was north of town along the bank of the Los Angeles River, far enough from the town's violence so they would feel safe. There were dry rolling hills and groves of trees on it near the water. It smelled fresh and clean.

"Isn't it wonderful, Abby?" Lucy twirled in glee, arms outstretched, long skirt billowing when Arlen showed them the spot on which he would build their house.

The place was an area Abby believed she had once passed on a freeway, then full of aging houses and no open spaces. But for now it was quite delightful. "You should be very happy here," she agreed.

"*We*, Abby," Lucy insisted, her expression suddenly worried.

"Of course," Abby responded, upset she had spoiled her sister's mood. Inside, her heart thumped with excitement. In a short while her family would be settled. Perhaps having a place of their own would help her father feel better.

Then she could return to Mike.

The family moved its camp to the homestead. As Abby had hoped, Lucius improved almost immediately; his plans for a farm that would take advantage of the temperate climate helped him leave his lethargy behind. He asked other farmers questions on plants and irrigation, then spent hours comparing the virtues of olives with walnuts, considering the possibility of growing grapes for a winery. One thing, he said, was certain: no orange trees for now; scale insects were currently decimating the crops.

Nearly two weeks after they arrived at the homesite, Abby decided it was time.

That morning she stooped to kiss Lucius, although he was preoccupied with directing his new hired help how to prepare the land for his farm.

Then she went in search of Arlen. As her new brother-in-law mounted his horse for the long ride to his job in town, Abby hurried over to him. "I want to thank you for everything you have done for my family," she said. She squinted up into the sunlight that poured from behind the man who now sat straight in his saddle.

Looking down at her, he wrinkled his brow in surprise. "We're all family now, Abby."

She smiled. Levelheaded Arlen would help her sister and father get over any renewed grief when she was gone. She watched as he turned his horse onto the dirt road.

She found Lucy sitting on a rock near the Danziger wagon. Lucy had acquired several new bolts of material. She was just finishing the sleeve on a new shirt she was sewing for Arlen.

"I'm going for a walk," Abby said. "Don't worry if I'm not back for a while."

Lucy's small features puckered in worry. "You'll be careful, won't you, Abby? You never know if one of the town ruffians will—"

"Here? In the very special homestead Arlen has picked for his bride? No one would dare! I'm just after some new medicinal plants." She bent to kiss Lucy's soft cheek and turned away quickly so her sister would not see the tears in her eyes. Then, lifting the hem of her beige skirt, she walked quickly away.

She would miss her family, but she believed they would be happy here. And she would find a new home for herself in the future. With Mike.

She hurried to the Wynne wagon and found her tote bag. Reaching inside, she made certain the plastic box was there; Arlen seemed fine now, and the box should not be left in a time before even its material had been invented. She assured herself she had her fossil rock.

The sky was leaden, the air more damp than on any other day since their arrival, perhaps portending rain. Dressed in her bonnet, a long skirt, and a soft green blouse, Abby headed across the nearly bare earth of the homestead site, away from the field her father planned, away from the river, away from any direction in which she was likely to be seen. She secluded herself beneath the bowed branches of a solitary willow tree.

She knew of no ancient sites about here that would contain the magic of the two places from which she had been catapulted from one time to another. She wished she had one of Mike's books that listed others. But surely her fossil rock would be enough. She thrust from her mind the possibility that the rock might only assist her in one journey through time.

Arranging her skirt beneath her, she sat in the shade, listening to the wind rustle the leaves on the weeping limbs. She thought of Mike. Would he be waiting for her? Would he still be angry? Nervously she pulled at the ribbons beneath her chin.

She would simply have to tell him the truth of why she'd returned to the past. He'd said he loved her. Surely he would forgive her.

She thought of his handsome face with its hollow cheeks and strong jaw framed by his dark hair. Of his expressive gray eyes that had confirmed how he felt about her. Of his tall, muscular body that had taught her so much about loving.

She would see him soon.

She would be changing history by returning to Mike, since Lucy's journal indicated she had remained. Was she committing a sin against eternity? She did not dare think so. Surely such a small variance would make no difference in destiny's grand scheme. And if—when—she succeeded, would that not be proof that she was fated to be with Mike?

Briefly she wondered where she would wind up in the future. So far, each time she had traveled through time, she had arrived in the same spot as she had left, only years earlier or later. As she recalled this area in the future, it was cramped and residential. She hoped she would not wind up in someone's living room, or, worse, in the middle of a freeway.

She pulled the fossil rock from the bag and placed it on her lap. Leaning back against the willow's trunk, she closed her eyes. "This may be totally selfish," she said aloud, "but perhaps it isn't. I think Mike needs me as much as I need him. Please let me return to him."

She braced herself for the tingling, the galelike sounds, the whirlwind that would send her into unconsciousness.

Nothing happened.

She did not open her eyes. Biting her bottom lip, she thought for a moment, then said, "If this is not an appropriate place of magic, then is it not a place of life? I am asking for a life with the man I love. Please let me go to him."

She clutched the fossil rock to her chest, squeezing her eyelids together. But the only breeze that touched her was the small one wafting through the trees.

Her breathing came in small gasps as she fought not to cry. "Please!" she shouted.

She opened her eyes and looked around. Nothing had changed; she was still in the mottled shadows beneath the willow. And beyond was the same near-empty landscape she had seen before.

"Please," she sobbed, falling to her knees. "Please." But she knew that she begged in vain.

Chapter Sixteen

A short while later, Abby meandered slowly forward, ignoring the hardness of the ground beneath her boots, the constriction of her skirt about her legs. Her random route took her near the river, where she saw Lucy sitting on the bank, writing in her journal.

Curse that volume! Abby had an urge to run over, seize it, and tear it into shreds. Its contents must be immutable. Abby could not change the truth of what it said. She would still be here months, perhaps years from now.

Maybe forever.

No! She stood still for a moment, taking deep, calming breaths, and realized she was shaking. Not from the coolness of the barely damp air, though: from the effort of holding back her tears.

"I'll find a way," she whispered. "Wait for me, Mike. Please."

As she continued forward, she realized what

she would have to do. She would return to the ancient Indian site in the mountains. That place had worked once. It would work again.

No matter that it would take up to a week to reach. At least on horseback, the journey would be shorter than in a wagon.

She would need an escort, though. Even if she'd had the precious maps she had lost in the future, she might not find the route on the paths of today. Besides, despite the fact that women in Mike's time simply hopped in their cars and went anywhere alone, that was not acceptable here.

But who could she get?

Arlen was busy planning the house and amassing materials when not working at his job at the hotel.

Lucius would not know the way. Nor would Abby wish to tax his health in that manner. Fortunately his enthusiasm for their new home helped his energy continue to improve. But he could not go with her.

Hunwet. Of course!

But where was he?

He'd said he was going back to his people, but he would soon look for others to guide. Surely he would come back to Los Angeles first. He would not go east in the wintertime; no new wagon trains would venture west till spring.

She would have to wait for him. For a while, at least. If she became too impatient, she would forget proprieties and find the place herself.

"Abby?"

Abby tried to paste a smile on her face as she

turned slowly to face Lucy.

"Is everything all right?" Lucy's head was cocked beneath the brim of her bonnet as she regarded Abby with concern in her eyes. Her journal was in her hand.

"Fine." Abby made her tone light. "I was not able to venture as far as I had hoped." That certainly was the truth. "I was tired, but now I feel better."

Lucy looked skeptical. "Will you sit with me near the river?"

Abby could think of no reason to refuse.

As they neared the water, Lucy began, "You've acted so unhappy since we got here, Abby. Even before. You have not told me why. And now you appear in the throes of despair. Please confide in me. What is the matter?"

Abby lifted her shoulders beneath her pale green blouse in a small shrug. "I daydream too much," she said. In her mind she saw the face of Mike Danziger.

Lucy pivoted to stand before Abby. Marriage had been good to her. Her pretty, petite features were enhanced by the twinkle in her dark brown eyes. Arlen seemed an attentive husband. Abby could not have asked for more for her beloved sister. She would no longer ask anything for herself, if only—

"Please, Abby, I want to know what is wrong." Lucy looked closely at Abby, her face now serious.

All the raw anguish Abby had been holding back suddenly broke loose, filling her with pain so intense that she clutched her stomach. "I can't tell you," she moaned.

Lucy led her to the riverbank, then joined her on the cool earth beneath a gnarled oak. Abby stared out over the silvery, flowing water. She had seen no flowing rivers in L.A. in the time when she longed to be. What had happened to them?

Now she might never know.

Like the river she watched, her tears began to flow. Then Abby heard a sob beside her and turned. Lucy was crying, too.

"I'm sorry," Abby cried, clutching her sister close. "I did not mean to infect you with my sorrow."

"You used to tell me about your powers, your visions, Abby," Lucy managed. "What did I do to make you stop trusting me?"

"I thought I was protecting you." Taking a deep breath to collect her thoughts, Abby blurted out her story, from her shared vision of shifting stars to meeting Arlen's descendant Mike Danziger on the desert. She told of some of the miracles of the future. Then she described her uneasy pangs that had portended danger, how she had saved Mike Danziger, and how Lucy's fourth journal had forced her to return to save the life of Mike's ancestor Arlen.

"What an incredible story!" Lucy said, her eyes wide. "But with your abilities to see things no one else can, and the way you simply reappeared from being lost just in time to save Arlen—well, I must believe it." She hesitated. "This man Mike.

There is a note in your voice when you speak of him. . . . "

Abby sighed, lifting her chin bravely. "I love him."

"Yet you came back to save Arlen," Lucy whispered. "Thank you, Abby. You gave up so much for me."

Abby's laugh was brittle. "You were in my thoughts, of course, but I returned for many reasons—and the most important was selfish. I couldn't live anywhere knowing Mike might never exist if I failed to act."

"I am still grateful. But now why do you not simply go back?"

There was no longer anything simple about it. Abby rose, suddenly aware of the sounds all around: the water's gurgle, the tune of a songbird in the tree above. Above, leaves rustled in the fragrant breeze, and a small bird with a long blue tail took flight.

"I tried," she finally said in a soft, choking voice. "Just now. And I failed. I believe I may be destined to remain here."

"Selfishly I should be glad," said Lucy with a wry lift of her lips. "But for you I am not. Why do you think that?"

"I could not read all of your last journal," Abby explained, "for it had been damaged over the years. But at its end, you say that I am in the garden of your new house with Papa."

Lucy's brow wrinkled pensively. "The way my poor Arlen is working, our house will not be finished for years—let alone growing its garden.

311

Perhaps you could return to your Mike then, but such a long time. . . . Poor Abby!"

"To try again, I need to go back to the mountains." Abby's voice sounded despairing, even to her. She lifted her chin and continued, "And for that I need Hunwet."

"What about Arlen?" Lucy offered. "He could—"

"He is just beginning to put your new lives here together. I will not make him disrupt that for the two weeks it would take to see me there, then return. No, it must be Hunwet." Or, Abby thought, she would go herself. But she dared not tell Lucy that.

"We'll ask Arlen to help you find Hunwet, then," Lucy said, her voice ringing with determination.

The next day Abby accompanied Arlen to town. They rode on horseback along a dirt path. Abby's full skirt was draped about so as not to expose her legs.

"Lucy told me you want to find Hunwet," he said, "and why." There was a skeptical catch to his voice. Abby could not blame him. Her story was not easily believable, even though he seemed to have accepted her visions after Lucy told him of them.

He urged their mounts to a slightly faster clip, and a warm, dry breeze blew against Abby's face. There had been rain the night before, and there seemed no threat of more.

Wanting to explain further, Abby began, "Arlen, I know that—"

But he interrupted. "Lucy believes, and that is all that matters. She'll be mightily upset when you go—wherever it is you're going—but she wants you to anyway. I could guide you back to the mountains, you know."

Abby felt grateful that, for Lucy's sake, Arlen had apparently accepted her story, though falling short of trusting it. "Thank you, but I will not allow you to take so much time away when you are needed here. No, I will seek Hunwet, but if he does not come soon I will hire someone else." That was not her true intent, however; she did not want a stranger to accompany her on so important a mission.

"Then I will help you find someone." Arlen reached up to straighten his suspenders. He wore a crisp white shirt and dark trousers for his job as cook, although Abby assumed the hotel supplied him with aprons. His gray eyes were bright and clear and reminded Abby so of Mike's. Arlen no longer seemed to have any residual effects from his ordeal with the bee sting.

As houses began to appear along the road, Abby dared to ask, "How long do you think it will take you to build a home, complete with garden?"

He glanced at her with both amusement and sympathy in his eyes. "A year, maybe longer, for the one I'm planning. In case your story's true, I promise I'll work as fast as I can. Perhaps I can hire your father's hands to help."

313

Abby smiled. "Thank you. You're a dear friend." She hesitated. "You know, of course, that you must grow no flowers in your garden, or at least that you must let others tend it while it is in bloom."

His look seemed puzzled.

"Bees," she explained. "You must do nothing to put yourself in their presence."

He laughed, then agreed. "I do not want to tempt the small villains to attack me."

While Arlen was at his job that day, Abby visited first the Woolcotts, who had dared to settle at the edge of town despite its reputation, for Jem Woolcoot had opened a tailor shop. They had bought a small adobe house from a man who had gone off to the gold fields, and two large dogs guarded its grounds.

Abby felt uncomfortable, as usual, around Emmaline, but she seemed to have recovered from her illusions about Arlen; her new beau was the owner of the dry goods store that sold her father cloth for his tailoring. They had not seen Hunwet, nor did they seem interested in seeing him again.

They did tell Abby where others from the wagon train might be found, including some survivors of the group that had splintered off. After leaving the Woolcotts, Abby sipped tea in the hotel restaurant and was grateful when Arlen found time to accompany her for several more visits. No one had seen Hunwet.

The sun had dipped low toward the horizon as Abby rode beside Arlen on their way back to the homesite. But on their hour-long ride the sky did not darken as much as did Abby's heart. Without Hunwet, her return to the mountains would be much more difficult.

She would find a way nevertheless. She had to.

A week passed, and then another. Abby visited town several more times, but still no one knew where Hunwet could be found. She would have to go without him.

She tried hard not to listen to the small voice in her mind that warned that simply returning to the spot where she had found the magic before might not help. One incontrovertible fact remained: Lucy's journal said that she stayed in this time until the garden in the new house was growing. And then it ended.

Maybe she would never get back to Mike. She could not be certain that even using both the fossil rock and the prehistoric Indian site would allow her to make another trip through time.

She talked to Arlen often about the landmarks they had passed on the last part of the voyage to Los Angeles. She remembered well the San Gabriel Mission and the town of El Monte. But she was not certain she could trace back the entire route to the mountains on her own.

She would try, though. Only another few days, and she would be off.

One evening Lucy approached Abby as she salted beef for her journey. "You're planning on going, aren't you, even if there is no Hunwet to guide you?" Her voice sounded small and sad.

Abby sighed as she nodded. She did not want to hurt her sister.

Lucy continued, "I don't suppose I could convince you to wait until your niece or nephew is born, could I?"

"Really?" Abby felt an enormous grin light her face. She embraced Lucy, but not too tightly. "Are you certain?"

"Almost."

"How wonderful! I'm so happy for Arlen and you." And for herself. Perhaps this was the child whose descendants would result in Mike.

Another thought struck Abby. She blinked at the magnificence yet simplicity of the idea. "Lucy, would you do me the great honor and favor of naming one of your children after me? Preferably this one, if it's a girl."

"Of course. I'd planned to do that anyway. Particularly if you're not here any longer." Tears flooded her eyes suddenly. "But why do you ask?"

"Your journal. I have been fretting over having to stay here for so long because its last pages seemed to mention me in the garden with Father. But it merely says *Abby* is in the garden. What if—"

"Another Abby! Oh, what a wonderful idea. When you leave, I shall simply write of my sorrow—and joy for you—that you have disappeared once more. And if this babe is not a girl, then I will simply keep making babies until I have one. That will not be a sacrifice." Lucy flushed scarlet beneath her shy smile.

Abby smiled back, pleased that her sister had

found happiness in Arlen's arms the way she had in Mike's. "Thank you," she whispered, pulling the slight form of her sister close.

"I'll miss you, Abby," came the broken yet determined voice in her ear.

Hunwet arrived early in the morning two days later, erect on the back of a gray horse. Abby saw him as Lucy and she finished washing the breakfast dishes. Their father was working with his men in the area cleared for his farm, and Arlen was in town at the hotel.

Hunwet dismounted, and Abby ran to him, her insides quivering. "Thank God you're here," she said. "How did you know to come?"

"Perhaps it is well to thank your gods or mine. I was with my people when I began to have bad dreams. They told me someone called to me. I consulted our *pul*—the shaman—and we determined that it was you." He tilted his head quizzically until his straight black hair touched his shoulder.

"It was. Oh, it was! I must return to the mountains, and I need you to guide me."

"You seek again the place of magic you found there?"

Abby nodded, unsurprised that she did not have to explain to the intuitive man.

Lucy had joined them. She wore one of the new dresses she had been sewing, as did Abby, but her bonnet was an old straw one.

"I know of another place of magic, much

317

closer," Hunwet said. "Would you like to go there instead?"

Abby's smile brightened. "Oh, yes! Can we go right away?"

Lucy looked at Hunwet, then Abby. "So soon?" She smiled bravely. "But no time is better."

The sisters found their father in his field. Abby hugged him tightly without explaining she was leaving forever, holding back her tears. Lucy said, "We—I—will be home late, Father."

"But—" Abby protested as they walked away.

Lucy's gaze was fierce. "I'm coming, too."

"Though within a day's ride and return, the place we are going is a long way," warned Hunwet.

Lucy's face was strained but brave. "Abby's way is even farther. I want to be with her as long as I can."

Abby went into the wagon and grabbed her precious tote bag, then examined its contents to make sure everything was there: the plastic box of the bee sting kit and, most important, the fossil rock.

Hunwet helped the sisters saddle their horses and mount, their long skirts tucked about their legs.

During their ride over low, scrub-covered hills beneath the gray sky, the three talked almost nostalgically of their time on the trail together. The conversation helped hours pass in the cool morning air, yet Abby grew impatient. When would they reach Hunwet's magical spot?

And then there it was, a large, overgrown

swamp filled with high grasses. The place smelled strongly of something pungent that gave Abby an excuse for the tears in her eyes. Instead of water and mud, the wetness was caused by an oozing, black substance.

"I do not have a name for this," Hunwet said. "But it is a place of magic. Look. There are bones of animals from many years past."

The material seemed to be similar to the pitch with which Abby had once filled cracks between the boards in their shed at home, but more viscous, even bubbling from beneath the earth. She saw the bones to which Hunwet referred, a few sticking straight out of the oozing mass.

Abby found a solid area on which to dismount. She looked up at her sister and her friend, feeling her eyes moisten again. Her voice was thick. "Thank you both. I'll miss you terribly."

Lucy slid down beside her, holding her tightly against her small body. "Oh, Abby." Tears rolled down her cheeks.

"Please give my farewells to Arlen," Abby told her.

Hunwet held Abby's shoulder awkwardly. "I wish you much luck in your place of tomorrow, Abby."

Lucy and Hunwet promised to wait over the nearest ridge for a while, in case the magic failed to work. She watched Lucy and Hunwet mount and ride off, one riderless horse led behind. As much as Abby loved them, she hoped not to see them again. But although she tried to be optimistic, she could not help but recall her failure the last time she had tried to return to Mike.

With a determined set to her shoulders, she looked about. She selected a grassy place to sit near a small lake, one from which a long and curved white bone protruded from a seep of the black substance at its edge. Closing her eyes, she felt the magic shift and curl about her like smoke in a breeze.

She found it hard to breathe, whether from anticipation or the terrible odor wafting all about. Her heart pounded in her chest like distant Indian drums.

Squaring her shoulders, she removed the fossil rock from her bag. She hesitated for a moment. She would never see her family again. And if Mike was still angry with her?

Quickly she cast aside the thought, closing her eyes, letting the magic flow through her. "Please," she whispered aloud. "Again my need is selfish, but I wish to go."

Her mind reached out for the magic, and she laughed as her skin began its familiar tingle. The fossil rock began to buck and burn, but she did not let go.

The world shifted, tossing her one way, then another, then spinning her with a crazy, reckless force. She tasted the black pitch as it pelted her. Her eyes opened, but about her was a void. She heard a growling in the sky above. Crying aloud, she was hurtled into unconsciousness.

Abby opened one eye, then closed it quickly again. The sun beat relentlessly, turning the inside of her eyelids a painful white.

Sunlight. Heat. When she had pleaded to go into the future, the sky had been gray, the air cool and moist. She forced herself to open both eyes and look around.

And then she screamed.

Towering above were two beasts resembling elephants, creatures she had only seen in sketches in books, one small but the other large with curling, threatening tusks. Out in the lake was a third, a rampaging beast, huge and brutal, its snakelike nose raised between long, pointed tusks as though to strike her, its expression wild and frenzied.

Caught in her long skirt, hampered further by the black, viscous substance seeping about her on the bank, Abby scrambled to escape—then stopped. The creatures nearest her were not moving. Even the one in the lake barely stirred, just swaying slightly without sound or forward momentum. All seemed frozen, as though time had stopped.

Her hand pressed to her mouth, Abby drew in her breath. *Had* time stopped?

What had she done?

And then a voice called, "Abby!" A wonderful, deep, rich voice that she had hardly dared hope to hear again.

Mike's voice.

She looked around. Before her was a pool of water oozing with thick, inky pitch. Behind her was a fence of woven metal.

And beyond the fence was the strong, solid figure of the man she loved.

"Mike!" she cried.

"Hey!" came an unfamiliar voice. "What are you doing there?" A officious-looking man rattled the metal fence behind the closest creatures.

Abby looked at them more closely. They seemed less threatening as they continued to stand silent and still. In fact, they seemed unreal, like effigies.

She pulled herself to her feet and slogged her way toward Mike.

Their fingers gripped one another's through the mesh of the fence. He was even taller than she remembered, and the handsome, firm features of his face, so much stronger than Arlen's, were stern. She recalled their last night of shifting stars. Was he still angry?

"Hello," she said in a shaky voice. He was here. She did not know how. But any doubts she had had about his forgiving her evaporated as he smiled—a warm, loving, welcoming smile. A current of happiness filled Abby, as quick and potent as the flash flood on the desert. Her delight exceeded her own sense of joy, for it was doubled. Once more she shared Mike's emotions.

She wanted to be with him. She had come such a long way, and yet they were still separated by the metal fence. She looked around for a way to reach him.

No one else was in the area with the seeping pool, though passersby peered in at her through the fence. She must look odd in her long, pitch-covered dress, her bonnet, her face that must be as streaked by the black substance as her arms and hands.

"Get out of here, miss," came the voice behind her.

She turned to the man in a blue jacket and gray pants whose bushy brows were drawn down in anger. His hands were filled with a chain, lock, and keys.

"Gladly," she said, "but I've lost my way. Can you show me how to get out?"

"Yeah, come on." He began to walk back the way he had come.

She noted through the surrounding trees the low buildings around her, one atop a hill; the density of other large edifices; cars on the street along the fence. If she'd had any doubts before, these were evidence that she had reached the future. The beasts on the bank remained unmoving, and she guessed now that they were models of creatures that had once roamed here and left their bones behind.

Pulling off her uncomfortable bonnet and jamming it into the top of her tote bag, Abby followed the man, picking her way carefully along the grass abutting the pool. He asked, "How'd you get in? The gates were all locked."

Abby tried to look helplessly feminine. "I don't recall."

He opened the nearest gate. "Don't do it again," he warned. "It's illegal."

Abby hardly heard. Mike had mirrored their progress from outside the fence. Suddenly she was in his arms.

"You'll get filthy," she whispered, her entire body quivering. "I am covered with that black pitch."

"Also known as tar," he said, his lips skimming her mouth. "This is the La Brea Tar Pits."

And then she was crushed against him. He was with her. Holding her. Not angry, but loving her.

She pulled away suddenly. "How did you know I was returning, Mike? I have never before been to the La Brea Tar Pits, so how were you here on my arrival?"

"Simple," he said, using her arm to keep her tight at his side as he led her along the path bordering the fence. "I read Lucy's last journal."

"But—"

"I located experts in reconstructing damaged books. People honed their skills a few years back after—"

"—the fire in the downtown Los Angeles Library," Abby finished. "Lydia told me."

"Once I gathered from Hannah that you'd felt compelled to go back, I did some sleuthing. You'd left the damaged journal in your bedroom."

"It was your family's."

He nodded. "When I first picked it up, I read what I could, including about Arlen's bee sting. Hannah confirmed your sudden interest in carrying your own kit. When I came to the end and learned you stayed with your family, I nearly wound up having Hannah call the men with the nets to come and get me."

"What?"

He laughed. "I mean I nearly went crazy."

Full of guilt for the sorrow she had caused, Abby cried, "Oh, Mike, if only—"

He put his finger softly on her lips. "Your sister's a smart cookie. I realized that after I had the journal reconstructed. She described in meticulous detail this 'magical' place to which Hunwet and she accompanied you. Once the journal was reconstructed, it wasn't hard for me to identify the tar pits. The only tricky part was the timing, but I guessed, based upon the amount of time you'd been with me before and comparing it with the time that had passed for your family. I've been hanging around here a lot for the past week."

"I'm so glad," Abby whispered. They had reached the Bronco in a parking lot, and she leaned on its sun-heated side for strength. "I was afraid you hated me. The first night I was back there I looked at the stars. I felt our special bond—and I felt you turn from me."

Sheepishly he lifted his dark brows. "I was angry till I understood. Then I had a hell of a time waiting for the journal reconstruction to be complete, and later for you to come back."

Abby heard a growling that she recognized as a jet. She pulled back to watch the silvery bird wing its way across the sky. "Will you take me in one of those?"

"Of course, anywhere you want on our honeymoon. You will marry me, won't you?"

She touched the hollow in his shadow-roughened cheek, so warm and firm and dear.

"Of course." But she could not help sighing.

He tipped her chin with his finger. "What's wrong?"

"I attended my sister's wedding not long ago—for me, that is. I only wish she could know that I am here and that I've found my happiness."

His grin was broad and fond. "She knows, Abby. In fact there are some cryptic comments in her journal that I expect are messages to you. But one thing I understood. She said that she hoped that, wherever her dear, disappeared sister may be, that she can be as blessed as she in knowing that her fertility will result in happiness for people in generations to come."

Abby laughed. "That sounds like Lucy."

"Now," he said, holding the car door open. "Let's go home."

As they drove off, Abby looked out the car window at the brilliant blue sky. She could hardly wait till that evening, when Mike and she could look at the nighttime heavens together.

The stars would never shift again.

COMING IN JANUARY 1996!

Love's Legacy

**THE GREATEST ROMANCE STORIES
EVER TOLD BY ELEVEN OF THE MOST
POPULAR ROMANCE AUTHORS
IN THE WORLD!**

MADELINE BAKER

MARY BALOGH

ELAINE BARBIERI

LORI COPELAND

CASSIE EDWARDS

HEATHER GRAHAM

CATHERINE HART

VIRGINIA HENLEY

PENELOPE NERI

DIANA PALMER

JANELLE TAYLOR

*ALL PROFITS WILL BE DONATED
TO THE LITERACY PARTNERSHIP!*

LEGACY OF LOVE

From the Middle Ages to the present day, these stories follow the men and women whose lives are forever changed by a special book—a cherished volume that teaches the love of learning and the learning of love!

JOIN US—
AND CELEBRATE THE LEARNING OF LOVE AND THE LOVE OF LEARNING!

ALL PROFITS WILL BE DONATED TO THE LITERACY PARTNERSHIP!

COMING IN JANUARY 1996!

MADELINE BAKER
"To Love Again"

Madeline Baker is the author of eighteen romances for Leisure. Her novels have consistently appeared on the Walden and B. Dalton bestseller lists, and she is the winner of the *Romantic Times* Reviewers' Choice Award. Her newest historical romance is *Apache Runaway* (Leisure; March 1995).

MARY BALOGH
"The Betrothal Ball"

With more than forty romances to her credit, Mary Balogh is the winner of two *Romantic Times* Career Achievement Awards. She has been praised by *Publishers Weekly* for writing an "epic love story...absorbing reading right up until the end!" Her latest historical romance is *Longing* (NAL Topaz; December 1994).

ELAINE BARBIERI
"Loving Charity"

The author of twenty romances for Jove, Zebra, Harlequin, and Leisure, Elaine Barbieri has been called "an absolute master of her craft" by *Romantic Times*. She is the winner of several *Romantic Times* Reviewers' Choice Awards, including those for Storyteller Of The Year and Lifetime Achievement; and her historical romance *Wings Of The Dove* was a Doubleday Book Club selection. Her most recent title is *Dance Of The Flame* (Leisure; June 1995).

LORI COPELAND
"Kindred Hearts"

Lori Copeland is the author of more than forty romances for Harlequin, Bantam, Dell, Fawcett, and Love Spell. Her novels have consistently appeared on the Walden, B. Dalton, and *USA Today* bestseller lists. Her newest historical romance is *Someone To Love* (Fawcett; May 1995).

CASSIE EDWARDS
"Savage Fantasy"

The author of fifty romances for Jove, Zebra, Harlequin, NAL Topaz, and Leisure, Cassie Edwards has been called "a shining talent" by *Romantic Times*. She is the winner of the *Romantic Times* Lifetime Achievement Award for Best Indian Romance Series. Her most recent title is *Wild Bliss* (Topaz; June 1995).

HEATHER GRAHAM
"Fairy Tale"

The author of more than seventy novels for Dell, Harlequin, Silhouette, Avon, and Pinnacle, Heather Graham also publishes under the pseudonyms Heather Graham Pozzessere and Shannon Drake. She has been celebrated as "an incredible storyteller" by the *Los Angeles Times*. Her romances have been featured by the Doubleday Book Club and the Literary Guild; she has also had several titles on the *New York Times* bestseller list. Writing as Shannon Drake, she recently published *Branded Hearts* (Avon; February 1995).

CATHERINE HART
"Golden Treasures"

Catherine Hart is the author of fourteen historical romances for Leisure and Avon. Her novels have consistently appeared on the Walden and B. Dalton bestseller lists. Her newest historical romance is *Dazzled* (Avon; September 1994).

VIRGINIA HENLEY
"Letter Of Love"

The author of eleven titles for Avon and Dell, Virginia Henley has been awarded the *Affaire de Coeur* Silver Pen Award. Two of her historical romances—*Seduced* and *Desired*—have appeared on the *USA Today*, *Publishers Weekly*, and *New York Times* bestseller lists. Her latest historical romance is *Desired* (Dell Island; February 1995).

PENELOPE NERI
"Hidden Treasures"

Penelope Neri is the author of eighteen historical romances for Zebra. She is the winner of the *Romantic Times* Storyteller Of The Year Award and *Affaire de Coeur's* Golden Certificate Award. Her most recent title is *This Stolen Moment* (Zebra; October 1994).

DIANA PALMER
"Annabelle's Legacy"

With more than eighty novels to her credit, Diana Palmer has published with Fawcett, Warner, Silhouette, and Dell. Among her numerous writing awards are seven Walden Romance Bestseller Awards and four B. Dalton Bestseller Awards. Her latest romance is *That Burke Man* (Silhouette Desire; March 1995).

JANELLE TAYLOR
"Winds Of Change"

The author of thirty-four books, Janelle Taylor has had seven titles on the *New York Times* bestseller list, and eight of her novels have sold over a million copies each. Ms. Taylor has received much acclaim for her writing, including being inducted into the *Romantic Times* Writers Hall Of Fame. Her newest historical romance is *Destiny Mine* (Kensington; February 1995).

Promises From The Past

Victoria Bruce

"Victoria Bruce is a rare talent!"
—Rebecca Forster, Bestselling Author Of *Dreams*

A faint scent, a distant memory, and an age-old hurt aren't much to go on, but lovely Maggie Westshire has no other recollections of her missing father. Now she finds herself on a painful quest for answers—a journey that begins in Hot Springs, Arkansas, and leads her back through the years, into the strong arms of Shea Younger. He is from a different era, a time of danger and excitement, and he promises Maggie a passion like none she has ever known. And while she is determined, against all odds, to continue her search for her father, Maggie doesn't know how much longer she can resist Shea's considerable charms, or the sweet ecstasy she finds in his timeless embrace.

_52064-8 $4.99 US/$6.99 CAN